FURNACE

Joseph Williams

Aidric Publishing

ISBN: 9798717952842

For Cathy

With special thanks to Mark Gottlieb

FURNACE

ROYAL SPACE ARMADA
DEPARTMENT OF INTERNAL AFFAIRS

REQUISITION FOR CLASSIFIED DOCUMENTS

(1) WRITTEN TESTIMONY OF RSA *FIRST LIEUTENANT CHALMERS, MICHAEL A.* REGARDING EVENTS OF *MISSION ****19JCE* (CLASSIFIED)

SUBPOENAED AS *EXHIBIT* C IN THE TRIAL OF THE CROWN VS. RSA *CAPTAIN GIBBONS, BARTHOLOMEW H.*

FILED BY REPRESENTATIVE *GALLAGHER, ELIZABETH A.*

*****PLEASE NOTE*****DISCLOSING CLASSIFIED R.S.A. DATA OUTSIDE OFFICIAL D.O.I.A. PROCEEDINGS IS PUNISHABLE BY EXILE WITHOUT APPEAL. SHOULD THE COURT FIND THE CLASSIFIED DATA SIGNIFICANTLY DETRIMENTAL TO THE R.S.A. AND THE DISCLOSURE ESPECIALLY EGREGIOUS AND/OR MALICIOUS, A TRIAL WILL BE HELD IMMEDIATELY TO DETERMINE WHETHER THE DEATH PENALTY IS WARRANTED.*****HANDLE WITH CARE TO AVOID SWIFT LEGAL RETRIBUTION*****

FURNACE

FURNACE

PRELIMINARIES

I screwed up. That's the only reasonable explanation I can come up with for the Furnace incident. No one else seems to see it that way though, no matter how deeply they wade in the muck and mire of data logs and survivor testimonies. The Crown even performed an inquest when we returned to Earth. The chief investigator assigned to the case claimed there wasn't a man or woman alive—excluding, maybe, the friends and relatives of the deceased—who would blame me for what happened to our ship in deep space. Beyond it, really. That's the worst part. We had no idea where the hell we were, and it was my job to know. Space is an infinite cesspool of misery with fresh horrors on every rock, but the Furnace incident was different than any so-called 'normal' complication on a hostile planet. A lot different. It wasn't a mission you would boast about to other soldiers when you dropped by Pluto or Mars Station. You wouldn't bother telling your next C.O. how you survived a combat zone unlike anything the fleet has ever seen, or how you climbed a little higher in the pecking order because of it. It's not worth it. You would never do it justice.

Furnace was hell. Surviving it was not a source of pride. It only meant you were a little weaker between the ears than the rest of your fleet brethren, and that maybe one day you would descend into utter lunacy while others enjoyed fat pension checks on luxury planets somewhere far from the war front.

For all his maddening nonchalance, the chief investigator meant well. He pointed out the same tired arguments I hear from people all the time, the ones desperately trying to vindicate me. He must have thought it would stick the more he beat it into my head.

"The ship's navigation controls malfunctioned," he reminded me with a shooing gesture during my report. The litany began shortly thereafter: Most of the crew had suffered complete mental breakdowns, including my commanding officer. All the coordinates I'd laid in were technically correct, and while certain aspects of my conduct were unbecoming of a fleet navigator, they were necessary in the face of such ruthless depravity. Eventually, probably after months of fleet-appointed therapy on the taxpayer dime, I'd realize that I was no more culpable for the deaths of my crewmates than the Crown was for sending us out to sea in the first place.

"You'll get over it," he added while ushering me out of his office, as though that were the final word on the matter. "Just take it one day at a time."

Sounds fantastic, doesn't it? A convenient way to disarm guilt and blame in one fell swoop. Fallacious, tautological arguments that elevate the fleet—and me, by proxy—above accountability. Above paying the piper.

None of that's comforting when I'm lying awake at three in the morning, staring at the night sky so intently that you might think I'm looking for bits of blood and bone from my fallen comrades floating in the moonlight. None of it seems true.

Night is always the worst. That's when I *know* I messed up. When the sky is nearly pitch-black like it was on Furnace and I see devils in the shadows and hear the clown king's bony knuckles rapping at my door. When I start obsessively running through my check-downs and coordinate logs searching for the hidden error that set everything in motion. The one that got almost everyone killed. I figure there's got to be an answer layered somewhere beneath thousands of encryptions, network codes, and technical jargon, right? I'm sure I'll find it eventually.

But maybe that's just guilt talking. Maybe I'm just seeking absolution for my sins on Furnace—the name we gave that planet past the edge of everything—so I can get closure. The chief investigator and my therapist seem to think so. Yet, in the end, it doesn't really matter what *they* think because *I* know I screwed up. It's all my fault. And it all started with a stop on Europa Station, where I let my guard down because of a girl I used to love.

But I guess I should introduce myself now, so long as I'm about to tell you the worst thing that ever happened to me. This is supposed to be therapeutic, but I've got a feeling it will be the opposite when all is said and done. For both of us.

I'm First Lieutenant Michael Chalmers, Fleet Navigator in the Royal Space Armada. Everyone just calls it the fleet though, lowercase and all. We jump around the galaxy transporting goods, protecting colonists, and picking fights, although the Crown would have you believe the latter is a lie. I don't officially have an opinion on it one way or another because I value my commission, but I will say that most of our 'misunderstandings' with other species have little to do with them invading *our* territory. Only the Kalak and Tsoul have been bold enough to enter our solar system with blasters blazing, and we all know what happened to them.

I put in two years with the infantry before they tagged me for navigation. I'd been looking to transfer since the girl from Europa—also a navigator—told me it was the thing to do. Every word she spoke back then was gospel to me, so I promptly volunteered to shadow some test missions on the side to learn the trade. After that, I fell deeply enough in love with either the girl or the work to never look back.

I saw plenty of unbelievable things during my two years in the infantry and even more between receiving my commission as a navigator and our surprise visit to Furnace, but those stories will have to wait for another time. If I don't tell this story now, I don't think I'll ever be able to get everything right. Time will strip important details from my memory. I may block it all out eventually for the sake of my mental wellbeing, or maybe the Crown will do it for me.

So, let me tell you about the worst mission anyone in the human fleet has ever run. I guess it all started on Europa.

EUROPA: AN INTRODUCTION TO FLEET LIFE

Believe it or not, the question I get most from friends and relatives about the fleet is focused on the stations between Earth and the Oort Cloud. They don't want to know what runs through your head when you're attacked by a nine-foot tall, six-hundred-pound alien. They don't care what a Kyzhaman orange tastes like or what physiological changes occur after hearing a Fronov female sing. They want someone to tell them what life is like for troops within our borders. How the other half lives. I guess I understand it in a sense. People aren't usually comfortable asking about the most traumatic events in your life. Like being shot three times through the ribs or watching your best friend bleed to death while field surgeons extract shrapnel from your back and sew you up to keep fighting. I get it, and I'm always happy to give some insight into how we ship-rats view the local facilities.

The first thing I usually tell them is that every soldier's favorite place to visit is Europa, and every soldier's *least* favorite assignment is Pluto. Europa Station is the last stop in the solar system where there's any fun to be had before a fleet ship enters the non-human portion of the galaxy. There are other stations between Europa and Pluto running through the Kuiper Belt —dozens of them, actually—but those are all doom and gloom. Usually, we only stop at one if we need an emergency refuel or have a problem with the ship's systems, in which case we might find ourselves on Pluto.

It's not just the scenery that makes Pluto a downer. The soldiers and scientists stationed in those labs are morose and irritable. I guess wasting the prime years of their military careers isolated on balls of ice and rock breaks their spirits (although you could say we are all in the same boat to some degree). As you can imagine, they're a real joy to be around in that state, but it's hard to blame them. They may have signed up for the fleet but almost none of them wanted babysitting duty. There's no adventure in it. No exploration, no furlough, no alcohol beyond what the supply ships smuggle in every few months. There's not even much in the way of rec activities to shake their cabin fever outside of SurReal World, and sometimes I wonder if the virtual reality does more harm for them than good. Maybe they just don't have enough imagination to believe what they're seeing under the holo-glasses is real, even for a little while. Did I mention most of them are a little insane? It's not surprising when you consider they live on desolate planetoids millions of miles from their loved ones. Hell, *anyone* who leaves Mother Earth for an extended period usually gets a little case of what they call the Parin Blues.

No matter how commonplace the reaction may be, though, it's still demoralizing to see people in such perpetual states of hopelessness, especially knowing they aren't leaving the solar system to risk their lives in the trenches. Probably they envy us for it, but what they don't realize is that they've got it easy. Some days, I think I'd resign my post in a heartbeat to share in their boredom and never again worry about being enslaved, tortured, dissected, or worse on an alien planet. I'd be giving up some action, sure, but to hell with it, right? I've barely been in the fleet three years and I've already seen enough of the killing floor to last me a dozen lifetimes.

Still, the grass isn't always greener. I guess it's good for me to think about the sad saps on Pluto from time to time. Their palpable frustration reminds me why I chose the risks of deep-space missions over a comfortable desk job in the first place. My willingness to apply for one of those posts is generally a good barometer of my disillusionment with the fleet on a given day, but I always arrive at the same decision. I'd rather die in the trenches than lose my soul to the Pluto labs.

Europa Station, on the other hand, is another animal entirely. Europa's got plenty of alcohol, not to mention gambling, state-of-the-art holo-training sims, and a feed with Earth programming so you can watch a ball game or catch up on your favorite shows while you're off-duty. Our onboard SurReal World holo-glasses have a lot of the TV stuff, too, but usually just from the weeks before we left. They haven't figured out a cost-effective method for updating the content real-time and it's (understandably) a low priority while we're still colonizing the galaxy and trying to avoid a second war with the Kalak lizards.

Europa is still a cold, desolate place though, and as the Crown's main arms-manufacturing site outside the Detroit factories, it's still a government station first and foremost. The truth is, no matter what I spout to inquiring civilians, I'm not sure *how* Europa became a destination for shore leave. The surface is every bit as miserable as any other moon station or planetoid (excluding the colonies). Maybe the first Europa crew was fun-loving enough to get the ball rolling and the reputation eventually became self-fulfilling. Who knows?

Anyway, when we arrived on Europa Station three days after we broke the Moon's orbit and about a week before everything hit the fan, the crew of our ship, the *RSA Rockne Hummel,* was in high spirits. And why not? We had two days to ourselves before we set off on a supposedly routine escort mission, and there were three other ships docked on Europa along with us, which was excellent news. The more ships on Europa, you see, the more soldiers wandering around looking for a good time.

I'd barely breathed a word to the rest of the crew, so I was looking forward to getting to know them all a little better. Six months can feel like sixty if you don't get along with your crewmates, even if you're in stasis for a good portion of it. Truth be told, there was another reason I was excited to arrive on Europa though, and she wound up playing a considerable role in my Furnace nightmare.

I was raised in the suburbs twenty miles from Detroit. I went to a good school. I got good grades. The general consensus among my peers and elders coming out of high school was that I had a bright future ahead of me, which of course meant I was destined to enlist. The economic climate five years ago was pretty much the same as it is today, and the most stable, lucrative career for any kid right out of high school is still the fleet so long as you survive long enough to reap the benefits. With humanity's reach ever-expanding across the galaxy through mining operations, incentivized colonization, galactic trade, and scientific research, there's no shortage of open positions whether you prefer a combat role, manual labor, or the real brainy stuff. Most assignments beat a cubicle job by a long shot, and a lot of them beat working in the factories and warehouses in Detroit. College would have been even worse. I saw no point to going seven-figures in debt for a check-mark on my public record and no real employment prospects, especially when I could be four to five years deep in a successful military career by the time I was out, and with no debt to boot.

So, I made the jump.

I bring this up not to romanticize my rapid rise among the fleet ranks but because I knew a girl (I guess she's a full-blown *woman* now as rightly as I consider myself a man) from my high school days who'd enlisted in the fleet around the same time I did, and she was stationed on Europa at the time of the escort mission. Actually, I more than *knew* her. We were an item for a couple years as teenagers and sent letters back and forth while we were both enrolled at the academy. It gave us something to look forward to, a distraction from the physical and psychological torture that is astronaut training. At some point I started feeling the old way about her again, even though we'd ended things shortly after graduation. In other words, I had more than drinking on my mind when we docked.

For reasons I don't want to get into, I'd like to omit her name and rank from this report, or whatever they decide to call this. I've already provided the chief investigator with her identity in case she's needed for questioning, but for the purposes of this account, her name is irrelevant. I also want to clarify right now that I don't blame her in any way for what happened on Furnace or prior to it. She suggested a course of action as a fellow fleet navigator based on her own experiences and theories, and I could have easily decided not to listen. The calculations still seem spot-on each time I run through them, and the chief investigator's team has independently verified their accuracy. It's not her *formula* that's wrong, either. Greater minds have tested it at Sol Facility for years. Yet that's the only deviation we made from our assigned flight path between leaving Europa and arriving in Furnace's orbit, so it's hard not to be suspicious of the so-called 'shortcut' even while acknowledging she's not to blame. After all, at least a thousand ships have made that exact same run between Europa and our extraction point, and not one of them has encountered our problem as far as I know. Maybe they just didn't make it back to tell the tale.

After we landed, I followed the holo-map to my assigned quarters and threw my duffel on the bed, turning back toward the corridor without bothering to flip on the light and scope out my accommodations. I like to think of myself as a fairly easygoing individual (at least, as easygoing as a navigator can be; our kind tends to freak out when life doesn't go exactly as we plan), but failing to unpack my belongings in favor of immediate debauchery was a little much even for me. Yet I was about to sleep for a month. I didn't plan on spending much time in my quarters. And as long as I didn't get so bent out of shape in forty-eight hours that I couldn't program a course for Marvek (the human colony where we were scheduled to pick up an ambassador), I figured I would be all right.

Before I reached Europa Center and The Captain's Quarters though, one of my crewmates intercepted me. The pilot, I quickly realized. Tymoteusz Wolski. We called him Teemo.

"Chalmers," he grinned, making his tight, brown stubble stretch across his narrow cheeks. He slapped me on the back and turned me in the opposite direction.

"Teemo," I answered.

I did my best to sound carefree and happy to see him, but thinking back, I probably did a poor job of it. As much as I wanted to get to know the man better, especially given that pilots and navigators are supposed to be like the rhythm section of a spaceship, I was in a hurry. It had been a long, long time since I'd held a woman, and the fleet wasn't exactly the best place to strike up meaningful relationships. In time, I knew I might get friendly with some of my shipmates. Myself included, there were seventy-four souls on the *RSA Rockne Hummel*, and thirty-three of those seventy-four were female. I hadn't gotten to know any of them well enough to calculate whether there was intimacy potential beyond a work relationship, but I was hopeful. It was going to be a relatively long mission for a mid-sized vessel, after all, and we would be working in tight quarters during our duty shifts outside of hyper-sleep.

The woman waiting for me in The Captain's Quarters, however, was familiar territory. I didn't want to blow it.

"Where you headed?" Teemo asked.

I knew him well enough to see there was mischief in his eyes, but not well enough to realize I should have run screaming the moment the smirk rose to his lips. Luckily, I didn't learn my lesson from him that night. Or maybe *un*luckily, I guess. Maybe if he'd dragged me off somewhere and I hadn't met up with my old flame, we never would have wound up on Furnace. Or maybe fate would have brought us there anyway.

"The Captain's Quarters."

He scoffed. "The CQ? That place is shit!" He waved both hands and shook his head emphatically to be sure his point was well-received. One thing I learned quickly about Teemo was that he was a consummate showman. Nothing was ever simple or boring for him, if only because he was determined to act as though it wasn't. "No," he continued, giving my shoulder a sharp tug. "You're coming with me."

I forced a grin and tried to slip his grip. "Is that so?"

He nodded. "It must be."

That was the other thing about Teemo. No one expected him to speak English (the *lingua franca* has been Galactic Standard since First Contact) and he wasn't great at it, but he tried anyway whenever he was off-duty around Americans like myself. I can't say why. I certainly never learned Polish.

Planting my feet, I finally broke free and started in the opposite direction. "I'd love to, Teems, but I've got plans."

"Plans?" he frowned. "What kind of plans? Am I invited?"

I laughed, and this time the good humor was genuine. I could feel that I was in the clear, and memories of the girl waiting for me—the one I'd been daydreaming about ever since learning our mission included a stop at Europa—were suddenly so suffocating that I had trouble holding my legs steady beneath me. "Not this time. Maybe tomorrow."

Teemo studied me closely for a moment, then his grin stretched wider than I'd thought possible. "It's a lady, isn't it? You're going to meet a girl?"

I turned away with a smirk and shook my head.

"You bastard! Take me with you!" he exclaimed.

I waved him away and he was courteous enough not to follow. I can't imagine how awkward the meeting would have been with Teemo at our table. It was plenty awkward without him.

I won't bore you with the details of my night out, mostly because I'm afraid I'll slip up and tell you more than you need to know. I'm a firm believer that those sorts of things should remain private. Call me old-fashioned.

Anyway, once we were finished and I self-consciously hurried into my rec clothes on the side of my friend's bed, she placed her hand on my shoulder and drew me back to her. Her touch was cold. It made goose-flesh prickle across my skin.

"Here," she said. "I want to show you something."

The light in the room from the viewport was even worse than it had been in The Captain's Quarters, but any navigator knows a coordinate datapad when he (or she) sees one.

"What's this?" I asked, accepting the chart from her outstretched hand. It took all my willpower not to look her in the eye, and even more than that not to look further south, but I was uncomfortable and the datapad was a useful distraction.

Sitting up in bed without bothering to pull the sheet around her, she kissed me softly on the neck and tapped the screen. A new menu opened on the display. Star charts. Constellations. It didn't take me long to realize the destination she'd programmed was Marvek, exactly where the *Hummel* was headed. It took me longer to notice that the simulation course she'd set was different than the standard flight path for fleet ships.

"Just a theory we've been testing here," she said, wrapping an arm over my back and resting her chin on my shoulder so she could scan the readings along with me.

I stared at the rainbow schematics on the display screen, trying to make sense of the rapidly reassembling solar systems as the simulation ran at high speed. I was too disoriented to follow, either from the rapid progression of the fleet craft on the datapad or from being half-dressed in the middle of the night with my beautiful—and naked—companion making too much contact. A girl I'd loved since before I knew how to love.

"A theory on what?" I asked, trying hard to hide how clueless and small I felt.

The question triggered a change in her. She lost the sexy, dark-haired mystique and vulnerability that had melted my brain into my gravity-equalizing boots. In their stead rose the look of an appraising, powerful fleet officer who might as well have been wearing seven layers of clothing beneath a full spacesuit. In the end, I felt equally overwhelmed. Lost. Amateur. Swallowed by everything about her. We started dating as teenagers, remember. When you know someone that long, I think you subconsciously revert to your old self in new encounters with them, no matter how hard you try to exist as a separate, novel entity. Which is all to say that, in relationships, some things never change.

"We think we can cut the duration of supply runs in half using these launch points." She swiped her finger across the datapad to restart the simulation, tapped the screen to pause, and then pointed at a set of tiny, flashing blue dots spread across the galaxy. "Basically, if you circle these stars with the right propulsion and time your orbit-break perfectly, you can use them as a slingshot to the next point. It's not just the mass relationship of the star with the warp bubble that drives FTL travel anymore. They've been testing propulsion with naturally-occurring gravity slip-streams and plasma tubes on the Sol facility."

I furrowed my brow and stroked my stubble absently, watching the simulation again with renewed concentration. "Why only *these* stars?"

"Like I said, the presence of natural gravity slipstreams with a unique energy spike. We've identified them around these specific bodies so far. You can use any one of them, or all of them if you want to go *really* far." She dropped the datapad on the bed and shot me a sly grin. "It takes an *expert* navigator to pull it off, though. The coordinates have to be laid in manually during the slingshot." She fell back to the pillow and pulled at my gray rec shirt with eyes that positively glowed in the starlight. "If you don't want to try it because you don't think you can pull it off, I totally understand."

"Oh really?" I glared at her, feigning an injury to my pride that felt all too real.

Then she giggled and I couldn't hold back.

Some two days later when we re-boarded the *Rockne Hummel*, I presented her suggestion to Captain Gibbons. Based on my personal recommendation, he accepted the proposal—no doubt eager to return home—and two-thirds of us went into hyper-sleep. The rest kept watch, but they never saw what went wrong. It happened in the blink of an eye.

By the time I woke again, we were already screwed.

FURNACE

BEYOND

"That's impossible."

"I agree, but that's what the ship's telling us."

"We must have fried the systems somehow. Does it show any temporary blackouts? Did we pass through an electrical storm or something?"

"No, sir. Everything appears to be in working order, except the sensors say we're trillions of light-years beyond charted space."

Captain Gibbons stroked his beard, frowning. "Damn..."

Teemo punched in a few commands on the control console but, evidently, wasn't pleased with the results. He rubbed at his neck. "What was the last checkpoint we hit?"

I consulted the computer readouts on the holo-projector and shook my head. "I can't tell. We passed Pluto Station three days ago, but we don't register anything after that."

"This is bullshit!" Teemo shouted at the viewport while he jammed on the flight controls. "Is the screen down? I can't see anything! I'm flying blind!"

"Calm down, we're still on auto-pilot," Gibbons told him, then turned in my direction. "Where are we?"

My stomach did a somersault. I felt like I was going to vomit, probably from being ripped prematurely from hyper-sleep. I prayed it would be the only side-effect. "Like I said, sir, I have no idea. We're beyond charted space, even using the Tsoul maps."

The captain sighed and approached my station, where he examined the readings on my console to verify my findings. The extra set of eyes wouldn't have done much good even if I was wrong, of course. Navigation is a highly skilled trade. Even captains, even *good* captains, rarely understand what they're looking at when we submit readings for review or file a report. They are almost entirely dependent on our skills and expertise.

"Where are the stars, Chalmers?" he whispered, trying to prevent the others from hearing. It was no use, though.

The entire bridge crew watched us intently, even the Master Gunner, Lao Gang, who should have been one level below in the *Rockne Hummel's* Weapons Command station. Everyone wanted to know what the hell had happened and why they'd been yanked early from hyper-sleep. Waiting to jump down my throat, too, in all likelihood. Detours aren't exactly welcomed when you're out on the black sea. Especially when the readings tell you that the 'detour' took you so far from home that there's no conceivable way back.

"I don't know, Captain. The only reading I'm showing is a planetoid directly behind us. If the scans are right, there's nothing else within a quintillion miles at least."

"Wolski, turn us around," Gibbons commanded, returning to the captain's seat at the center of the bridge. "Our scanners are damaged. We'll have to fly manually until we find somewhere to make repairs. Chalmers, you said there's a planetoid behind us, right?"

I nodded before I realized he wasn't looking at me for a response. "Yes, sir. About eighty thousand miles off. Technically, it's not a planetoid, though. It's not orbiting anything."

"Can you land us there, Wolski?"

"Yes, sir."

"Then let's lower the shields and get a look out the window with our naked eyes. Lao, I expect you to be down at Weapons Command five minutes ago. You know protocol."

Lao Gang glared at the captain but slipped into the elevator before he could be rebuked.

Gibbons didn't seem to mind all that much. "Rosie, where are you? I need a damage assessment on our scanners. Maybe on the FTL drive, too, while you're at it. I want to know what the hell went wrong here."

I was itching to speak up, mainly to clarify to the captain and everyone else that I hadn't even *attempted* my lady friend's slingshot approach yet because we hadn't reached the star where I was supposed to try it. I may have altered our course toward the first glowing blue dot in her simulation, but I hadn't diverted beyond that in any respect. It was supposed to take us a while to get there. The captain knew that, I'm sure, but that didn't mean the rest of the crew did, and I didn't want to make a bad impression. A very thin layer of confusion was all that kept them from storming my station. I only had to glance at Sergeant Ronia Salib's scowl to know *she* was out for blood. The squad leader for our modest infantry complement (twelve soldiers who were essentially on a 'rest' mission after a prolonged period of heavy combat) wasn't one to cross, and that was on her good days.

"Bringing us about, sir," Teemo said.

Even in the throes of anxiety, I couldn't help but notice how perfect his Standard was in contrast to the way he usually butchered English. It made me wonder why he even attempted English at all. I guess it's not my problem.

"I want you heavy on those dials, Chalmers," the Captain told me. "If you catch so much as a fart on the scanners, I want to know everything about it."

"Yes, sir."

"In position," Lao Gang's voice boomed over the comm line. "All weapons prepped."

I winced at the Master Gunner's purposeful omission of 'sir' or 'captain'. Lao was the only one of us with balls big enough to act like he didn't give a damn about rank. Excluding, of course, the Crown Representative assigned to our mission, Elizabeth Gallagher, who bore the title of Quartermaster by default as long as she was hitching with us. She was a politician, though. A Crownie. Lao was fleet through and through, and most officers would have confined him to quarters for not addressing them properly, let alone doing it on purpose.

Not Captain Gibbons, though. Gibbons scared the hell out of me (which is a very good trait for your commanding officer to have) but he was a reasonable man who made allowances for protocol slip-ups during high-pressure situations. It seemed like most of those allowances were made for Lao by necessity, but that was no skin off my ass. I was perfectly happy keeping my head down until my name was called.

"Thank you, gunner," Gibbons replied. "Stand by."

It was clear this wasn't a combat situation so we all knew Lao would probably wind up standing-by for a very long time, twiddling his thumbs. But protocol was protocol, and it was there for a reason. It only took one slip-up with an enemy vessel nearby for us to punch our tickets to the great nothing, and our scanners couldn't always detect hostile crafts. Especially when they were malfunctioning.

"Sergeant Salib," Gibbons called, stroking his beard and turning the chair to face his staff sergeant. She was watching from the door with her trademark scowl hanging off her lips like an overused catchphrase. "Please wake the rest of the crew from hyper-sleep and make sure your troops are combat-ready."

"Yes, sir," she said, stepping through the doorway to the main corridor.

The captain turned to me and shrugged. "You can never be too careful."

"No, sir," I agreed, then turned back toward the viewport to do my job. I hadn't done so hot on the mission so far, and I was determined to make up for it if and when I was needed.

The moment my eyes focused in on the planetoid outside the window, though, a huge heat flare whipped up from the surface and slammed into the port bow of the *Hummel*.

I clenched my teeth. *Shit, The viewport shield is down*, I thought.

"Fuck!" Teemo shouted. He braced himself against the rebellious ship-controls. I was distantly aware of a sound like snapping branches from his station, and then the ship shook violently and I couldn't hear anything at all.

Warning lights started flashing. My display screen lost power momentarily and then flickered back to life. It may as well have died altogether for all the good it did me. Even if it had been functioning at maximum efficiency, I'd pointed out myself that there was only one ball of rock within a quintillion miles, and we could already see it with our naked eyes. For once, the consoles were useless.

To their credit, though, my nav scanners did pull one final reading from the planet's surface before gasping out completely, and it was a fairly useful one. It analyzed the atmospheric conditions of the planetoid, which allowed us to manually calibrate our shields for the emergency descent. It also helped us prep our suits for the ground mission, although that, too, turned out to be a pointless luxury. The planet adapted to *us* more than we adapted to *it*.

But that's getting ahead of myself. At the time, we thought we were finished. The idea of the surface had been driven from all our thoughts the moment the bridge went dark. Of course, the bridge was *always* dark in the sense that the only lights were some old movie theater-style dots on the floor and ceiling along with the glow of data screens at each station, but even those modest tubes went out in the wake of the fiery whip that struck us from the surface.

"Was that a goddamned *solar* flare?" the Captain asked incredulously, calmly pulling himself from the floor to reclaim his seat.

It wasn't technically a solar flare, but it sure as hell affected the *Hummel* like it was. Royal Space Armada (fleet) ships are built to withstand a hell of a beating, so the fact that our secondary shielding hadn't done shit to protect us—especially with our navigation systems down—was frightening. Whatever energy had caused the whip to reach so far off the surface packed one hell of a punch.

No one answered Captain Gibbons because no one had any data readings to confidently say one way or the other, but the confusion on the bridge was short-lived nonetheless. We were experienced fleet astronauts, remember. Not rookies. Not civilians. Each one of us was an expert in our respective field, otherwise they wouldn't have sent us out on a political mission in the first place. This was new territory for us, but almost every mission broke new ground in some way or another. In the grand scheme of things, after all, we're still in the early days of space exploration.

"Is everyone all right?" the captain asked.

A few anonymous voices confirmed that they had no major injuries, and then Teemo cursed and inhaled sharply. "I think I broke my arm, sir," he groaned.

Gibbons leapt from his chair and crossed the bridge to the pilot's station in two seconds flat. Before Teemo could protest, he yanked the controls from his hand and pushed into the chair with his hip. "Let me take us in, then," Gibbons told him. "Go have the doctor give you a look."

"Which one?"

The question was understandable (we had three crewmembers on board with the designation of 'doctor' and none of them were strictly medical) but Gibbons wasn't in the mood for hand-holding.

"I don't give a shit which one. Just get the hell out of my sight before I crash this goddamned ship."

Teemo staggered past me, looking wounded in more ways than one.

"Go see Sillinger," I whispered when he was close enough to hear it.

"Isn't Sillinger one of Ronia's brutes?"

"He's also a field medic. He'll fix that for you no problem. Besides, I don't think our esteemed doctors are awake yet. You might be waiting a while."

He frowned but nodded appreciatively. "Thanks," he told me.

I nodded back, then turned my attention to the captain. If we were going to land on that planetoid in the middle of nowhere, he would need all the help he could get whether my systems were functioning or not. I wasn't sure I'd be able to do anything at all, but I couldn't just sit on my hands and watch as we hurtled to our deaths.

"How we looking back there, Chalmers?"

I glanced down at my screens even though I knew they were blank. "I've got nothing, sir. All my systems are dead."

"Then why don't you get your ass up here and use your eyes?" Gibbons said calmly. He didn't look up from the planetoid.

"Yes, sir."

As I moved up toward the pilot's chair, I noticed the debris field between us and the atmosphere.

"You see that?" Gibbons asked.

"I see it." I squinted at the viewport, trying to discern what sort of debris we were dealing with. "What do you think it is?"

The Captain said nothing, and that worried me. If it was something as simple as a broken-up meteor caught in the planetoid's orbit, he would have reassured me right away. The fact that he didn't answer—and that he pointed out the field at all—told me he thought it was something else altogether.

And then I realized what we were looking at, probably half-a-minute behind the captain's realization.

It was a ship. Or *pieces* of a ship at least. It was impossible to tell what make it was or how long it had been out there, but it was undeniably ship debris, and undeniably alien. And there were more of them.

"Holy shit..." I muttered.

Luckily, the captain had more composure than I. He easily maneuvered our dying vessel through the debris field with minimal impacts. I didn't help at all. I merely gaped.

"The surface, sir."

"I see it, Lieutenant."

"It looks like it's *burning*."

Gibbons once again said nothing, and once again I took it to be a bad sign. A sign that he didn't know *how* to respond. He did, however, turn to me when we were about to enter the atmosphere of the dull-orange planetoid, which eerily reminded me of the view above Mars. "Why don't you go down and suit up with Ronia's squad?" he said. His hawk-eyes narrowed. His grip tightened audibly on the controls. "I've got a feeling we'll need a repair team on the double if we survive the landing. Might as well take Rosie with you, too, if you can find her."

I took a deep breath and flexed my palms to keep my voice from faltering. "Yes, sir," I said, and then left the bridge without another glance out the viewport. I didn't want to see the planetary-mass object any more than I was required to under the captain's orders. It was an ugly rock, and it wouldn't be long before I discovered just *how* ugly it truly was.

"All hands prepare for an emergency landing," Captain Gibbons' voice echoed down the corridor. In the darkness, with nothing but the backup lights to guide my way, he sounded devilish. Haunting. Mischievous. Grating. Every negative emotion I'd felt in my entire life balled into one miserable weight in my stomach.

In other words, I had a bad feeling about Furnace the moment we laid eyes on it. And it only got worse from there.

CASUALTIES

"Get a doctor!" Martavius, the shipswain, yelled.

"Which one?" someone responded. I can't remember who.

"I don't fucking care! She's not breathing!"

The stasis chamber was crowded. All of Sergeant Salib's soldiers had run from the armory across the hall to see about the commotion. They were trained to search for wounded on the battlefield, and to their credit, they responded swiftly and efficiently despite being in various states of surface-detail prep. It wasn't their fault they were too late.

Marty's wife, Latricia, never woke from hyper-sleep. Neither did Patrick the sous chef (a generous term for someone who heats frozen blocks of protein), or half the engineering team. The ones who'd been left in their pods a little longer because there was nothing they could do to help our situation.

Later, I would reflect on the seven deaths that occurred in the stasis chamber and realize that the hyper-sleep tubes had probably fried at the same time navigation went offline, but it doesn't really matter. There's no justification for senseless death. It's just a part of the experience in deep space. You grow numb to it, and you thank God that, this time, it wasn't you. That may make me sound like more of an asshole than I'd like to be, but it's the harsh truth, and it's my only comfort now.

Before I could process the flurry of activity around me, before even my extensive combat training kicked in and drove me to my wounded crewmates, Sillinger pushed roughly past me and squatted beside Marty's wife. Apparently, he'd already patched up Teemo's arm.

"She won't wake up?" He wiped sweat from his brow with the sleeve of his undershirt. He was a pale man. Always in the throes of some illness or another, whether it was a cold, flu, or general disagreement with the artificial atmosphere, but there was no doubting his skills as a field medic. He was equally artistic with a rifle and a laser scalpel, but the latter was often more useful. Like most of Ronia's squad, he was a rookie in terms of experience, but his composure rivaled most fleet officers I've served under.

"She's not even breathing!" Marty yelled, grabbing Sillinger by the shirt.

Marty was usually a cool customer, as far as I could tell. In his right mind, he would have realized how stupid it was to physically accost the one man on the ship capable of saving her life, but he was understandably shaken.

Sillinger pushed Marty away and unfastened the medical scanner from his belt. "There's a med-kit in the armory with an auto defibrillator."

Charlotte Rayford, a lanky, fair-skinned sniper from the infantry, nodded emphatically and exploded through the doorway to the locker room across the hall.

"Marty, I need you to hold Latricia's head up, okay? She swallowed a lungful of stasis fluid when the systems shut down and I think it's solidified in her chest. We need to keep her upright and try to break up the fluid so she can breathe."

Marty calmed considerably, glad to have something to keep his hands occupied. Glad he felt like he was doing something to save her. One look into Sillinger's eyes, though, and I knew it was too late. And not just for Marty's wife Latricia, who I hadn't spoken a word to since we'd launched from Earth. No one had even *attempted* reviving the others from stasis. I guess we were all scared the same thing would happen again. It turned out that our instincts were correct, but that doesn't excuse the fact that cowardice was primarily responsible for our paralysis.

Anyway, we all knew Latricia was dead. If she wasn't breathing, then she'd aspirated the stasis fluid into her lungs. Even if she could have been revived at that point, she'd either wind up dying of pneumonia or suffer such extensive brain damage from the lack of oxygen that she'd be in a vegetative state indefinitely.

To his credit, Sillinger did everything he could. Mostly for Marty's sake. Charlotte reappeared with the med-kit shortly after, and the rest of us just gaped in stunned silence while they tried the defibrillator before turning to a few less archaic field treatments from the kit. Nothing worked, and Marty's desperate pleas to no one in particular grew higher-pitched and more gut-wrenching with each passing moment. I felt like I'd swallowed a bowling ball, but I couldn't take my eyes off him.

I left before it was over. Not because I was too yellow to hear Sillinger's pronouncement or because I wasn't a good enough man to help Marty through the ordeal, but because I had a job to do. If we didn't figure out how to fix the ship soon, I reasoned, we'd all be following Latricia into the great nothing. I was determined not to let that happen.

And I'd never been so scared in my life.

I found Sergeant Salib waiting at the airlock door, SX rifle at the ready, flanked by a half-dozen soldiers in combat suits eagerly awaiting active duty. Combat gear, mind you, is considerably less cumbersome than the bulky plates set aside for the ship's navigator. It's not so bad once you get used to it—hell, I actually *prefer* it to the infantry reg suits nowadays—but I still wasn't used to it then. I made a mental note to let *them* do most of the actual work, since my hands wouldn't grip the relay conduits as well as they could with their mildly adhesive gloves. The infantry gloves are designed so soldiers can steady their rifles easier and rattle off accurate shots, but everyone on the ship winds up using them at one time or another, whether for something actually practical like staying attached to the ship on spacewalks, or as a tool for bad practical jokes. I'll let your imagination do the work on that rather than take the time to explain, but I will say even a mild adhesive can pull off a hell of a lot of body hair.

"What are *you* doing here?" Sergeant Salib scowled.

"Captain's orders, sir," I answered.

"Captain's orders? How the hell is a nav rat gonna fix the ship?"

I shrugged because I wasn't sure about it myself. Probably the captain just wanted me off the bridge for a while so he could think, or maybe he'd seen my record in the infantry and wanted an extra gun in case something bad went down. I couldn't imagine *why*, actually, but I guess that's why he was the captain. "He says you could use the help since half the engineering crew is down, sir," I lied, careful to avoid the word 'dead' even though I'd just seen the vitals on the stasis pods up close and personal. I don't think Captain Gibbons even knew about them yet, but it seemed logical enough to me.

"Fine," Salib relented. "Just stay at the back of the line. We're running a tight perimeter until we know what's out there. The goddamned sensors are blind."

No shit, I thought. "Yes, sir." Sometimes people forget that the navigation systems are only slightly lower on the power relay hierarchy than life-support and helm controls. If *my* screen goes dark, *everyone's* screen below bridge level should be dark. It's just the way the fleet prioritizes. Life support so you're around long enough to get creative on escape routes, then helm control for evasive maneuvers in case you're under attack, then navigation so your getaway ride doesn't crash into the side of a moon. From there, the list is up for a little more interpretation based on the computer's assessments. You know, whether the situation necessitates weapons, electropulses, etc. All that's to say that the grunt workers are a low priority while the ship is off the ground, especially aboard the *Rockne*. We had two measly shuttles and no fighters, all damaged in the flare, so even combat pilots wouldn't have done us any good.

Salib's twelve soldiers formed a tight line in front of me. They listened intently as she ran through her check-downs and assigned mission priorities, which mostly consisted of singling out the half-dozen boot-troops too slow with a hover-wrench to perform repairs, then instructing them to just watch for trouble and make sure their weapons were pointed away from the ship. Real rousing stuff. I didn't pay much attention to the logistics because I *was* good with a hover-wrench, but Salib's delivery had exactly the amount of invigorating venom and irritation you would expect from a Sergeant addressing her troops.

"Nav rat," she shouted back to me once her speech was complete and her troopers had begun powering their weapons.

"Yes, sir?"

"Stay the hell out of the way and do whatever you've gotta do in a hurry."

"Yes, sir."

She glared at me with dark eyes that could have swallowed me whole. They might have with another moment or two. I was given a reprieve, however, when she pressed a button on her shoulder and the arch of the glass-domed helmet snapped into place over her head.

The countdown on the airlock began. Fifteen seconds until the surface.

"Thirty minutes, fuckwads," Salib shouted. "Any dicking around and I'll shoot every damn one of you myself."

I'd like to say it was an empty threat for the sake of the fleet's image, but that's not really accurate and I'm aiming for full disclosure. The ugly truth is that officers kill their subordinates with alarming regularity during deep space missions if it helps them prove a point, and the soldiers are more than willing to keep their mouths shut about it so long as it isn't their corpse on the other end of the rifle. Shit happens in deep space. Tensions rise. Small mistakes can cost an entire crew their lives. There's little tolerance for fuckery of any sort, and especially little during a critical ground mission on an uncharted planet. In those situations, God only knows what fresh hell awaits once the airlock doors open.

"Five seconds. Helmets on. Weapons armed. Feet moving."

I was about to find out.

FURNACE

GROUND

When the airlock hissed open and hot dust exploded into our line of troopers, my first instinct was to reach for the ghost of the SX rifle I'd carried during my infantry days and take cover until I spotted an enemy target through the cloud. In the confusion, even Salib's troops—fresh on the heels of their Sergeant's death-threats toward anyone who lost control during the mission—ducked reflexively and sought shelter against the airlock walls.

Damn, I thought. It was going to be an uphill battle getting to the surface, even though the ramp was on a downward slope. The wind tore through us so violently that it was difficult to keep my footing even with the gravity-equalizing boots holding fast to the steel.

Those first few moments were chaos. In retrospect, we weren't even *close* to prepared for the surface conditions. But in our defense, we went in blind. It's easy to get rattled that way, even for combat vets. The success of a mission, Gibbons used to say, is predicated on the preparedness of the soldiers. Knowing the enemy. The weather. Where to look and what to look for. We had no idea what we were getting into.

The debris that pinged loudly against our spacesuits was unsettling on its own, but what really put everyone on edge was the grating, persistent screech riding on the wind. It was so loud that I couldn't hear Salib's voice over the comm link even though I saw her lips moving. I tried to cover my ears, forgetting my helmet was locked and also that I was carrying a charge-pistol in my right hand. Others, maybe soldiers with more sensitive eardrums than my own or maybe ones who'd just left the volume too high on their comms and had to deal with the amplification, fell straight away, dropped their weapons, and started screaming. As with Salib, I couldn't actually *hear* their screams, but I *saw* them well enough.

Salib stomped back up the ramp and grabbed one of the soldiers by the forearm. She was livid. Her squad looked weak and she wouldn't stand for it, even if it was understandable given the circumstances. I couldn't tell who she'd singled out at the time because his back was to me, but I discovered later that it was Ensign Tomas Chara. For the sake of this report, it should be noted that he was the first field casualty on Furnace, although I'm not sure what the official designation is for a soldier who kills *himself* before the bullets start to fly.

Poor bastard.

Salib shook him a few times, kicked him in the stomach plating, and then tapped his helmet with the barrel of her SX-60, trying to get his attention. It didn't do much good. He just kept writhing around the airlock ramp, clutching the sides of his helmet like he was trying to dig to his eardrums.

I'm not sure what pushed him over the edge. No one else is, either. It happened too suddenly.

We all watched in horror as Chara rolled onto his stomach and convulsed until his momentum and the shuddering contortions of his body worked him into the fetal position. At first, I didn't consider it much more than an overreaction or hypersensitivity to external stimuli, which is common on an unknown planet. Maybe the strain of space travel had been too much for him and this was just a manifestation of deeper problems. God knows it's happened enough in the fleet to justify the notion. But then, he started clawing at his helmet so violently that at least two of his fingers snapped inside his gloves, and that's when I knew it was something worse than minor agitation. He'd crossed the border into full-blown psychosis.

I stumbled in his direction, probably shouting, "Shit!" or something equally eloquent, but the comm log is either lost or indecipherable so I guess there's nothing to corroborate that particular detail. Matter of fact, we don't have anything to prove the incident itself other than anecdotal evidence. Our sensors were offline, so no one has been able to verify whether or not Chara suffered any fractures before he pulled the plug, but I guess it doesn't matter to anyone but me. Knowing would help me make some sense of it, I suppose. Sometimes, though, we just aren't given that luxury.

"Tom!" I *know* I shouted that out loud, because I remember thinking how strange it was that I'd never used his first name until that moment, and I still couldn't get it right. Like Teemo, Chara was proud of his heritage. Under other circumstances, he would have kicked my ass if he'd heard me call him anything other than Ensign Chara or Tomas.

Salib was busy cussing him out when the first trickle of blood fell from his earlobes, and she still hadn't finished by the time he pressed the retrieval button on his helmet and the glass dome slid back into his suit. After that, she shut up completely—a rare feat for Salib when her troops were performing below her expectations—and the entire squad, even the ones who'd been doubled-over in agony, scrambled to reverse Chara's fatal mistake before it was too late.

But it wasn't a mistake, and we *were* too late. And, lacking sensors, we didn't understand the composition of the atmosphere at that point so we didn't know to stay away from him until it was too late to avoid another unpleasant surprise. In many ways, it was the worst part of all.

Within moments of lowering his helmet, Chara's head exploded, showering the entire squad with blood, bone, and brain-matter from head to toe. Even with my helmet firmly locked over my face and my body covered in Kevlar and metal alloys, I flinched when the splash hit. I don't know if it was revulsion so much as utter shock, but I had trouble opening my eyes again for a few moments. I didn't want to see the aftermath, and I still hadn't fully grasped the gravity of the situation.

I was frozen, ruminating on how we'd been obliviously coasting through neutral space only an hour earlier, our minds occupied by anything and everything other than the possibility of watching a fellow soldier's head explode on a scorching, desolate planetoid in the middle of nowhere.

It was sobering. It was surreal. It had me on the verge of utter hysteria, and it didn't take much imagination to realize I wasn't alone in that regard.

I might never have moved from my crouch at the foot of the ramp if Salib hadn't punched me straight in the chest. Even in a full suit, the impact jarred me out of combat shock. With the infantry's electrical arm-bolt charges and the sergeant's considerable strength, she packed a hell of a punch.

My eyelids snapped open immediately. Salib stood less than a foot away, motioning frantically toward the dust-veiled, dull-orange tundra. Evidently she'd realized that she couldn't out-voice the screeching wind, but also knew she needed to get us moving to shake the paralyzing effects of Chara's death. And it *was* a paralyzing event for us, especially on the heels of watching Marty's wife die in the stasis chamber. I can personally attest to that.

No matter how hardened you become against death at sea and in the trenches, exploding heads and spousal farewells always melt your heart and your composure. If they don't, you don't have any business serving in the fleet in the first place, because you've clearly lost sight of why we do what we do. I know how *ra-ra* that sounds, and I certainly have my own issues with the fleet, but a cold heart goes well beyond regulations and combat training. It's an issue of humanity, and it's easy to lose it among aliens even without brushing it aside yourself.

Anyway, Salib avoided a major catastrophe by getting us all focused again, even if it was only a temporary fix. I calmly engaged the sight filters on my glass helmet and ran through my noise-cancelling sub-programs until I found one at the right frequency. After that, I could think a little. Not to maximum capacity, but enough to effectively remove my head from my ass.

There were still a couple soldiers on their knees along the ramp or on the ground scrambling to calibrate the systems in their suits, but nine other squad members had regained their nerve and were taking defensive positions around the ship. We had to move quickly. There was a lot to do still and the squad hadn't requested assistance from engineering with the mechanical work, which struck me as odd. Maybe because half the engineering crew had perished in the crash.

I figured Salib was supposed to perform the evaluation herself, in that case. She was the only member of her team even remotely qualified to diagnose ship malfunctions from the outside, after all. But since the captain had sent me along for the ride and Rosie (better known as Lieutenant Iglesias, our engineer) was nowhere to be found, I grabbed the repair kit from the extended airlock ramp and hustled to the surface.

Damn, I realized halfway down. *It's my fault. I was supposed to get Rosie from engineering before we pressurized.*

I'd fucked up again. Salib should have known that and reminded me, of course, but that doesn't vindicate me. Having comm systems damaged ship-wide certainly contributed to my negligence though, and that's not an excuse so much as a frustrating fact. If the comms had been operational when I'd exited the bridge, I could have called down to engineering and Rosie would have known to meet us at the airlock. But my head had been a mess then and I'd forgotten once I reached the lower decks.

The death of Marty's wife shook me, which I guess makes me a good little human. Looking back, it's amazing I even remembered to initialize the oxygen and gravity equalizers on my suit before exiting the *Rockne* in that mental state. As far as this particular mission goes, though, forgetting to fetch Iglesias was a relatively minor offense. It's low on the totem-pole even among my personal indiscretions. Besides, I'm sure Rosie had her hands full in engineering, though I never thought to ask her. It's a reasonable assumption, I'd say. There was more than enough damage on the inside to keep her busy.

With the dust swirling around me, I never got a good look at the lay of the land during that disastrous recon and repair. By the time I reached the bottom of the ramp and worked my way behind the line of soldiers to the exhaust ports for the FTL drive, my adrenaline was pumping so furiously I could barely grip the emergency repair kit, and that wasn't like me at all. Like I've said, I saw plenty of crazy shit during my infantry days. I stared down the white eyes of death more times than you could ever imagine during the Kalak War. I bagged thirty-seven lizards in the Battle for Titan and was held captive by Tsoul terrorists for six weeks orbiting Mars before I grifted one of their spacesuits and hopped out an airlock (no thanks to the indifferent Crown for that escapade, who refused to negotiate with 'terrorists' while I was left to foot the bill for their principles).

I'm not mentioning these things because I want you to marvel at my galactic conquests or sterling fleet career. I'm just trying to paint you a picture that I was no first-term recruit with cabbage behind the ears. For me to quake with adrenaline when there were no enemies in the immediate vicinity and with no less than twelve trained fleet soldiers watching my back, it was clear something wasn't right. It does make a certain kind of sense, though. I'm a navigator, and navigators as a rule don't like to lose their bearings, especially when there isn't a star visible and yet the ground beneath our feet is burning hot. On top of that, for all the missions I'd run out in neutral space, I hadn't arrived on an uncharted planet until that day. The possibilities were terrifying. Exciting too, I guess, but mostly terrifying.

I could have been fine, though. I could have held it together in spite of my overwhelming paranoia and sense of displacement. In fact, I even managed to set the scan and repair kit down on the warm, dusty rocks and unbuckle three of the four clasps before I felt a presence behind me and my fingers locked up.

"What ..." I gasped.

I guess I was a little jumpy. With good reason, as it turned out.

I turned slowly, alarmed but attempting to save face in case it was just a soldier taking position to shield me from the wind and the theoretical hostile natives. Part of me is still sure that's what it was, because that's the trust they drill into you during training. You'd think it would be the other way around to keep us on our toes, but there have been far too many missions on peculiar planets where soldiers get a little too excited and shoot to kill. That's why they discourage trigger-happy behavior in Basic. The death toll on excursions to uncharted planets is about ninety percent friendly fire. Usually, if there are potential hostiles on the surface, we know well in advance of landing.

I kept my head about me as well as I could, but when I looked over my shoulder, there was no one around. Not any more, anyway. I did spot something, though. It was there one moment and gone the next, but it chilled me ten times more than watching the death of Marty's wife and seeing Chara's head explode combined.

It was my mother's severed head, rolling across the dull-orange earth like a macabre tumbleweed.

"Jesus Christ..."

My stomach rose into my lungs. I fell against the side of the ship and stared at it with wide-eyed horror.

And then, it was gone. I was left trembling beneath a smashed FTL drive with blue smoke billowing from the starboard exhaust vents.

"All right, Sergeant," I said into my (finally) functioning comm link, deciding then and there that I'd had enough. "Scanner's broken," I lied. "There's nothing we can do from the outside until we get it running again." My voice was surprisingly level. Thank God for small favors. I couldn't think of anything more traumatizing than recounting my experiences between the stasis chamber and the severed head in detail. Even then, I knew it would cause my mind to fracture. "I'm heading back."

Salib cursed under her breath but she must have felt something, too, because she was already waving her troops back up the ramp.

I re-buckled the kit and followed the squad before I heard the order. It was the first of many direct fleet-reg violations I committed during my approximately twenty-six hour visit to Furnace.

I don't think I've ever run so fast in my life.

DAMAGE ASSESSMENT

"What's the status of the engines, Rosie?" the captain asked.

About a dozen of us were seated around an anchored steel table in the tactical briefing room. Everyone was on edge, Salib most of all. I think seeing her that way got everyone else wound even tighter. Salib didn't rattle easily, especially in combat situations. You might have been able to catch her stammering if an officer quizzed her on fleet protocols beyond combat directives, but in all other situations, she was stone-cold steel.

Rosie sighed and rubbed sweat from her brow with a grease-smeared palm. "I couldn't tell you. As long as the sensors are off-line, we're running dark. We all know what we're doing but we can't say for sure how close we are to fixing the FTL drive until we can verify it with the scanners, and we don't know how background systems are being affected by the repairs we're making. I've got most of my crew working on bringing critical systems back online, and then we'll see where we're at."

Gibbons frowned but nodded. Rosie's report must have been exactly what he'd expected, but it looked like he'd held out hope for a better prognosis anyway. Hearing 'I don't know' from his Engineering Officer probably didn't make him feel very good. It sure as hell didn't make me breathe any easier.

"We need the long-range comms running again immediately," Elizabeth Gallagher interjected from across the table. Rosie stiffened and Gibbons shifted uncomfortably in his chair at the sound of her voice. The rest of us remained completely still and silent.

Gallagher was the Crown Representative for our mission and also the acting Quartermaster, remember, meaning she was charged with ensuring every action we took was in the best interest of the Crown. There's one of them on every RSA ship, but Gallagher is by far the highest-ranking rep with whom any of us had ever flown. She was assigned to our mission because Rep. Dirlika Heindorf—the politician we were scheduled to extract from a backwater colony so the two reps could negotiate a trade alliance with a Fronov delegation—was even a few rungs *higher* in the Crown hierarchy than Gallagher, and that was saying something. They carried a lot of weight, and Gallagher wasn't shy about letting the crew know it. Basically, if we fucked up, she made it clear that the fleet generals would hear of it. We'd probably be relegated to desk-jockey duty on Pluto.

So I'm betting you can guess how popular she was with the crew.

I liked Gallagher from the start. She was elitist, no-nonsense, and abrasive, but there was a weightlessness about her expressions which was endearing nonetheless. Her intellect and grasp of ship operations impressed me from the moment we left port, and I'd been hoping to get to know her a little better ever since she'd reported me to Gibbons for failing to complete our Europa landing log until our departure checks. I'm not sure what this says about me, but her sheer disregard for the feelings of our crew made me want to matter in her eyes even more.

Of course, it didn't hurt that she was goddamned beautiful, although I suspect some of her allure was just the constant reminder of her status. You couldn't even look at her without thinking there was a chance she would someday wind up in the Big Chair wearing the Crown, and who doesn't want to be the one sleeping beside the most powerful woman in the solar system?

"Agreed," Rosie said diplomatically, shrugging off Gallagher's command. "Long range comms are definitely a priority. We'll work as quickly as we can."

I wonder what it's like to date a politician, I thought.

Gibbons watched me closely while my mind wandered, though I didn't realize it was wandering at all until Elizabeth looked me in the eye and caught me staring. Luckily, the captain interjected before I fumbled out an apology that would only have increased the tension in the room. We were all uncomfortable.

"Chalmers," he said. "Once we get the engines up and running, what will you need to get us out of here?"

I cleared my throat and leaned over the table, watching the imprint of my palm fade from the surface. "Well, to be blunt, I need to know where the hell we are, sir. Even a general constellation to point us in the right direction. I don't see a planet or star or *anything anywhere* with the naked eye, and that's all we've got to go on right now." I shrugged and leaned back in the chair. "I mean, it's amazing the surface is even illuminated and north of absolute zero, let alone *hot*. When you think about it, that should be impossible."

"I'm aware of the situation outside, Lieutenant," Gibbons said softly. "What I need to know is which *exact* systems you need operational in order to get us the hell out of here. Now pull your head out of your ass and tell us how we can help you do your goddamned job."

I gaped at him. The entire room froze around me. They were staring in my direction to see how I'd respond.

Shit...

I'd never seen the captain look at me with such stern, unyielding contempt in his eyes. I'd always been one of his favorites, so it was more than a little jarring to see him call me out like that for no greater fault than nervously rambling in the face of extreme stress. More importantly, in the wake of watching people die on an uncharted planet while I stood idly by, unable to help them in any way. It was the sort of thing for which I'd normally receive a week of recup time just for seeing outside a battlefield, and *two* weeks under Captain Gibbons. I never would have expected to be confronted before the *Hummel's* officers for a simple nervous reaction. I was goddamned tired, after all, and goddamned sure I was about to die without ever setting foot on Earth's humble shores again.

But the fleet doesn't *really* give a shit about that, anyway. They don't care what we see or what happens to us out there. Not once we're far enough from investigative journalists that they don't have to worry about PR. Besides, they know that a soldier like me with an eye on advancement would never breathe a word of dissent. The risk of subtle but thorough retribution is far too high. Like I've said many times before, I've never been keen on working Pluto Station or mining some godforsaken asteroid in the middle of nowhere with no hope of seeing real combat unless the local colony starts an uprising.

No thank you, ma'am.

Anyway, Gibbons' snap reaction was a clear indication to me—and likely to everyone in the room who'd served under his command for more than five minutes—that he was starting to crack.

Gibbons? I thought, checking myself. *No way.*

Of all the miserable captains I've had the pleasure or misfortune of meeting during my service in the fleet, he was the last man I ever thought would cave to pressure so early in the game. The situation was dire, of course, but we hadn't even been grounded for three hours at that point. I knew Gibbons, and that meant I knew he was made of harder stuff.

Hard enough that I couldn't truly believe he was flipping his can while I (somewhat) held it together in spite of all the shit I'd seen. That—more than anything—made me hesitate before I responded.

"I'm sorry, sir," I finally managed through tight, dry lips and a curtain of heavy stares. "I guess the most important thing for the time being is just to get the engines running and life-support stabilized. Once we have all that taken care of and the hull breaches are patched up, I can jump us a safe distance from...whatever this place is...and we can start figuring out how to get back."

Assuming we can get back, I thought.

As a navigator, the complete absence of starlight in space was considerably troubling. Hell, *more* than troubling. It shook me to the very core, and it still does. Before I saw it with my own eyes that day, I would have told you there was no conceivable point in any universe where at least a *distant* star wasn't visible. I guess that may still be true considering the way things turned out, but it still bears careful consideration going forward. At the very least, the absence of constellations told me that we were far beyond the reach of any fleet ship in the history of human spaceflight, and that the chances of us returning home before we died of old age— even with the stasis tubes—were not very good.

My assessment passed without comment from Gibbons, and that slipped my already foul mood from bad to worse.

"Agreed," Elizabeth finally said, just to break the silence. I could see that she was fuming, but I didn't understand why until much later when I found out she was just as terrified as the rest of us. "For the time being, we'll have to focus on patching the ship from the inside."

"Damn right," Salib cut in. "No fucking way I'm going back out there."

"And Captain Gibbons," Elizabeth continued as though she hadn't heard Salib's comment at all. God, I admired her.

"*Would* have provided that assessment himself, were he in his right mind." She paused, allowing the accusation to sink in. "For the sake of this ship, Captain, and the wellbeing of all her crew, I strongly suggest that you return to your quarters and read over fleet regulations on what's expected from a captain at a time like this in order to survive."

Her voice quivered ever so slightly over the last four words. So subtle I don't think the others even noticed. They were too shocked by her audacity, anyway. Probably annoyed, too. After all, whether she was right or not, she worked for the Crown. The infuriating, out-of-touch dictators who commanded us to perform suicide missions with no comparable payoff while they farted around in Geneva pulling each other off and writing speeches. Gibbons, on the other hand, had been through Hell and back on the front lines like the rest of us. Gallagher really had no right to talk to him that way, and especially to lecture him on the virtues of captaincy.

And, in spite of my dedication to Gibbons, it made me like her even more.

For a moment, we all watched the captain struggle to keep hold of himself while he decided whether or not to contest the point. Whether or not, in other words, duty and hierarchical constructs were worth honoring when the universe itself had slipped right out from under us. In the end, he must have decided that the lives of the crew were, in fact, more important than proving a point to some bigwig who would probably beat us all to the fiery clutches of death on that strange new world.

"My apologies, ma'am," he told her with a contemptible grin. "The strains of the situation have clouded my judgment. It won't happen again."

I remember thinking he probably wouldn't get a chance to prove it.

To break the tension, and also subtly reaffirm her support for the captain, Salib rose and stepped between Gallagher and Gibbons. "What are your orders, sir?" she asked with a stiff salute, using her back to block Gallagher's view of the rest of the table.

Gibbons grinned ever so slightly and stood to return the salute. "Have your team comb the ship and make sure all hull breaches are sealed." He paused and frowned in deep thought. "Also, it wouldn't be a bad idea to get someone to take a roll call. Matter of fact, bring everyone we have on board to the gymnasium and have them sound off. We don't want anyone wandering off until we know the dangers of the planet."

"I don't think we'll need to worry about anyone *voluntarily* leaving the ship at this point," Gallagher remarked.

Stepping around Salib, the captain hovered over the Crown Representative with a look of naked disdain. "I'm not worried about what's *outside* of the ship, Representative. I'm worried about what might have found its way in when we opened the airlock. Something could have crawled in through the vents, or any one of the dozens of hull breaches Rosie's conjectured." His eyes were squinted with fury but his voice was remarkably reserved.

It was interesting to watch him draw back into himself in the silence that followed. Like watching prey recoil after a defensive strike to intimidate a predator, only I couldn't imagine someone as battle-hardened as Gibbons saw a Crownie—even Gallagher—as anything but a nuisance. A harmless fly.

Towards the end of the diffusing silence, Gibbons caught my stare from across the table, and when he spoke again, it was like he spoke directly to me. The words and his intense gaze sent chills up and down my spine.

"Something bad might have infiltrated the ship. Something that can kill all of us. An alien, a pathogen. Maybe not. Who knows? Either way, we need to gather everyone together to make sure it *won't* happen if it hasn't already. I don't give a damn if anyone on this crew decides they want to leave the ship, but I sure as hell won't be picking up any hitchhikers." He paused thoughtfully, then turned for the door. "I've been down that road before."

I wasn't sure which mission he was referring to, but I didn't want to ask. I was afraid the specifics would stray a little too close to our current situation.

Have I told you I've always known I would die at the hands (or tentacles or stingers or teeth) of some hideous, alien monster on a planet far away from home?

No?

Well, maybe I'll get there eventually. I guess Gibbons and I had more in common than I ever realized.

ASSIGNMENT

An hour later, an hour which I spent nervously pacing the gym and trying to look busy while carefully avoiding all matters of consequence, the captain changed his mind.

"Teemo. Chalmers," he called into the all-purpose gymnasium through the open doorway. His voice echoed across the court to me yet somehow had a small quality to it that made my stomach clench. If even *his* voice was trivialized within our ship, I reasoned, what did that say about our place in the universe? "My quarters. Now."

I glanced around the room as I followed Gibbons, trying to spot Teemo and get a read on his reaction to the summons. I couldn't find him anywhere, though. Probably he'd already followed the captain out, I thought, or else he'd returned to his seat on the bridge after getting his arm patched up. I've learned over the years that fleet pilots are practically incapable of relinquishing control of anything once they believe they're responsible for handling it, and nothing about my previous interactions with Teemo made me think he was an exception.

Halfway to the door, I felt a firm tug on my arm and whirled around reflexively, ready to lash out for no good reason. Like I said, I was on edge.

It was Gallagher. Her blue eyes were wide with something that wasn't quite terror. Maybe suspicion with a touch of hopelessness. Maybe I'm confusing her emotions with my own.

"What is it, ma'am?" I asked once I realized she was looking past me through the open door. Probably making sure Gibbons wasn't standing in the shadows, watching.

"Chalmers, right?" she asked when she was sure the captain had moved on.

"Yes, ma'am," I answered, only slightly offended that she hadn't known my name well enough not to ask.

"Nice to meet you," she said stiffly. We'd met about a half-dozen times before that, but I let the comment slide with a little more understanding than the name thing, which I guess is counterintuitive. Something about the follow-up, though, made me realize she had noticed me enough to at least recognize my face. That was good. She'd met a whole lot of fleet monkeys since she'd boarded the *Rockne Hummel*, after all, and apparently, I'd made a lasting impression. Even in the face of certain death, I took it as a small victory.

"Yes, ma'am."

Her eyes narrowed and she touched my right hand lightly. "Do me a favor, will you?"

"Ma'am?" I tried to act like I didn't notice her touch at all, but I have a feeling I failed miserably.

"Come see me as soon as you're done speaking with the captain. I want to know everything he has to say."

So that's *what this is*, I thought. *She wants me to spy on my own goddamned captain.*

I didn't like the idea at all. What sort of fleet soldier would I be if I tattled on my captain to a Crownie?

"May I ask why, ma'am?"

Her fingers slipped from my hand abruptly and she took a self-conscious step back, like she hadn't realized we'd been touching at all. "I need to know his frame of mind to evaluate whether or not he's fit to command this vessel through a crisis."

I hesitated, glancing over my shoulder at the open doorway. Like her, I wanted to be sure the captain hadn't seen me conspiring. It didn't feel right at all, especially considering how I'd specifically requested a position on Gibbons' crew and he'd offered me the job, overlooking a half-dozen more qualified candidates who'd been relegated to supply missions instead.

Aside from that, her request made me especially uncomfortable because it was *my* fault we'd wound up on that godforsaken planetoid in the first place, and *my* garbled calculations that had presumably led to the captain being unfit for command, though I never truly bought that assessment from Gallagher. Not until later, anyway, when my chance to prevent his rampage had already passed. Yet another thick coat of blood on my hands for my failures on Furnace. At the time, though, Gallagher's suspicions seemed more than a little hasty considering Gibbons hadn't yet made any irrational or psychotic decisions.

But I couldn't articulate all that to Gallagher on the spot and wouldn't have wanted to anyway. "I'm not sure I'm comfortable with that, ma'am," I said instead.

I knew it was a mistake the instant the words left my lips. She was a goddamned Crownie, after all, and one of the bigshots at that. You don't refuse a direct order from someone like her unless you're prepared to fix sewage leaks on civilian luxury spacers, or spend ten to fifteen years in a forced labor camp in Bali. But she caught me off guard, and I was worried someone would overhear us.

As it turned out, there was no need to fret. Gallagher was kind in her own way. Understanding enough of the position she was putting me in, at least, though presumably not enough to spare me the headache.

"I understand, Lieutenant," she said, eyeing the insignia on my sleeve to catch my rank. "But I'm not asking you to make that determination for me. I'm simply asking you to report back on what he has to say, which I am *legally* authorized to find out for myself if I choose. I have the authority to go anywhere on this ship that I damn well please, *including* the captain's quarters. If I wanted to make a big scene about it, I would have. Instead, I'm asking you to simply report the facts after your conversation. Are you able to do that?"

I nodded slowly, feeling small. "Yes, ma'am. Sorry, ma'am."

She smiled and patted me softly on the arm. "Thank you."

We locked eyes for a moment, then she turned away before I even thought to salute.

Once she'd passed through the doorway, I took a quick look around and realized that practically everyone in the room was staring at me. Some with suspicion, some disdain, some merely bored or scared or desperate for a distraction from the waiting game, no matter how trivial the distraction proved to be. I can hardly blame them, but it made me feel a lot worse about talking to Gallagher, and I worried they'd seen right through my half-hearted protest against reporting on my captain to anyone other than fleet command. More than that, I worried they'd noticed how small I'd felt in Gallagher's presence, whether it was a result of her rank or my own insecurities.

I hurried down the corridor without stopping to acknowledge the repair crew, even when a couple soldiers from Salib's team tried to flag me down to assist. I wasn't about to keep the captain—or Gallagher—waiting any longer than I needed to, and time truly was of the essence with life-support running out and given our lack of progress in finding a way home. I hoped Gibbons had regained his wits since the meeting and formulated a better plan of attack, but one step into his quarters assured me that he hadn't quite regained that level of sanity.

"Shut the door," he told me.

I did.

Teemo stood at full attention in front of the captain's wooden desk. His hands were glued firmly to his sides despite the cast on his broken arm. His stare rested somewhere between the ventilation ducts and the top of Gibbons' head. Like a good little soldier. That wasn't anything like Teemo. I could tell he was scared.

"Yes, sir?" I asked. I glanced at the door control to make sure it remained unlocked in case things went bad, then took my place beside Teemo.

"I want the two of you to join Salib's team for a surface mission."

I swallowed hard. My stomach dropped. I couldn't believe what I was hearing. "Sir?"

Gibbons gave me a sharp look and sat back in his chair, picking thoughtfully at a loosening splinter on his desk. "You heard me. Meet Salib by the airlock and get suited up."

"I thought you said you didn't want anyone on the ground again, sir?"

"*I* didn't say that. *She* did."

Damn. He knows.

I couldn't imagine how he'd heard about my talk with Gallagher in the absence of comms, and it didn't seem likely that he could have overheard us and then beat me to his quarters, but my guilt got the better of me. Whether he suspected I was evaluating him or not, I was jumping at shadows.

The captain stood and pushed his chair in slowly. I tried not to notice Teemo subtly shifting his weight away from me to avoid association now that I'd chosen to challenge the captain's orders. It's not the sort of thing your fellow troops typically encourage. Not unless they like the prospect of being court-martialed or tried for mutiny once the mission ends.

The thing is though, by then, I was already more than a little suspicious that the mission never *would* end, and if it did, that I would never again take a deep space assignment. I'd seen enough of the universe to last a lifetime.

Besides, what the hell kind of commanding officer sends his only pilot out on a ground mission with a broken arm while stranded on a potentially hostile planet? I guess that should have tipped me to his degrading mental state, but I was too close to the situation to see it then. Too much had happened.

Should have kept my mouth shut, I thought.

Gibbons rounded the table. He didn't look happy.

Fuck.

He stopped so close in front of me that I could smell his horrible stasis breath. The glowing green grime hadn't quite washed off his skin. I wondered if I looked the same.

He smiled wide. "I'm going to *pretend* you didn't just question me twice in my own goddamned quarters when I gave you a direct order, Lieutenant. I'm going to chalk it up to the 'extraordinary stress' of being stranded on a planet that shouldn't fucking exist beyond contact range of any of our fucking deep space installments."

My muscles locked and I stared straight ahead, careful not to meet his gaze or even flinch. Anything might set him off, I realized. Anything might push him over the edge. It was becoming more and more apparent that he teetered on the brink of some personal catastrophe. His *words* were typical Gibbons, but the *smile* threw everything else out the window.

I'd never seen the man so much as smirk.

For a moment, he stood with his nose a few inches from my face. Staring me down. Waiting for me to crack. Then, the smile abruptly vacated his lips and he turned toward Teemo.

"The fact is we need to know the lay of the land here before we take the next step. We *all* know we're running out of time."

I almost followed up with another question but caught myself at the last second. Maybe he was right, after all. It wasn't like me to speak out of turn so often in front of a superior officer. Or at all, really. I didn't know what the hell had gotten into me. Maybe it was just the thinning oxygen levels, or maybe being trapped on the planet on the heels of rocketing through endless space was too claustrophobic. Lots of soldiers have that same problem when they return home and hang up their gravity-equalizing boots. Especially navigators, because we're the ones who understand how truly massive the universe is.

"We need to know whether or not there's a place anywhere on the planet that's capable of supporting life. It doesn't seem likely—*impossible*, really—but we have to know our options. I'm not looking for a five-star hotel with breathable air and a vending machine, but it sure as hell would be nice if we could shield ourselves from burning alive."

Is burning any worse than dying of thirst or starvation? I thought, but didn't dare say in front of the captain. I didn't dare say it in front of myself, either. Hearing talk of death aloud—even from my own lips—would have been too much.

"We need to know what sort of resources are nearby. Anything we can use to expedite repairs on the ship." He turned back to me, this time with a deep frown. "Locals," he said, letting the word hang between us long enough for me to catch his meaning. "I want to know if we have any friends in the neighborhood."

"Yes, sir," Teemo said.

I hesitated a moment, but not because I didn't agree with the logic behind the ground mission. I just wasn't sure how it would go over with Salib, or whether or not it was the best decision to separate Teemo and me—the two most important specialists for getting us the fuck out of there, one of whom was already injured—from the ship. Without a navigator and a pilot of Teemo's ilk, the *Hummel* wouldn't get very far. And if they somehow got the ship up and running for a short burst and we weren't there to guide them, our team would wind up stranded and the ship would wander off into deeper nothingness outside the planet, having shot blindly for home with no real hope of reaching it.

Not that my presence necessarily made the odds much better, but it certainly didn't *hurt* them to have me around. If any one of us was capable of making sense out of gravitational fluxes, meteor paths, etc. (assuming that we would even encounter them), it was me.

"Chalmers?" Gibbons cut into my thoughts. He was standing in front of me again. I hadn't even noticed him move. My mind was even more clouded than I'd realized.

"Yes, sir," I answered, mostly because there wasn't anything else to say unless I wanted to wind up in a holding cell, or, if the captain was feeling especially generous, confined to quarters. I wouldn't be any good to the mission *there*, either.

Maybe, but at least you won't have to run a suicide mission on the surface. You know *what's down there.*

I didn't *really* know, I guess, but I knew it was something I wanted to avoid. Hell, even Salib had felt it, and she was about as impervious to irrational fear as any creature I've met in this universe.

"Good. Now hustle down to Salib. You've wasted enough of everyone's time already."

In the heat of the moment, I wanted to snap back at him with some kind of meaningful retort, but of course that was a fantasy. The situation would have to get a lot more fucked up before I'd risk mouthing off to my commanding officer in a possible combat situation.

So I saluted him with clenched teeth and turned back toward the hallway, thinking that if we ever made it back to the ship alive and somehow—against all odds—figured out a way off of the planet, I would file a report with the fleet about Gibbons' conduct during that particular mission.

Maybe.

Even then, I knew it was bullshit. I knew I wouldn't have the balls, and I knew Gallagher would beat me to it.

TAKE TWO

After futilely searching the passages outside Gibbons' quarters for Gallagher, whom I'd expected to be eagerly awaiting my report, I caught up with Teemo and followed him to the winding stairs at the rear of the ship where we descended to the lower deck. By the time we reached Salib's squad—or what was left of it—they were already suited up and sorting ordnance by the airlock.

"About goddamned time," Salib muttered once we were within earshot. "Better use combat suits this time, boys. Just in case."

I could tell the words pained her as she spoke, especially the last three. It took me a while to understand why.

From the corner of my eye, I noticed Marty was still kneeling beside his wife's corpse. He didn't look at me. I didn't expect him to snap out of his stupor anytime soon. I didn't blame him, either. After all, what was the point? We were already dead as far as most of the ship was concerned. In light of his wife's death, I didn't think he'd be any more optimistic than the rest of us. Probably worse, in fact.

"You should head up to the gym with the others," I told him. "The captain ordered everyone up there for a head count."

Marty turned to me with a vacant stare. "Fuck you," he said weakly.

I shrugged and began strapping Chara's combat gear to my lower body. It was still warm and a little wet from being hosed down. "Fair enough."

Glancing to my right, I saw Teemo examining the body armor he'd been assigned from another wounded soldier that wouldn't be joining us on the surface.

"Everything all right?" I asked.

He looked up at me, startled, as though he hadn't realized anyone else was in the room with him at all, let alone someone who might notice his wide-eyed appraisal and realize it was something out of the ordinary.

"Sure," he told me. "Everything's fine."

But his eyes darted nervously back to the scuffed shoulder plates, like the ghost of Chara or some other damn thing was about to jump up and wrap itself around his head. Once I started thinking a little deeper about the blood-spattered chest plates and arm-guards I was strapping on, though, I got a little chill, too. I'd watched Chara die, after all, so his ghost was more than just a vague unease born from someone else's past. It was a tangible memory for me. Almost a physical presence. His death was still very real in my mind, and I couldn't help feeling that wearing his equipment so soon after the fact was somehow wrong. Even if there were no other spares I could use to protect myself against God-only-knew-what on the captain's scouting mission.

It's all bullshit, anyway. This whole mission is pointless.

I wasn't about to say so to Salib. I could tell she was even less excited about venturing back into the screaming atmosphere than I was.

"All right, assholes," she shouted from the airlock door. "Make sure your noise equalizers are properly calibrated before that hatch opens or you're going to be in for a hell of a bad time." She glanced at my bloody armor without realizing she'd done so. I was the only one who noticed. The others were too preoccupied with imagining death on the other side of the airlock. And, oh, how right they were. "We don't know what exactly we're looking for and our scanners are still on the fritz, so we're going to split off into teams of two and cover the area by sight. Partner up and pick a direction. We'll meet back here in one hour."

The whole squad simultaneously programmed the holo-displays on the arms of their spacesuits and set the timers for one hour so we would know when to head back. I wasn't convinced the measure would be effective considering we'd have no way of gauging how long the trek back would take us (other than just turning around after thirty minutes), but it wasn't like the ship was going anywhere. Whether we took one hour or one week, I thought there was a good chance we'd find the crew in exactly the same place as we'd left them...assuming they hadn't killed each other first. That wasn't necessarily a given. Space fever can lead to all sorts of violent behavior. 'Visions of Parin' they call it out here, but I thought there was a better chance that starvation or mutiny would rear their ugly heads before space sickness became a factor.

"All right," Salib continued. "You spot anything worth mentioning, send up a flare before you go any further. We'll all converge on the site for backup as soon as we see the lights."

She locked eyes with me and I nodded self-consciously, tightening my grip on the SX rifle I'd grabbed from Chara's gear. Whether or not I'd seen what I *thought* I saw on our first foray onto the planet's surface—I was leaning more and more towards the vision being some sort of stress-induced hallucination in the wake of the ear-splitting, screeching wind—I still had a feeling that there would be trouble once we split into smaller groups. I couldn't quite put my finger on what it would be or why, but it made me squirm a little in my spacesuit.

"Count from ten," Salib told us over her shoulder. She had her hand pressed against the door controls but not hard enough to open it yet. She wanted us all ready in case the shit hit the fan again from the get-go.

Here we go, I thought.

I had no idea why I was so nervous. I'd faced down much worse shit than an uncharted planet with no signs of life. I guess the saying is true to some extent, though. The greatest of all emotions is fear, and man's greatest fear is fear of the unknown. Or something like that. And who the hell said that, anyway? Lovecraft? I guess it doesn't really matter now, but at the time it seemed like an issue of devastating import.

"Five," Salib said.

I could sense the other soldiers tensing against the walls, bracing for a cosmic impact which would have little to do with their bodies and a whole hell of a lot to do with their mental wellbeing.

God, it was hot in that suit.

"Opening."

I took a deep breath and gripped the SX rifle even tighter. The gloves already stuck to my sweaty fingers.

The door gasped open and the protective shield on my helmet shot down immediately, dimming the blinding glare of the planet's surface before it could permanently damage my eyes. Only that wasn't quite true, because it couldn't possibly have been that bright, and it wasn't that bright later on. The planet just hadn't adapted to us yet.

"Partner up," Salib reminded us. She was already descending the ramp with Sillinger at her side.

Sure, take the only goddamned medic with you, I remember thinking. It was standard protocol but seemed incredibly selfish at the same time. Fear does that to the best of us.

"Are you single?" Teemo asked me with a grin. He favored his broken arm but the miracle cast seemed to be doing its job, otherwise he wouldn't have been able to grip the butt of the rifle at all. "Looking for a partner?"

It was good to see him smile again. It settled my nerves a little, but it was also an eerie grin. A killer-clown grin, although I don't know why that particular image came to mind.

"I don't know," I said. "Are you offering to buy me a drink?"

He scoffed. "I don't buy drinks for anybody. Buy them yourself."

We both laughed uneasily even though it wasn't particularly funny, then started down the ramp with more nonchalance than we should have, in retrospect. If I'd had the slightest inkling of what we'd find on that planet once we crested our impact crater, I'd probably have killed every single one of the troopers right then and there before turning the SX on myself. It wouldn't have been any worse than what we endured. I can't think of anything that *is*.

Teemo and I were at the very back of the line, so we didn't have much choice on the direction we headed. We just angled for the lone open stretch of the slope and started walking the pale, orange landscape.

The land was like something out of a half-remembered childhood nightmare. Huge. Twisted. Open, scorched, and ominous. From the bottom of the crater, I could see grain waving gently above, and it made a chill prickle over my arms. The wind was too severe for the stalks to sway so lightly, even if they were thicker than they appeared. The gusts should have uprooted them completely. In fact, by my reckoning, the entire landscape should have been a complete wasteland.

Except it wasn't.

It just hadn't adapted to us yet.

As we reached the top of the crater and looked out over the encroaching land, my mouth went dry and my legs turned to rubber. If Teemo hadn't reached out to grip my shoulder,

I might have tumbled all the way back down the crater to my death, and it wouldn't necessarily have been the worst thing to happen that day.

"Do you see it?" Teemo asked.

His grip on my shoulder was so tight that I felt it through the spacesuit's armor plating.

"Yeah," I told him, shrugging out from his grip. "I see it."

"Do we send up a flare?"

Flexing my trigger finger and switching off the safety on the SX, I squinted down at the ruins in the distance. "Not yet. Let's wait until we see what's out there."

It wasn't the worst call I made that day, but it certainly wasn't the best, either.

INTO THE CITY

"We should send up a flare," Teemo said firmly.

Our backs were pressed against a giant boulder forty feet or so outside the city gates (if you could call the rusted husks leaning drunkenly against the stone walls actual gates). We'd walked about a mile, maybe more, since reaching the top of the crater and we'd decided to investigate the ruins before getting others involved. We had cover, but a steady, chilling cacophony of voices had broken through the constant howl of wind, maybe because our noise equalizers had blocked out the worst of that particular pitch. My hands had begun sweating so profusely that I could barely hold the SX steady even with the gloves.

"Not yet," I told him again.

I'm not sure why, but now that we were off the ship and away from the sobering reminders of death, the adventurer in me had resurfaced. I wanted a closer look at the city. I wanted to find out what sort of creatures had built the heinous eyesores leering down at us. I wanted to get a sense of the city's culture, which seemed so utterly alien in their buildings and yet chillingly familiar at the same time. And I wasn't even consciously aware then that there *was* a culture behind the buildings' construction. For all I knew, the whole city could have been just another severed head bouncing past me in the wind. A hallucination. A vision.

Except Teemo saw it, too, and I needed him there with me to verify the find before the others came and stole it out from under us. I wanted to be first. Again, I couldn't tell you *why*, considering it goes against all fleet protocols for a ground mission when scanners and comms are down, but I wanted to see it myself.

Come on down, Mikey, a voice whispered inside my head. *Let me give you a tour of the old home place.*

I bit my lip and pushed tighter against the rock.

"Are you all right?" Teemo asked.

I nodded and shuffled away from him until I could see on an angle down the right side of the city street.

"Five minutes," Teemo told me. "Then I'm sending one up."

I waved him away with my elbow. My hands were too busy holding the SX to bother with him. I could barely contain my excitement.

Then I saw the creature for the first time. The ringleader, as it turned out. The one responsible for the deaths of my crewmates.

"You're a goddamned idiot," Teemo muttered. He hadn't spotted the thing yet.

"Shh. What's that?"

Every ounce of common sense at my disposal demanded that I jump to my feet and sprint as far away from the ruins as I possibly could, but my sudden, inexplicable fear was too paralyzing to muster anything but that simple question to Teemo. I'm not sure whether I wanted his opinion on the creature or if I just needed confirmation that I hadn't completely lost my head from watching Chara and Marty's wife die. "Do you see it?"

Teemo craned his neck around the massive boulder and frantically withdrew, dropping his rifle with a sudden jerk. It looked like his broken arm was acting up. "Shit!" he hissed, wincing back a startled exclamation. "What the fuck *is* that thing?"

"Try the comms," I said hoarsely. I would have tried them myself but there was no *way* I was about to take my finger off the SX trigger for even a moment, especially now that my only back-up was unarmed.

"Fuck you!" Teemo shouted hysterically. The sight of the creature was too much for him to take. He didn't give a shit about tact any more now that he'd lost his weapon. "Do it yourself!"

He scrambled to release the flare gun from his utility belt while I slowly peeked around the edge of the boulder at the soulless creature making its way down the dusty, haunted street. Its imposing gait unnerved me. My jaw went limp and my stomach dropped.

"Teems...it's looking at me..."

He never heard me. By the time the words had left my lifeless tongue, he'd managed to unhook the flare gun from his waist and pumped three charges in fast succession, which was the entire magazine for the emergency gun. They used to only carry *one* flare, and then we really *would* have been screwed, because as it turned out, the last blaze was the only one Salib's crew saw. The others were swallowed by the atmosphere. It didn't make much difference for me, but it may have prolonged Teemo's life.

"Come on!" Teemo yelled.

He yanked me to my feet and I stumbled, dazed, among the rocks and razor-sharp wheat stalks.

"Your rifle," I said, not sure why the protest was on my lips. I felt the giant creature behind me, calling to me, strolling nonchalantly between the houses of a damned race. Maybe its *own* damned race.

An entire race of those *goddamned things?* I thought. I couldn't imagine something so god-awful.

"Screw the guns!" Teemo shouted. "Let's get the fuck out of here!"

Over the years we'd both spent in the service (not nearly as many as Gibbons, but a respectable amount considering the volume of action compressed within them) we'd seen plenty of aliens, ranging from cute and cuddly to outright horrifying. Some with man-eating reproductive organs (not an exaggeration) and some that taught you the very definition of euphoria through the psychotropic compounds released in their sweat. Therefore, it might seem like our initial response of running at the prospect of first contact was an overreaction, but only if you forget to consider what had happened in the preceding three hours, and also if you've never seen a twelve-foot-tall demon thundering towards you.

It was hideous and terrifying.

Twisted horns on its head, a sliced-open smile, seared flesh with open sores, and what appeared to be crude clown makeup smeared over its face. And that's without mentioning the tight muscles on its naked body that expanded and contracted in hypnotic rhythm with each step. It looked strong enough to pull both of us apart limb from limb through our spacesuits, and also like it wouldn't waste a drop of flesh if it got hold of us. If I hadn't been scared shitless, I might even have admired the creature as the epitome of ugliness and depravity.

"*Run!*" Teemo yelled.

He was already a good thirty feet away and had only just begun to reach top speed, but my feet were still locked behind the boulder with the creature creeping closer and closer by the second.

Where are you going, Mikey? it called out to me.

It wasn't even looking in my direction, and I wasn't facing it. I heard its voice nonetheless.

Some force pulled me back to the city even as my feet moved toward Teemo, who gestured frantically for me to follow but didn't make an effort to wait up. It's not his fault. We were dealing with the same level of terror, just a little differently, and that's about as common among a group of soldiers as it is in ordinary people. Just like Gallagher and Gibbons back on the ship. Gallagher was dealing with the knowledge of certain death by attempting to control the situation as much as possible. Gibbons coped by relinquishing a little bit of order in his life to face the cold, hard facts. For Teemo and me, the difference was that Teemo was rattled enough to run and I was rattled enough that I *couldn't* run even if I'd wanted to. The ultimate example of fight versus flight.

Sometimes, I've learned, what's portrayed as bravery on the battlefield is simply paralyzing terror, and the self-preservation instinct that sends people running is actually a superior intellect and quicker reflexes.

I guess it all turned out okay, but only because I'm alive to file this report. It turned out okay for *me*, I should say. Except really it didn't, and I think you already know why. All those sleepless nights. Guilt. Nightmares. Distrust. Writing this. It's no way to live.

"What the hell is *wrong* with you?" Teemo's voice found me over a great distance, and I realized that it wasn't coming through the atmosphere but through the short range comm that was kicking in and out with a crackle of static.

By then, I knew my decision had already been made. I could feel the ground shaking slightly beneath my feet and sensed the shadow growing at my back. The creature wasn't far away. It had spotted me. Not *just* spotted me, either. It had singled me out for investigation. The hunter had become the prey, and I had no hope of escaping the demon's elongated stride.

"Relax," I said into the short range comm, not knowing whether or not the message would reach Teemo. "I've got the SX."

I wasn't convinced it would be any use against the monstrous alien, but there was no point appealing for help. If

Teemo came back for me, I thought, it would only lead to his death in addition to my own, and he didn't deserve to go out that way. He'd wanted to send the flares up immediately and I'd told him not to.

On legs that seemed to weigh somewhere between eight hundred and a thousand pounds—could have been the gravity equalizers on my boots giving out or just the effect the creature had on my physiology—I turned back to the boulder, cowering into futile refuge even as I caught movement from the corner of my eye. It's embarrassing to admit in retrospect, but at the time, I fully subscribed to the childish theory that as long as I didn't look at the damned thing, it wouldn't be able to touch me. I guess stranger things have happened than an alien ignoring a lesser life form, but I knew deep down I'd have no such luck.

This is it, I thought, checking the safety on the SX to make sure I'd remembered to flip it down while bracing for the inevitable confrontation. It's funny to me how the reality of death never set in during those few moments, despite my proximity to Death incarnate. I didn't have full context then, though. I lacked perspective. If you dropped me into that *exact* situation now, I probably would have popped open my helmet and let the atmosphere suck the life from me before I'd ever allow myself to be desecrated by that abomination. Who knows it if would have worked.

Luckily for me, I had no idea what was on the other side of that rock aside from a very brief glimpse of the monster's exterior, so I didn't get creative with suicide options.

"Get the fuck out of there!" Teemo screamed. I only caught part of it through the short range comm but I understood the sentiment.

I brought the SX to bear, leapt up to face the last place I'd seen the monster, and started firing.

Too late, though.

The creature was already on my side of the rock, and when I turned to face it, I managed three wild shots that missed the target completely before it screeched, lifted me clear of the ground, and drew me toward its mouth.

"Shit shit shit shit shit..."

Its jaw expanded obnoxiously wide, revealing a black, rotted tongue and rows upon rows of razor teeth. Then it clamped down on my helmet and the glass shattered.

The wind tore at me immediately. I felt the breath leaving my lungs.

Then its teeth pierced my neck in a wide ring and everything went black for a while.

Even in my dreams, I heard Teemo's screams.

DARKNESS

The crew's real nightmare began sometime between the horned clown biting through my helmet and when I awoke inside one of the city's abandoned buildings. I wasn't actually around to witness Salib's first encounter with the creatures that chased her squad from the ship, but I've gleaned bits and pieces from survivors since then. From what I've heard, I was one of the lucky ones, but only in the beginning. Only in that I survived and was unconscious during the initial slaughter. You know a mission was bad when the best you can say about it is that you weren't awake to see your crewmates massacred.

I woke up terrified, not knowing exactly where I was or what awaited me in the darkness. I could tell right away that, aside from a few shards around the base, the glass shielding on my helmet was gone and the planetoid didn't have an oxygen atmosphere. A big problem, to say the least. I spent a few frantic moments visualizing the air rapidly draining from my lungs, then realized I was still breathing somehow and felt my fear cautiously subside. I figured the atmosphere must not have been as toxic as we'd initially suspected. I should have known right away, but it was a forgivable miscalculation with our scanners on the fritz. The notion of an oxygen atmosphere seemed impossible after witnessing Chara's death, but I couldn't think of a better explanation for my sudden ability to breathe with a malfunctioning suit.

Unless I was still dreaming. The idea occurred to me as I sat there working through the mammoth headache between my eyebrows and a general cloud of grogginess, but everything seemed too *actual* to be a dream. Utterly concrete, including the walls. The only thing that kept me from dismissing the notion entirely was just how bizarre the mission had been from the moment I'd been pulled out of hyper-sleep. *Everything* about it was bullshit, not just the crash or the city or the alien. It was unlike anything I'd ever heard about before, even in whispers of Aidric Squad's deep-space missions, and those bastards see *all* the weird shit the universe has to offer.

These weren't the sort of mission hazards we prepped for in Basic. Then again, Basic has never been much help when it comes to the chaos of battle. It's a systemic failure, really. In Basic, a can't-hack-it sergeant runs you into the ground to get your endurance up real nice, degrades you a hell of a lot, and maybe teaches you how to turn the safety off on an SX. If you're lucky you get a few survival drops on inhospitable moons, too. Other than that though, I'd argue Basic actually stifles a soldier's development in far too many instances to make it a viable training program. For the amount of risk we assume on the battlefield, we deserve better.

I guess that's my inner disgruntled-soldier showing. But hell, I think I'm allowed to hold one or two dissenting opinions about the fleet, considering my last mission saw nearly my entire crew butchered and I still haven't been cleared to resume active duty in spite of repeated requests. They're pushing me toward desk-jockey duty on Pluto Station while I recover from the trauma, I guess. *Pfft.* No thank you, sir. I can't think of a bigger fuck-you after everything I've been through than serving on Pluto Station.

Neither here nor there.

The room where I awoke on Furnace was small with absurdly high ceilings that made me dizzy to look at. The dusty stone floor was grooved with age. Pools of water collected in a dip at the center of the room beneath a chandelier carved from bones. They were too big and too complex for a humanoid and some were darker than the ivory hue I'm accustomed to, but I didn't look too closely at them. There were too many other things to worry about, and the last thing I wanted to do when I was already neck-deep in a bad situation was freak *myself* out.

What now? I wondered.

The obvious answer was to come up with an escape plan, but I didn't see any doors nearby or depressions in the wall that might have disguised an exit. All I could see was a rectangular window to the pitch-black sky about fifteen feet off the ground. There was no way I could reach it without any tools at my disposal. The creature had emptied my utility belt when it took me along with both of my ammunition clips. So that was out. Besides, I wasn't about to rush into the open without knowing the exact whereabouts of the crazy clown-looking wraith, especially without knowing what he had in store for me. I couldn't imagine it was anything good—I wasn't *that* naïve—but I was at least composed enough to realize he would have killed me right away unless he had a plan for me.

It wasn't much of a consolation, but it reminded me that I had a little time to make a proper analytical decision before I ran off and did something stupid. I'd lost my SX (I verified it was gone three times with a quick search of my utility belt and the damp floor) but I figured the weapon wouldn't have been much use, anyway. The monster was too goddamned *big* to be dropped with SX bullets. I needed a fucking short-range missile launcher or something at least on the same branch of the Destruction family-tree to have a shot at overpowering the creature, and I've dropped into enough battles to know pure brawn isn't always the best course of action. At that point, I didn't even know whether or not there were other beings like the clown walking around. For all I knew, a whole army of them was watching me that very moment.

I continued to puzzle over escape scenarios for a few minutes but eventually found myself back at square one, feeling much more helpless—yet more awake—than before.

That's also when I realized that even though I *thought* I'd checked the room thoroughly, I wasn't alone.

To this day, I'm convinced the creature materialized sometime after I awoke. Otherwise, there's no way I would have missed something so imposing in such tight quarters even with the bizarre, funhouse shadow-play from the gently swinging bone-chandelier.

"Oh boy…" I whispered, slowly crab-walking away from the figure.

As far as I could tell, it was the same creature who'd broken my helmet and dragged me off to captivity, though it was difficult to say with any certainty while it squatted in the shadows. I thought I saw horns, though. Its head hung squarely between its knees. Its arms dangled so low that its knuckles scraped the stone floor.

Well, I thought, *I'm fucked.*

I'd known it before, of course, but this knowing was worse. The fear was nothing like it had been when I'd first spotted the son of a bitch striding through the city like an undead carnival reject on steroids. The first time around, I'd had a weapon, another soldier with me, some idea of my location in relation to the crew, and a whole lot of open ground to work with in case I needed a quick escape. The end result may have been just as bad, but at least I'd felt a little more in control of the situation then.

This time, I was utterly helpless, and I knew it. We *both* knew it.

The walls didn't just press in around me, they dove at me. A chilling reminder that the distance between my living breath and the afterlife was finite. My stomach churned in such violent waves that I wasn't sure whether I'd vomit or shit myself first when the bastard moved. Thankfully, neither wound up happening. I'm still not sure how.

Focus. You've only got one shot to get out of here.

I scanned the room again, clinging to the theory that if I'd overlooked something as huge as the horned monster seated directly across from me, I could have missed a blatant opportunity for escape, as well. Like a doorway. Or a bazooka. Anything.

But there was nothing to be found, and no hope for salvation. Nothing to defend myself with if the creature decided to attack again. Not even the glass shielding on my helmet.

I pressed against the rear wall and gripped the flat surface for purchase, trying to maintain my composure while the creature slowly unfurled itself.

"Back off, asshole," I said weakly. I tried to add some volume to my voice to throw the creature on its heels, but it was a futile attempt made worse by the lack of conviction in my delivery. The feint did little more than accentuate my fear.

The diseased, clown thing stood to its full height, tilted its head to the side, and grinned at me with wide, bloodshot eyes. Its neck twitched in creaking spasms that made me shudder. With one massive stride, it crossed the room then stopped an arm's length from me. I didn't see any other options, so I ducked away and rolled to the corner of the room, trapping myself in an even tighter spot in the process.

"What do you want?" I asked.

Somehow, my voice was a bit steadier this time around. I think eluding the creature's grasp to that point made me feel more in control. Like maybe my fate *hadn't* already been decided and I *wasn't* completely at its mercy, though the situation was clearly dire.

In response, the clown leaned forward until its horns nearly touched my forehead and wagged its tongue at me, splitting the black, fish-like appendage over its razor teeth. Dark blood flowed over its chin and dripped to the floor.

Jesus Christ...

It reached out with scabbed fingers to grip me by the neck. I barely ducked away again, this time with much less room to spare.

The room started stretching before my eyes. Reality itself seemed in flux, but I felt lighter. The spacesuit still weighed me down, but not as much as before. The glass from my helmet wasn't all that heavy, but the gear on my utility belt was, and being relieved of both added some speed to my movements. A little more maneuverability. I started sensing daylight in the creature's blind-spots. Started thinking maybe I was better off in an enclosed space like that one, after all, rather than out in the open where its long strides would have easily overtaken me.

The clown-thing lunged at me again but I'd pre-emptively side-stepped its attack. It reared back and growled forcefully enough to shake the walls, then laughed a piercing witch's cackle. The contrast in pitch was startling, but not half as startling as the sound that followed from its wide mouth.

"There's nowhere to run," it told me in a low, mocking lilt.

I froze in my tracks for a split-second, shocked to hear Galactic Standard from the lips of an alien trillions of light years from the nearest human settlement. My hesitation, though, provided enough of a window for the creature to skewer me through the stomach above my right hip. Its hooked nails worked their way roughly through my skin and out my lower back.

I shrieked until I ran out of breath.

The pain was all-consuming. I could picture the thing's rotting skin inside me. A million cells of alien bacteria poisoning my bloodstream from the entry wound alone. I may have said I knew before then that I was totally and completely fucked, but that was really the moment I accepted it. There was no going back from a wound like that while I was cut off from any form of medical supplies. Worse, I knew the bastard wasn't finished. I could tell by its wide, maniac grin and the way the purple blood flowed over its bleach-white face.

It was salivating.

It was hungry.

I gasped and slammed back into the wall reflexively, separating myself from its knife-like fingers but tearing more skin in the process. I fell to the floor on the verge of unconsciousness, wishing that the demon would finish me quickly so I wouldn't have to endure any more pain.

And then an odd thought occurred to me as the clown thing lifted me off the floor and slammed me against the stone wall with little effort, causing the bone chandelier to swing in a peculiar, high-gravity rhythm which was deeply unsettling and oddly hypnotizing at the same time.

The screams, I remembered. *They're gone.*

I could hear plenty of other noises in the distance but my helmet was broken, meaning the noise equalizers in my suit were offline. Without them, my eardrums should have exploded from the screeching sound that had driven Chara to suicide. At the time, I didn't even consider the idea that I'd been taken to a separate location with similar technology built into the structure itself (as was the case with the *Hummel*), or far enough away that the sounds didn't reach us at all. It wasn't much of an observation and didn't seem particularly important as I struggled within the monster's grip, bleeding out and hoping to die by strangulation before being eaten alive. Coupled with the realization that I could breathe without my suit in a non-oxygen atmosphere, however, it raised a red flag. It could have been the creature's dwelling itself, but something told me the likelihood that the clown demon both required oxygen for breathing and also had severe auditory sensitivity was slim.

And that got me wondering just how much of the experience was real. I stubbornly held out hope that I was still dreaming.

In the moment though, it felt as real as anything. It hurt. More importantly, I was about to be eaten.

Fight it, I told myself, trying to muster every last ounce of will in my dying moments to pull off a daring escape.

As the creature's grip tightened around my throat and I felt the last breaths vacating my lungs as poignantly as I felt my windpipe collapsing, my battle instincts took over. Out of stagnation arose the hunger I'd known during the Kalak War. With the colossal, adrenaline-fueled determination of a soldier on his last rope, I roared, slammed my fist into the creature's nose, and swung my legs up to kick it in the throat at the same time. Neither blow inflicted significant damage, but the resistance itself stunned the creature enough that it dropped me to the floor.

I landed hard. The impact snapped my mouth closed and my teeth locked down on the tip of my tongue. I was up and running before the demon recovered to snatch me back up, though. I had no idea where the hell I was headed. My survival instincts had assumed control over every thought and action.

The clown thing laughed again and clawed at the back of my head, tearing streaks through my neck and the top of my suit.

"There's no hiding place," it told me again. "No refuge."

I continued running a serpentine pattern around the room, looking for any glimmer of daylight I might use to escape no matter how horrible the alternative. I could only think of the immediate danger, and the putrid smell of the maniacal clown demon at my back spurred me on.

"Wherever you go, I will find you," it told me. "You are my vessel."

Suddenly, the wall in front of me vanished and I was running over the planet's surface with miles of flat earth surrounding me.

Alone.

"Jesus..." I muttered, gasping for breath.

I fell to my knees and dug my hands into the dusty ground, shielding my face from the wind while I collected my thoughts.

My hands shook. My stomach screamed in agony. The back of my neck was aflame and damp with blood.

It was real, I thought, touching the wound on my stomach with a wince and flexing my jaw. *This is* all *real.*

For a while, I wondered where exactly that left me, and then I got to my feet, picked a direction, and started running again. One way or another, I knew I didn't have much time.

WASTELAND

I don't know how long I ran over the faded orange expanse. Long past the rendezvous time Salib set for her squad to compare notes. I didn't know where I planned on going. I just knew that if I didn't get back soon, either Rosie would fix the ship's engines and they'd jump from the planet without me (even if they didn't know what came after), or I would run out of food trying to find them. Admittedly, it was a shortsighted mindset. Water was, by far, a more immediate problem than food. Sweating out my short supply of fluids wasn't exactly the smartest thing to do, in that case, but I wasn't in my right mind. Truly, hunger and dehydration should have been the least of my worries.

I almost passed out from pain and blood-loss a half-dozen times, and that forced me to take several breaks along the way against my better judgment. I tried not to think too much about the clown thing. I didn't see what good would come of it, but I couldn't help myself. I had no control over my thoughts whatsoever, so images fired into my brain at random. My mind simply couldn't process everything that had happened with a rational perspective while the whole universe was imploding around me. I had no clue what was real and what wasn't, or if I was even still alive. For all I knew, I'd never actually woken from stasis. Furnace could either have been the worst nightmare I'd ever experienced or a glimpse into the terrible afterlife that awaited me.

Each time I took a break to skirt the black curtain of unconsciousness, I chewed over a thousand questions and doubts. Each time, I decided that it didn't matter whether I was dead or not. The face of the clown demon and its weeping sores kept hijacking my thoughts.

There's no hiding place, its hideous face reminded me. *Wherever you go, I'll find you.*

Even in my head, the voice manifested with a full choral accompaniment. Mad harmonies echoing from deep within its hollow chest. The effect was chilling.

It was always at this point that I'd start running again. As long as I kept moving, I figured I'd find answers sooner or later. Either I'd die or I'd find some form of refuge from the wind and maybe quell the endless parade of questions, like how I was able to breathe on the surface without a helmet, or how I survived the supposedly scorching atmosphere with only a malfunctioning suit protecting my delicate human skin. It was ground I'd already covered, but at least when I was in captivity (or something like it) I was able to rationalize the phenomenon as the city's life-support measures to protect its inhabitants. Out on the open land, I couldn't fabricate any answers at all.

So I kept running, and gradually the scenery began to change.

By my rough estimation, I'd run at least five miles when I first saw the open flames whipping out from the ground ahead of me. I could see orange-red mountains in the distance by then with clouds of colorful gases hovering in their midst. Somewhere between the fires and the mountainside, I thought I saw some trees and other forms of plant life, but I was too far away to say with any certainty. I may have detected movement as well, but with heat baking the earth over the lakes of lava, it could have been a mirage or even a humidity distortion.

I stopped running again, this time because I recognized that I had a decision to make. Did I want to continue toward the lava and the mountains, or run parallel to them in either direction? I didn't want to turn around and run back the way I'd come. I knew exactly where *that* led me, and I also knew I might be dead before I retraced my steps.

Yet looking off to the left and right, I didn't see landmarks for a long way, either, and my throat already felt like sandpaper. The idea of running aimlessly again—possibly in the wrong direction—was completely out of the question. The steady, burning pulse in my stomach told me I'd be dead if I stopped to rest as well, and might not even make it to the mountains. My best bet was to forge ahead and hope that I'd run into some stragglers from Salib's team or stumble onto the ship along the way. If I was lucky, I'd find a hidden stream in the mountains and buy myself some time.

Needless to say, natives were about the furthest thing from my mind at that point. They wouldn't be for long.

I was a couple hundred yards from the nearest lava lake when I saw the figures standing around the shores, then the shadows squirming frantically in their arms. There looked to be about two dozen of them in all, but they were too busy to notice me from that distance.

What now? I wondered.

I sure as hell didn't want to venture any closer after my last encounter with a native, but I didn't think I really had a choice, either. It was a wonder they hadn't spotted me already with the endless miles of wasteland as a backdrop. I stood out like a shambling sore thumb on the orange-hazed plateau. I couldn't very well escape in *any* direction without one of them eventually seeing me. And if they were even half as tall as the horned clown thing, they would overtake me in no time, even if I wasn't seriously wounded or several miles into a jog in light atmosphere.

Guess I'll have to take my chances.

I kept moving. As I approached, I noticed the figures were dipping the squirming shadows into the lava. Based on the frantic splashing the victims made in the shallows, they were having some difficulty with it, too. How they could step into the lava without burning alive was beyond me, but it was hardly the strangest thing I'd seen that day. I didn't even flinch.

I assumed that they would chase me down and try to eat me just like my clown friend once they spotted me. This time, I vowed to be prepared if it came to that. One more significant injury would be my last straw. I'd fight to the death. And if there was nothing I could do to stop them, then at least I wouldn't have to deal with the fleet's bullshit anymore. I'd be going out on my own terms.

Screw the fleet.

I started thinking about the *Rockne Hummel* as I broke into a run again. I remembered how I'd left without reporting to Gallagher. How Gibbons had eyeballed me for questioning his orders in a crisis. How Marty told me to fuck off while he mourned his dead wife, and how the damaged spacesuit I wore had been Chara's just a few hours earlier.

Suddenly, I wasn't in such a rush to return to the ship.

But what was the alternative? I wasn't dumb enough to believe I would last on the surface, and I wouldn't have wanted to even if I could. The fleet may be a heartless death-machine, but it's the only heartless death-machine I know. I knew I'd have it better if we survived.

Drunk on pain, thirst, and exhaustion, I called out to the figures with delirious good humor. "Hey, fuckheads. You hungry?"

The ones closest to me stopped what they were doing to investigate. I still couldn't make out their features. The way the scenery doubled and trebled with each step, I couldn't focus well enough.

"I'm a little spoiled, but I shouldn't be too bad. I'm sure you've had worse," I told them, laughing weakly.

I wiped sweat from my eyes and fell to my knees, unable to brace against the impact with the rough earth. A few jagged rocks cut me hard enough to bruise and draw blood, but I barely noticed. It was nothing compared to the wounds in my stomach and neck and I was on the verge of passing out, anyway. Or maybe dying. I couldn't tell which. "At least I'm warm," I whispered.

I stared up into the starless sky and closed my eyes, defeated. I listened as the figures approached and wondered how the vile planetoid beneath me could exist. How there wasn't a visible star within at least a hundred trillion light-years and yet the planet was still hot. And not *too* hot. Habitable for humans, apparently, but at least as sweltering as the Arizona desert.

It's not real, I remember thinking. *You're either dead or dreaming. None of this is possible.*

I believed every word of it, but my body had reached its absolute limit. Rational arguments no longer had any real sway on my psyche. I've never ascribed to the old wives' tale that if you die in your dreams, you die in real life, but this was one scenario where it seemed the only logical outcome for me. Another modified cliché seemed to fit as well: What came first, the death or the dream?

It's not real, I told myself.

But the footsteps were getting closer and closer, as if in direct opposition to my weak assurances. Each footprint in the dusty earth pounded through my skull, sending shockwaves of pain into my neck and stomach.

"Just kill me," I muttered.

My lips were so parched I could barely form the words. They had already split from wincing a hundred times over during my run.

How has it come to this?

By my reckoning, it hadn't even been a full twenty-four hours since we'd emerged from our FTL jump. I didn't understand how the situation could have degraded so quickly. My physical health, sure, but not my spirit. Not my psychological health. Not the mental state of the *Rockne Hummel's* crew. I hadn't even engaged in true combat yet. I hadn't been tortured beyond a solitary (though lethal) wound and a bad scratch. I never would have guessed an abdomen puncture and a few hours in a desert was enough to utterly break me, but there I was. I'd been trained for far worse, and yet the idea that my death would never even be marked, that it would remain a mystery written off to the tragedy of the *Rockne Hummel* which no one would care to explain because the situation itself was inexplicable, was completely unbearable. Especially on Furnace, as we came to call it. The soulless planet. It was a fate far worse than death.

And the footsteps pounded closer.

"Just get it over with."

The creatures were near enough that I could feel heat radiating off them as they closed the final gap.

This is it, then, I thought. *I guess it could be worse.*

I opened my eyes and stared up at the hazy, starless sky, wondering how far I'd wandered from the *Rockne Hummel* before my legs gave out along with my will to survive. I wondered, too, whether or not Teemo had gotten away in time or if he'd suffered a similar fate at the hands of the clown demon. I guessed I'd never know, and somehow that was comforting.

"What an asshole..." I moaned.

A massive hand dragged me to my feet and shook me so hard I felt my brain rattling against my skull. A bald, muscular creature with no eyes and tar-black skin pulled me close to its blunt yellow teeth.

At least this one won't eat me, I thought. It was huge and seemed strong enough to tear me apart effortlessly, but its teeth were worn beyond the capability for even a liquid diet, let alone one that required gnawing flesh from bone.

Death is death.

I was still steeped in agony. My prospects for survival didn't look good. Worst of all, I could hear more of them approaching, and I knew the others might be a little hungrier and a little more capable of feeding on me than my new friend.

Although, I thought, maybe he had his own way to consume me. A method I couldn't even imagine.

Only one way to find out.

The monster's rancid breath beat down on my face. The heat was unbearable, but the gases rising from its belly were worse. Sulfur mixed with other nasty elements I'd only encountered on asteroids. They were particularly pungent. One whiff and I was fully awake and ready to vomit.

I may have been thirsty, starved, overheated, and nauseous to the core, but it was the smell that finally pushed my body over the edge. I was spent. Before I could even upchuck into the creature's face, though, it let out a grating, soul-shattering screech that stifled my gag and made me scream back instead. It threw me to the ground so hard that the impact knocked the wind out of me.

As if I needed something else stealing my breath.

What the hell are you doing? a voice cried out inside my head. *Fight this asshole! If you want to die,* make *it kill you!*

It was sound suicidal logic, if such a thing exists, but I didn't have the energy for it. Instead, I lay completely still and watched the freak-show of demonic horrors continue its procession toward my beaten, bloodied body. They'd almost reached the tar-skinned monster's side by then, and yet they seemed to float further and further away from me at the same time. Like I was seeing them from somewhere outside myself. It's well-documented that many people have out-of-body experiences when they are close to death, but this was unlike anything I've read about. I was actually *there*. Present in every way possible, yet also able to see a great distance behind me. I could even see the thing following me through the desert. The horned demon.

Christ...

And it was looking for more than just a quick taste of flesh. It wanted to make me suffer. It wanted every part of me. Maybe to mount on its wall as a trophy, or to fashion into a new bone chandelier, or to frame my corpse wherever the bastard displayed its most cherished conquests. Maybe torture was just the only thing it knew. You can never account for alien culture or taste, least of all in hellish wastelands beyond the reach of the living.

It's coming.

The vision of the grinning clown stalking me across the desert gave me a new urgency and I snapped back to reality. I may have been ready to die, but not at the hands of *that* sick fucker.

So I guessed that meant I *did* have something to live for after all. Even if it was just dying in a more complete and agreeable manner somewhere down the road rather than being skewered in the rotting clown's lair while it pulled out my intestines. I figured I would rather bleed out or die of thirst in the shadows than become the centerpiece of his collection, or worse, one of the asides leading up to the main event.

I guess that's the point of survival for all of us, though. To keep living so we can die a different kind of death. On our own terms, if we're lucky. But it's one thing to know Death in an abstract sense and quite another to be in a position where you truly have to decide between the lesser of two evils. Especially when 'lesser' is hardly an appropriate term to describe either one.

I got an unwelcomed reminder of that thin distinction when I turned my attention back to the gathering horde of natives and felt my heart stop completely. They were terrifying. Each one of them was a nightmare beyond my wildest imaginings, and no two were alike. In terms of physical composition, most of them didn't even appear to be distant cousins. Yet they were vaguely familiar in the same breath, like they'd crossed over into our reality somewhere along the road.

A white-eyed witch with oily, disheveled hair patting over her dark skin like moss and vine in a swamp. The sort I used to imagine peering out of my closet at night, only this one wasn't quite human.

An olive-skinned monstrosity with tentacles for its mouth and large, lidless eyes boring into me with a deep, insatiable hunger.

A scrawny winged creature with a hairless, flesh-toned beak yet otherwise humanoid features.

A purple alien nearly the size of the horned clown with half its skin rotted away and its lips burnt off. It was standing beside a one-legged humanoid creature with a bat's head and pincer hands.

They were awful. And they kept coming.

An ape-like creature as big as Sasquatch with blood-red hair and five-inch incisors.

A bipedal fish with wide eyes and a mouth slung open in slack-jawed hunger.

A red-skinned, yellow-eyed demon straight out of Renaissance paintings that snarled at me as it approached, still carrying something (or rather, some*one*) under its arm.

And most glaring of all, though I didn't understand why at the time, was the hooved creature in the middle of everything. A beast that was half humanoid and half goat. A faun, as far as I could tell, but he reminded me of the clown somehow. His eyes locked onto me with a peculiar disinterest, like he was looking *past* me into something else. Lost in his own thoughts. Daydreaming.

In the middle of all this? I thought.

But I guess it was a commonplace occurrence for him, because it looked like he was just going through the motions. I'm not sure why that disturbed me so much, but it did. At least I could write-off the savage hunger and frenzy of the other creatures to sheer starvation. But the idea that slaughtering helpless, wounded strangers demanded the same level of attention as taking a shit would for a normal person chilled me to the core in spite of the overwhelming heat.

Get up! my mind screamed.

It's difficult to listen to the rational part of your brain though when everything happening around you is decidedly irrational. Somehow, I wanted to laugh at the sheer impossibility of the freaks approaching me, but then I thought of the clown following me across the desert, how it was bound to arrive any moment to scare away the (somewhat) lesser evils and drag me off for its own grotesque whimsy.

After that, my legs got moving in a hurry.

As the tar-skinned creature stooped to lift me again, I scrambled to my feet and started punching at its arm. Each blow went wide or glanced futilely off its rock-hard flesh, tightening the beast's grip around my throat, but I managed to struggle free anyway when a leopard-headed monster plowed into us. The beasts growled at each other and started fighting over the warm-blooded meal. I didn't stick around to find out who won.

The moment my feet touched the ground, I started running. I still didn't have a plan. But there was really only one direction to go, so I lowered my shoulder and charged into the swarm of oddities. It may seem ill-advised in retrospect to dive into belly of the beast (with a lake of fire beyond them to boot), but I saw paths between the lava leading to the mountains. It was the best chance I would get.

I managed to pull about two-dozen feet closer to the lava before the first freak grabbed hold of me. Even then, I kept fighting for purchase in the dry earth. If I couldn't make it to the mountain, I decided I could at least hurl myself into the lava and get dying over with before someone else did it for me. It wouldn't be easy. A pincer snapped onto my left bicep and I shrieked in pain. I didn't fall, though. I drove my legs forward until I was free of both creatures and stumbled another dozen strides from the crowd.

Once I was close enough to the lava to shrink away from its heat, I saw what work had occupied the devils before I presented them with a more enticing project.

"Holy shit..."

Dozens more creatures were scattered between the lava lakes, which were actually ponds sealed from each other by a network of earthen pathways. The sight of the narrow path was demoralizing enough on its own, but what really shook me up was seeing live aliens of varying species being dragged and dipped into the lava piece by piece. Mercifully, their screams were drowned out by the roaring crackle of the lake and the screeches of the abominations surrounding them, but watching their expressions was gut-wrenching. Every agonized gasp tore a piece from my soul, and every alien mouth twisted with dumb amazement ground it into the dirt.

That's when I realized that my fate was completely out of my hands as long as I was stuck on that godforsaken planet. I was surrounded by creatures with physical and psychological advantages over me, and I was on unfamiliar terrain. Even if I'd had the strength to get away, I had no idea whether or not there was a safe place on the entire planet where I could hide out, let alone how to get there.

"Holy shit," I said again.

My voice was weak. Defeated. Parched.

I forced my eyes shut so I wouldn't have to watch the alien captives tortured with lava. It helped a little.

Take a deep breath, I told myself. *There's nothing else you can do. Just wait for it to end, and try to go out with dignity.*

I felt a rough hand on my shoulder and flinched, almost scrambling away before my stubborn will asserted itself and I fell still. It was pointless to keep fighting. I was too injured and too goddamned tired. My focus abruptly shifted to appeasing the demons as much as possible in the foolish hope of reprieve from their perverse, insatiable appetites.

As if to remind me I had no leverage to strike a bargain, the creature that held me screeched in my ear and shook me violently. Try as I might, I couldn't keep my knees from buckling. I dropped to the ground again, this time convinced I would never again rise from that poisoned earth among the living.

Fuck it, I thought. *I always knew it would end like this. On some fucked-up planet at the hands of some fucked-up alien.*

It's the best you can hope for in the fleet, I guess. In fact, the concept of a lonely death on alien soil is so propagandized that recruits actually *pray* for it. Like they'll gain some Badass points for their legacies by dying. The problem is that, most of the time, people don't wind up knowing whether you died eating spoiled food with alien bacteria, charging enemy fighters, falling out an airlock, or committing suicide. They don't know whether you died in a trench or an alley. Casualties in the line of duty are so plentiful at the front lines that it takes an almost supernaturally heroic act to get noticed by anyone outside your commanding officer. Unless, of course, your death suits the needs of the PR machine. Most don't, because it's better PR to pretend there's no such thing as death.

Anyway, I was still somewhat under the illusion of the Glorious Death in the Line of Duty during those first hours on Furnace, so I tried to convince myself I was *lucky* to die in a (sort of) battle, like some great Viking warrior or an explorer from a bygone era.

So I accepted my fate. Braced for it. Tried self-consciously to reflect on a life ill-spent in the cold, damp corridors of a dozen fleet vessels.

And then there was another screech beside me, followed by a low grunt. The latter made my ears perk up and my eyes snap open.

What the hell's going on? I wondered. I was surprised none of them had claimed me yet when I could heard them so near. I reasoned that maybe they *knew* they had me trapped and wanted to savor the moment, or maybe they were still fighting over the right to burn me alive limb by limb.

When I heard *human* voices though, quickly followed by the unmistakable reports of heavy IO pulse rifles in the distance, I began to have my doubts.

Salib? I wondered, struggling to my knees to see through the waves of heat and the writhing swarm of bodies.

IO pulse rifles aren't standard for a peaceful mission of exploration on an uncharted planet, which is absolute bullshit as far as I'm concerned. When else will you need your heaviest artillery except when you have no idea what you're up against? Hearing them told me all I needed to know about the state of the squad. Things must have gotten bad while I was gone.

Really bad.

"Chalmers?" a voice called to me between pulse-rifle reports.

After the initial blasts, my hearing went away for a while. The last thing I remember before I started alternating through degrees of consciousness was an unrecognizable fleet soldier (I think it was Sillinger, but I'm not sure to this day) dragging me along the terrain to a hover-gurney and sprinting me to the mountainside. We entered a cave at some point and someone said, "Jesus Christ, he looks bad," before shoving a pill down my throat and shooting me up with a tranq.

Then I was gone a while.

But alive.
I guess I should be grateful.

THE HOLDOUTS

Never once during my marathon through the desert or my encounter with the carnival of horrors at the lava lakes did it occur to me that I had gotten off easy. It was impossible, really. My entire life prior to that mission told me so. And yet, as Salib relayed the events between the clown-thing crushing my helmet and when Sillinger performed emergency surgery on my stomach in the cave darkness, I realized that it could have been a hell of a lot worse for me. Namely, I could have been with the rest of the ground crew when the first wave of natives attacked.

"How many survived?" I asked Salib.

Her perpetual scowl deepened and she stared at me like she couldn't tell whether or not I was joking. I'm not one to make jokes of any kind during combat, though. Least of all about recent KIAs from the company that just saved my ass. It took her a moment to draw that conclusion—we didn't know each other very well—but eventually she must have decided I really *was* as clueless as I sounded. In retrospect, I'm almost embarrassed that there was even a sliver of doubt in her mind. I must have come off like a complete asshole to her in our limited interactions.

"You're looking at everyone that's left," she told me.

Her voice was hoarse, probably from shouting directions to her troops when the comms went out. Not that it would have done much good. Once the creatures attacked and the bullets started to fly, there was little chance they could have heard her over the noise.

It took a few seconds for her words to register. Blame it on the drugs from Sillinger's emergency procedure. By the time I realized her squad had lost more than *half* its complement just in the time we'd been separated (four to six hours by my estimation, maybe more), I was speechless. I couldn't even offer an empty condolence to her for losing the soldiers she was charged with protecting, losses which I could tell weighed heavily on her just by the way her eyes locked onto the darkness and refused to release their grip.

I kept quiet for a while. It seemed like the right thing to do.

After patching me up with some adhesive first-aid foam to close the wound front and back, then sticking some medicated gauze on the cuts along my neck and left bicep, Sillinger began working on one of the soldiers holed up in the shadows near the cave-mouth. I couldn't see who exactly was left alive, though, and I was afraid to ask while the literal and figurative wounds were still so fresh. Eventually, however, the silence hanging between myself and Salib became too uncomfortable to endure.

"Was it the group outside?" I asked, carefully omitting the second half of the question. I didn't need to explain what I meant. "The ones by the lava?"

Salib stood and dusted off her pulse rifle. "No. There's others closer to the ship. We ran into *these* motherfuckers trying to get away from the first group." She swallowed hard and adjusted her utility belt, trying to look official and preoccupied though I could tell she was really trying to stifle the memory of the massacre that had driven them over the mountains. It didn't look like she was winning. "The others are worse."

"Worse?" I shuddered at the idea. I guessed I really *had* gotten off easy. Then again, nothing they'd described so far was quite the same as the razor-toothed grin of the clown corpse pursuing me across the desert. I wasn't sure how or why, but I knew it was still following.

He, I thought suddenly. *It's a he.*

I pushed the notion aside for the time being.

"You're lucky we found you. If we'd headed back to the ship five minutes earlier, we'd be gone and those bastards would have eaten you alive."

She leaned back against the cave wall with a thoughtful expression that I didn't like. I could see the wheels turning behind her eyes and recognized how her grief-stricken rationale was veering toward a very dark place, particularly regarding her opinion of me. It made no real sense, but I've seen soldiers who've recently lost squad-mates blame civilians or troopers they've saved after sustaining heavy casualties, even when the two occurrences were only tangentially related at best (or worst, depending on your view).

The truth, of course, is that I could very well have died (and nearly did) before they rescued me, but it wouldn't have had any bearing on whether the others in Salib's squad lived or died. I saw the cogs of her grief-arithmetic spun inside her head anyway. She was weighing my life against the others.

As if to confirm my fears, she moved her gaze in the direction of the wounded troops near the cave-mouth. "If we hadn't found you, the rest of my squad would still be alive," she said softly.

"So what's next, sir?" I asked quickly, trying to lead her away from any resentful thoughts, while also subtly reminding her that she was still in charge of the survivors and we were holding out between two groups of flesh-eating devils. Not the ideal occasion to indulge personal grudges. "How far away is the ship?"

Scowling, Salib turned her attention back my way and started walking briskly toward me. "What the fuck does it matter? We were attacked right outside the goddamned door of the ship, Lieutenant. There's no way the captain and the rest of the crew survived. And even if they did, we have no way of getting back to them. We're stuck here." She leaned over me, cords of misdirected, helpless anger standing out in her neck. "We're fucked," she whispered.

I guess she may have whispered so the wounded wouldn't hear the grim pronouncement, but at the time, it sure as hell seemed like she was aiming for some spitefully dramatic emphasis. Blaming me for the loss of her crew, I thought, then adding insult to injury by reminding me our situation was hopeless. It was, but it wasn't my acting C.O.'s job to tell me so. *Her* job was to figure a way out of the impossible for us, or at least lead us to believe there *was* a way out as long as we had breath in our lungs.

Sillinger tapped her on the shoulder and nodded toward the other troops. "We've got to get them out of here. I can stop the infections for the most part and try to patch them up, but a couple of them won't make it regardless. The wounds are too close to major arteries." He paused for a moment, swallowing hard and clearly suppressing a grimace. "The teeth cut them to the bone."

Salib nodded slowly, thinking, then pointed her rifle at me. "What about *this* asshole? How come you were able to save him?"

Eyes widening defensively, Sillinger shrugged. "I don't know, sir. His wounds weren't as serious."

"He was cut through the stomach all the way out his back. You want to tell me that none of *his* internal organs were damaged, but every goddamned one of my wounded soldiers is going to *die?*" Salib hissed.

It was clear there was nothing I could do or say to appease her. I had unwittingly assumed the role of scapegoat for her helplessness and failures as a commanding officer, and Sillinger realized it, too. The very breath in my lungs offended her. She was out for blood, and mine was the easiest to spill because I wasn't one of her own.

Worse, I had the audacity to live when others had died.

Time to go, I thought.

While her attention was still focused on Sillinger, I slid along the wall in the opposite direction until I was completely covered in shadow. If she wanted to shoot me, I thought, she'd have to find me first. I couldn't imagine things escalating to that extreme with her squad significantly depleted already. But twenty-four hours earlier, I couldn't have imagined a single goddamned thing about that planet or what would happen to me there. For all I knew, my life was even *more* expendable to her now that death was a certainty for all of us. If she'd truly lost hope, what did fleet regulations matter to her? What the hell could the fleet do to her if she killed me? Court-martial her corpse? And even if she *did* survive the ordeal and make it safely home to be questioned by the Department of Internal Affairs, she could easily say that I—like dozens of others—had been killed while valiantly combatting the natives. Nothing was preventing her from killing me.

"Sir, I..." Sillinger started. He did his best not to look in my direction so she wouldn't follow his gaze. God bless him for that.

"Why is *he* still alive?!" Salib shouted, gripping the back of his neck. Spittle flung from her mouth and slapped against his cheek, but Sillinger didn't notice. He was too scared and confused to answer, or really do anything but stare wide-eyed and hold his hands up defensively.

"I don't know, sir!" he protested.

She drove him back against the wall. "What about the infection?"

Sillinger began stammering an answer or excuse, but he never finished. Salib tightened her grip and slammed his head against the cave wall with enough force to make me groan.

"You're fucking useless," she said.

I squatted quietly in the darkness, afraid to move in case the sound drew her attention. Sillinger was still alive, but barely conscious and bleeding from the base of his skull. The damage may have been little more than a concussion, but I thought it was more likely that his head had cracked open. Either way, Salib wasn't about to leave anything to chance. Apparently, she truly believed the only trained field medic left on her team was 'useless' and expendable. She brought the pulse rifle up to bear and blew his head off without hesitation. Bits of bone and gore flew everywhere, showering Salib and splattering against my shins. The smell of scorched flesh was almost as bad as the clown demon's breath.

What the hell do I do now? I wondered.

I was stunned by my lack of emotion at Sillinger's murder, but I'd seen a lot of shit that day. As far as deaths and nightmares went on Furnace, in fact, Sillinger's murder was one of the easier ones to witness. Ashamed as I am to admit it now, the most pressing concern for me right then was where I could go to avoid Salib, not how I could sneak up behind her and avenge the death of the man who'd saved my life twice in the preceding half-hour. Salib and the survivors from her squad stood between me and the cave-mouth, and I had no idea what lurked in the shadows behind me. All I knew was that if there were monsters like the demon clown in broad daylight, then it stood to reason that there would be even more formidable terrors where only darkness lived.

What will it be, then?

It sounds awful, but I had to admit that fighting humans—even fellow soldiers—was far more desirable than fighting monsters. Was it worth the shame, though? Was it better to let Salib kill me than take advantage of my brothers and sisters bleeding out in a cave hundreds of trillions of light-years from home?

Damn it, I thought.

I was only a couple hours removed from wishing for the quick release of death on the planet's surface, and yet there I was, plotting the murders of fellow humans. And for what? Another chance to face the nightmares outside the cave? To live another hour or two in the grating wind before they subjected me to torture far worse than the receiving end of Salib's pulse rifle? It was absurd. I'd like to chalk up that initial reaction to irrational fear, or even the drugs Sillinger gave me after surgery. The truth is, though, I was thinking the same way any human would have in that situation. That's not an excuse, either. It's just fact. We're all instilled with survival instincts from birth which (occasionally) overwhelm our senses of honor and duty. Otherwise, our species never would have risen to supremacy on Earth, let alone advanced to the point of spreading humanity's seeds across the galaxy. It still makes me cringe, but in that moment, I was consumed by the hard-coded desire for self-preservation, no matter the consequences.

Then again, it had been a while since I'd seen the clown demon. I guess I'd lost perspective on just how steep the consequences could be for leaving the cave.

"CHALMERS!" Salib suddenly screamed. Her back was turned to me. She gripped the pulse rifle tightly and examined the remnants of her squad. "YOU'RE A FUCKING DEAD MAN!"

The testicle-shrinking boom of her voice made me jerk backwards so hard that my head slammed against the cave wall. I cursed under my breath. Just loud enough for her to hear it.

"Damn it..."

She swiveled around to face me.

"Damn it," I repeated.

The first blast from her pulse rifle exploded into the wall three feet behind me. A minor miscalculation on her part, and one I couldn't count on again now that the cavern had lit up long enough for her to spot me.

Fuck fuck fuck fuck fuck fuck...

We locked stares. My courage withered beneath her cold resolve. I knew by the look she gave me that she was prepared to kill me without further parley. If I was lucky, she'd use the pulse rifle. From what I could tell, though, she wasn't against finishing me with her bare hands.

I scrambled deeper into the cave, trying to make as little commotion as possible but with little success. I had all the subtlety of a hurricane.

"Sir!" I shouted over my shoulder, wholly negating the small measure of stealth I'd won in my escape bid. "Calm down!"

"Fuck you," she growled through clenched teeth.

I could practically feel the heat of her combat-breath searing the medicated gauze on the back of my neck. She was close.

Damn it damn it damn it...

I struggled to unclasp my armor plating so I could move more freely through the tight, winding corridors ahead, but it wound up slowing me down and the noise made me easier to track. I eventually gave up and just started running as fast as I could while feeling my way along the wall.

Right up until I ran face-first into a rock and dropped like Kalak bomber, that is.

The world erupted in white light momentarily and I realized that another shot had been fired behind me.

Oh no...

I didn't feel pain right away so I figured she'd just missed me, but then the nerves in my cheeks and chest lit up like livewires and I cursed loudly. Contorting my face only made things worse, though, and I forgot all about Salib and her pulse rifle while I writhed back and forth on the wet ground.

When I opened my eyes again, I saw that the wall directly above me was smoldering from a pulse charge. The impact had saved me, then. If I'd dropped a moment later or kept running, the shot would have caught me in the back of the head and my brains would have exploded across the cave like Sillinger's. Instead, Salib's blast smacked the wall, and a moment later, the cave lit up again with white light.

Only this time, it hadn't come from Salib's rifle. It was Charlotte Rayford who'd fired. She was bleeding from a crooked nose. The right side of her face was torn to shreds and her teeth were exposed where her cheek had burned away. She looked like absolute shit, and I knew immediately that she'd been one of the troopers Sillinger pronounced a lost cause before Salib blew his head off.

I forced myself up on my left elbow for a better look.

Salib stared at me with such palpable venom in her eyes that I jerked back again, as though the intensity of her hatred alone could incinerate me. I held her gaze for a moment, frozen with indecision, and then the muscles in her face slackened and she leaned against the cave wall. Her feet gradually slipped out from under her and she hit the ground with a graceless thud that made me wince. I could hear bones and cartilage crack in her face with the extra force of the planet's gravity on top of them. Charlotte had caught her in the back of the head, but she'd also hit the life-support controls on her suit, which must have shorted the gravity equalizers.

I watched her die, then turned to Charlotte. Her helmet light was on and glared directly into my eyes, but I could still see she only had an hour left to live at the very best. She was braced against the wall with one knee on the cave floor and her head hung down so her chin touched her chest. I gave her an inquisitive look and she shrugged half-heartedly.

"Sillinger," she said.

I nodded and struggled to my feet. I didn't care that she'd saved my life only to avenge Sillinger's unjust death—I would have done the same regardless of who Salib was trying to kill—but I *did* care that she'd used her last bit of energy to do what was right...at least in my judgment. I wanted to help her if I could, but I wasn't sure how.

"Thanks," I said. The word felt lame rolling off of my tongue. Lonely, too. Considering the stakes, it was a poor sentiment of gratitude. I might as well have thanked her for showing up to a kegger or telling me my haircut looked nice. "What can I do?"

She didn't answer.

I walked a few steps beyond Salib's body, then stopped.

"Char?" I whispered, raising my hands in the universal gesture of surrender.

Her rifle was pointed at me. "Fuck off," she said.

I stood frozen for a moment, trying to decide whether or not she really meant to shoot me. I didn't want to make any sudden movements that could rattle her or tighten the grip of her trigger finger. I'm not stupid.

After a few seconds, her head fell against the cave wall out of sheer exhaustion. I decided to let her die in peace. Nothing I said to her, even a heartfelt expression of gratitude, would ease her passing. It could only mess things up, and maybe even get me killed.

"I'm sorry," I told her anyway, not knowing exactly what for but knowing I owed her that much, regardless.

I made my way towards the cave entrance without another word, giving her as wide a berth as possible. I still passed within arm's reach. She didn't raise her rifle again, though. I don't think she had the strength, or maybe she was already dead. Either way, I shuddered once I passed her. It had been one hell of a close call, but so had everything else on the planet so far. It was a miracle I was still alive, and I wasn't sure it was the kind of miracle I actually wanted. I kept wavering on that front.

Stepping between the wounded soldiers at the cave entrance was much more difficult than passing the bodies of Salib, Charlotte, and Silinger, though. The remnants of Salib's squad were still agonizingly conscious. They moaned. They reached for the unraveling strands of life with shaking fingers. A couple of them would survive, I thought, but they weren't in any shape to hike across a hostile planet without food or water, let alone with an army of monsters stalking them.

Where did those other species come from? I wondered distractedly. I remembered the scene around the lava, where demons forced seemingly innocent captives into fire for their amusement.

At the time, I hadn't thought about it much because I was on the verge of death myself. Suddenly, though, the distinction seemed important. Those aliens hadn't been Salib's troopers or even other personnel from the *Rockne Hummel*, and we hadn't seen any other ship during our arrival. Our systems had been malfunctioning, of course, but the likelihood that there was an active ship near enough to have its crew captured and tortured by the locals was slim, at least in my calculations.

So what did that mean? Were the other aliens locals, too? Or had they crashed like us? Was it possible that the clown demon and his minions had traveled to another planet and kidnapped them?

I didn't care all that much for the wellbeing of those creatures (at least, not as much as myself or my fellow humans from the *Rockne Hummel*), but if alien ships had crashed or landed intact on the surface, or if the natives indeed had the capability of space travel, there were likely ships nearby that we could hijack to escape.

Don't get ahead of yourself.

At the very least, though, it merited some consideration. If I ever made it back to the *Rockne Hummel*, I would demand that Captain Gibbons take another recon team to investigate the matter. I would lead it myself if possible, although I didn't expect him to allow me back on the surface a third time with an enemy on the loose. I was his navigator, after all, and even with his mind on the fritz as it had been since we'd dropped out of FTL in the middle of nowhere, I'd like to think the captain knew enough not to needlessly put me in harm's way a third time. Believe me, I don't have a huge ego or any delusions about my self-worth, but the fact of the matter is that a ship needs a navigator and there wasn't anyone left on board who could fill in well enough to plot our way back home.

As that thought occurred to me, I realized for the first time that there might be those among the *Hummel's* crew that didn't *want* to make it home. Not with any conscious resistance, but with another force working at them. It sure as hell hadn't seemed like Salib wanted to get back to the ship and blast off of Furnace. Maybe because she'd lost most of her squad, but maybe not. The notion forced me to examine the wounded soldiers sprawled over the cave floor with more than a little suspicion.

You'll still need all the help you can get.

It was true. They had more weapons than I could carry on my suit and more eyes to spot the enemy. Aside from that, they were humans and my crewmates. I wasn't about to leave them behind if I could help it.

"Come with me if you want a chance to live," I told them.

They stopped groaning and three of the four struggled to their feet. The fourth was completely unresponsive and, like Charlotte, may have already passed on by then.

"Good," I said. "Let's go."

I didn't know where the hell I planned on taking them, but I knew we couldn't stay in the cave any longer, if only because the decomposing bodies of Sillinger, Salib, Charlotte, and the other soldier I hadn't identified would eventually drive us mad. Maybe even push us past the brink of self-preservation into the realm of outright lunacy.

We had to go *somewhere*. We had to do *something*.

So we stepped out of the cave back onto the killing floor.

And some of us lived to tell the tale.

MOUNTAINS

I'll be the first to admit I wasn't in any shape to lead the group when we set out from the cave, and yet I was still our best hope for survival. I had three soldiers with me—Aziza Mbutu, Katrina Mnatsakanov, and Brendan Flaherty—and they were all worse off than I was.

Aziza had a chunk missing from her left cheek where one of the creatures had bitten to the bone. Her eye was swollen shut, maybe even gone completely. I couldn't tell.

The right side of Katrina's suit had been crushed and she barely had use of her arm and leg. Her limp was slow and inefficient, but I wasn't about to tell her to stay behind.

Brendan had it worse than any of us, though. His right arm had been severed just above the elbow. The backs of his legs were ripped to shreds, with long claw marks standing out in sickening clarity like red exclamation points. His armor plating was torn below the ribs and loose bits of flesh flapped there as he moved. I don't know how he managed a single step while bleeding through the almost comically insufficient gauze pads Sillinger taped to him. I can only guess that whatever drugs he'd been given to cope with the pain were tiny, encapsulated miracles. Maybe Zylos? Numb-ers? I'm not sure. Either that, or the prospect of dying was just too scary for Flaherty, although that doesn't seem to fit. He was a deep-space soldier, after all. He had to know deep down that life would only get worse for him from there. I guess it's that same hard-coding in all of us that makes us fight to survive even when we know death is the only true release from pain.

We exited the cave about fifteen minutes after Salib killed Sillinger. At first, we stuck to the shadows along the winding mountain paths as much as we could. I heard demons screeching in the distance as we walked but didn't risk a glance over the rocks. I didn't know whether or not they'd stuck around the lava, but I knew stealing another look would only slow us down. Worse, it might sap the already dwindling resolve from my companions. We needed all the hope and focus at our disposal, and gazing into the eyes of utter despair isn't conducive to either. Instead, I gripped Salib's pulse rifle tightly and kept moving until we found a path leading to the peak.

"Stay low," I told the others. We were on the verge of exposing ourselves to every creature within ten miles and I wanted to avoid detection as long as possible. Even with a generous head-start, I knew we still might not get very far if the monsters spotted us when we began our ascent.

Katrina nodded back at me, out of breath but not as physically or psychologically broken as I'd expected. Aziza was predictably stoic and not breathing hard at all, though that was likely because each breath stretched her torn skin and, in turn, stretched her mouth into a deeper grimace of pain.

Flaherty—also predictably—was struggling. He didn't look like he'd make it another five feet up the mountain, let alone all the way to the peak and down the other side.

"You all right, Flaherty?" I asked.

He couldn't even raise his head to tell me yes or no. He couldn't even put weight on his legs anymore.

"He's done," Katrina told me. Aziza said nothing.

"Flaherty?" I called, a little louder this time. I wasn't worried about being overheard. The wind and hiss of lava were plenty loud to cover my voice. I glanced back over the miles of rocky wastelands anyway. Just to be sure.

Flaherty still didn't answer. His shoulders slumped further south and his good arm (I use that term lightly) slipped clumsily from the rock he'd used to brace himself. He fell forward in a graceless heap, unable to break his fall because his support arm had betrayed him.

"Jesus," Katrina winced.

I leapt to him a split-second too late but still managed to catch him before major damage was done. Once I had a firm grip, I propped him against a boulder.

"Flaherty!" I shouted into his ear.

I thought about slapping him in hopes of jolting him awake, but I could tell by his complexion that it would have been useless. He was either dead or would be within five minutes. Maybe fifteen if he really fought for it. I couldn't see why he *would*, but it wasn't my life.

"Leave him," Aziza told me flatly. She'd never struck me as the emotional type, but the finality in her voice still gave me a chill. It wasn't supposed to be easy leaving a brother or sister behind. At least, not out loud.

"There's nothing we can do," Katrina echoed. Her tone was a little softer but I could tell it had been manufactured to placate me. She kept anxiously eyeing the road from the lava to the mountain path.

I turned back to Flaherty and shook him, knowing the movement would domino ungodly amounts of pain through his nervous system but also knowing that pain might be my only chance of bringing him back. He didn't stir at all, though. His eyes were half-open and his cracked, bleeding lips slung crookedly to the right. I couldn't hear any breath, but the wind was heavy on the mountain.

So what was I supposed to do? His own squad-mates wanted to leave him behind, and maybe the fact that they *were* his squad-mates justified the abandonment. He was one of *them*, after all, and as long as *they* were the ones who made the decision that he was too injured to continue without risking the entire group, I figured it was all right to let him go. Of course, I guess there's always the possibility that he was just an asshole and they weren't broken up over the prospect of his death. But considering they'd just lost the rest of their squad including their commanding officer, I'm sure they were a little desensitized, and that was probably the overriding emotion (or lack thereof) that allowed them to cut the cord. It made the grief a little easier to swallow.

Regardless, I agreed with their assessment. There was no way Flaherty would make it up the mountain, and the chances we'd be spotted during our ascent were significantly higher if he did because we'd have to help him the whole way up. Besides, he was probably dead already, right? I don't know for sure. I would have needed to disengage a significant amount of armor-plating on him to verify beyond the shadow of a doubt, and I didn't have that kind of time. *We* didn't.

Truth be told, I didn't want to know if he was alive, anyway. It only would have made things more difficult if he was. At least now I can comfort myself by assuring everyone around me that Flaherty had already passed by the time we left him. Usually, that's enough to assuage my guilt. Sometimes, it's not.

I rose and took two steps away from him, swallowing back cotton-mouth and checking to be sure the pulse rifle's safety was disengaged.

"Wait," Aziza said, gripping my wrist. "Don't shoot him. They'll see it." She nodded down to the lava lakes and I followed her gaze. The monsters were little more than hulking, abnormal shadows in the distance and so were their victims, but her point was well taken. If the purpose of leaving Flaherty's body behind was to avoid detection by the creatures, it was stupid to fire a pulse rifle unless absolutely necessary. A pulse charge would be visible—and perhaps audible—from several miles away on a bad day, even if it was filtered by trees and battle smoke. On a clear mountain landscape, however, we would be found the moment the shot was fired.

It was also a waste of ammo, but none of us chose to point that out even though I'm fairly certain we were all thinking it. It's how they train us in the fleet, especially soldiers like us who are accustomed to battle and deep space excursions. When you're cut off from the rest of humanity, every resource is precious. Especially bullets and pulse charges.

I switched the safety back on the pulse rifle and sighed. "All right," I said. "Let's get the fuck out of here then."

Over the years I've been an active fleet soldier both in the infantry and as a navigator, I've had to leave a lot of brothers behind. A few hours earlier, I'd left Chara to die. Hell, I'd let Sillinger and Rayford die for saving my life, and I'd watched Salib die while trying to kill me.

But for some reason, Flaherty's death hurt the worst. I think because it was the first time I'd *knowingly* left someone when it wasn't their request and when his fate was far worse than a normal passing. If the creatures discovered him out there and he had even one breath left in him, he would suffer. Not for an hour or a few years, but forever. Whenever I reflect on the ways that Furnace broke me (which is often indeed), I think that particular fracture was the most profound. It was the *change* that it sparked. The subtle shift in me which completely altered my self-worth. Suddenly, I knew I was capable not just of leaving a soldier behind, but of deciding to prolong his misery for the sake of conserving ammunition. A single goddamned pulse charge, which didn't wind up doing me any good anyway.

That's the kind of shit that messes you up for good.

"What's the plan, sir?" Katrina asked.

I shrugged and strapped the pulse rifle to the holster on my back. I needed both hands to negotiate the terrain. "We hope to God we find the *Hummel* before we die of thirst." I paused, thinking about the clown demon stalking me across the wastelands. "Or something else."

Aziza groaned with effort as she followed. Katrina fell silent for a while, which I'd gathered was rare for her from our brief conversations during boarding protocols at Serenity Base.

The mountain wasn't particularly tall as mountains go, but it felt like an eighty-five degree slope as we scaled it. The gravity-equalizers on our suits were starting to malfunction as our energy sources ran dry, too. For a trio of wounded strangers in a strange land with nothing left in the tank, it made for one hell of a climb. I didn't look back to check on Katrina or Aziza at all, mostly because my arms were trembling and I thought I'd lose my grip if I was startled even momentarily by the view behind me. But I heard how much they suffered along the way. There was no shortage of grunts, moans, curses, yelps, or cascading rocks in my wake, and I'm pretty sure they both stopped to rest at least twice while I continued on without them.

Yet somehow, roughly an hour later, the three of us were within reach of the summit and none of us had sustained further injury (excepting, of course, the sheer exhaustion of climbing a mountain while recuperating from life-threatening wounds). It wasn't until we reached the top that I realized I hadn't expected all of us to make it after leaving Flaherty to rot on the killing floor. Somewhere in the back of my mind, I'd figured that at *least* Katrina would have phoned it in before we reached the halfway point. Let alone the summit. It wasn't over yet, though. We still had to make it down the other side without incident, but I had no doubt we could manage now that we'd gotten through the hard part (or so I thought).

I sat down a few feet from the mountaintop and turned back to them.

"Do you remember how far the ship is from here?"

Aziza touched her cheek gingerly and winced. The blood beneath her eye had begun to coagulate in a strange cluster with yellowish-gray fluid. It looked rife with infection. I tried not to let my revulsion show, but I still nearly vomited the meager contents of my stomach at the sight.

"I have no fucking idea where the ship is," she said. "I thought *you* did. Wasn't that the whole point of climbing here?"

Katrina grabbed the last handgrip before the peak and gasped. "Stop," she said between gulps of air.

I didn't know what she was referring to but I felt awful seeing her struggle so badly while I perched above them and effectively blocked them both from proceeding.

"Relax," I told Aziza. "We'll figure it out. It's better up here than what we would have had to face back there." I nodded toward the lava lakes and the endless wastelands beyond them. "I've already been out that way. We'd all be dead before we found food or water."

"Still might be," Aziza muttered.

"Maybe," I said. "But at least there's hope."

Even Aziza couldn't argue that point. Not until we looked over the other side of the mountain, anyway, and saw what fresh horrors awaited us.

"You've got to be fucking kidding me," Aziza scoffed. She was exhausted to the point of delirium. I could see the ghost of a smile rising on her lips, and that was plenty bizarre for the situation. It was Katrina's response that really caught me off guard, though, and I'm not sure why. As soon as she saw the fields of corpses below us and the abominations prowling the dull, moss-green and cadaver-gray landscape, she dropped to her knees in prayer.

Aziza collapsed backward so violently that I thought she'd fainted initially, right up until she scoffed and shook her head at Katrina. "That won't help us," she said. "*He* doesn't live here. *They* live here."

"Shut up," I snapped, more because I felt a need to lash out than I actually cared about protecting Katrina's religious freedoms. "It sure as hell won't hurt anyone." I glanced at Katrina, trying to avoid glimpsing the land ahead of us until I came up with an alternate escape plan. Her prayer was old Russian, a dialect I figured must have pre-dated Standard by at least a milennium.

"We're fucked," Aziza said.

Katrina finished praying and we sat in silence for a while with downcast eyes, intent on ignoring our predicament.

What do you do now? I asked myself for seemingly the hundredth time since we'd crashed on Furnace.

Choose the lesser of two evils.

I was getting good at it, I guess. Escaping the city. Running through the desert. Attacking the demons rather than fleeing. I don't know how I was ever convinced one evil was lesser than the other.

Have you forgotten what followed you through the wastelands?

For a moment, I actually had. The recollection made my blood run cold and my fingers tingle.

Forward, then. Always forward.

I thought of Flaherty's body at the foot of the mountain. Charlotte's. Salib's. Sillinger's. I swallowed and shook my head.

There's no other choice. You can't look at them again and you can't look at the clown demon, either.

Some superstitious part of me was convinced that merely gazing upon the horned demon in his crusted, bleach-white clown skin would suck the soul right out of my body, dragging my heartbeat and breath along with it.

"I can't do it," Aziza said. Her voice pulled me back. The sensation was awful. Like a drill sergeant throwing you from your bunk to inform you of a surprise survival drop on Venus. "I'll just stay here and wait. You two can do whatever the hell you want. Get eaten by one of those bastards, or a whole fucking army of them. I'm not moving from this spot no matter what."

"Zeez," Katrina pleaded. Her eyes were wide with shock and terror she never would have shown in battle, even facing an entire battalion of Kalak.

"There's no point. We won't survive. I don't know about you, but I don't have enough ammo to take out more than one or two of those things before I'm bone dry. And that's *if* I hit my targets." She gestured to her face and arm, moving so slowly it was difficult to even connect the two motions. "I'm pretty sure my marksmanship isn't what it used to be."

Katrina struggled to her feet and wiped sweat from her forehead with the dry, dusty metal of her forearm plating. "No," she said firmly. "You're coming with us."

Aziza's tone immediately soured. I was surprised it hadn't already. She glowered at Katrina like they weren't best friends who'd spent over a year together in the trenches. "Fuck you, bitch. It's my choice. I'm not going anywhere."

"Your duty's to the fleet and the captain. Not yourself."

"My C.O. is rotting in a cave because of *this* asshole. My duty's not to anyone but myself. A soldier has the right to die in battle."

"This isn't battle," Katrina countered.

"*This* is," Aziza snapped, pointing to her swollen, pus-covered cheek once again. "And *this* is what will kill me. I can already feel it spreading."

"They can help you back at the ship."

"Who can?" Aziza demanded.

"What do you mean 'who'? One of the goddamned doctors!"

"We're not going to find the ship. We don't even know if we're going in the right *direction*."

"We are," I interjected.

"How do you figure?"

"I don't know. It just feels like it, doesn't it?" She didn't answer. "Plus, I can see the top of a huge crater ahead," I said, pointing over the land on the other side of the mountain. "It looks like the impact from our crash landing."

I was telling the truth. It *did* feel like the *Hummel* was off in that direction, although I may have just felt that way because our greatest obstacle so far was stretched before us and I expected formidable opposition before victory. Blame the soldier in me.

It also seemed like the crater to the lava was a reasonable distance for the squad to have traveled since we'd split into pairs searching for supplies and refuge as our life-support waned. I never would have thought the atmosphere was breathable, but I would have preferred the most toxic atmosphere imaginable a thousand times over to the bloodthirsty aliens on the prowl.

"Shit," I groaned. "You *should* remember where the hell the *Hummel* is. You just came from there, didn't you? How could you all wind up together with no idea where you left the ship?"

"Same way you did," Aziza snapped back. "We all wound up here like you said, so why don't *you* remember?"

She had a point. It shut me up for a while.

Luckily, Katrina wasn't ready to give up the fight just yet, because I didn't have any arguments left and I was starting to care less and less whether or not she accompanied us.

"You're pathetic," Katrina suddenly chimed in. I was shocked to see genuine disdain in her eyes. I couldn't tell if she truly meant what she said or if she was just trying a different tactic to convince Aziza to come with us, and I don't think Aziza could, either.

"What did you say?" she asked, more incredulous than appalled.

"You're a pathetic piece of shit. This is the craziest action you've seen in your entire life and all you can do is whine.

Weren't you the one complaining how boring a political escort mission would be? Weren't you the one who said you wanted a real fight to get your blood pumping?"

Aziza glared back but said nothing. Katrina was still struggling to catch her breath, but there was a flash of wildness in her eyes that assured me she'd find the air to go on no matter how weak her lungs felt or how badly her wounds burned.

"That's what I thought. All talk." She leaned forward dramatically and spat at Aziza's feet. "You're a spineless piece of shit and that's how we'll remember you when we get back home and your body's rotting out here. I'll tell everyone you love that you didn't make it back because it was too *hard* for you. Because it *hurts*." Katrina's eyes narrowed with scorn and she spat her cotton-mouthed saliva onto Aziza's cheek, as if she was convincing herself with each word, as well. "You should be ashamed of yourself."

As you can imagine, that didn't go over well.

Before I realized what was happening, Aziza had pointed her rifle at Katrina and pulled the trigger. The shot only missed her head by two inches. Maybe less.

"Watch what you say to me, asswipe," she growled with her finger flexing on the trigger-guard.

Katrina's eyes widened again. She backed away slowly with her hands held up in the universal gesture of surrender. I think she realized at last that her best friend was capable of killing her just for questioning her honor, and maybe hitting a little too close to home with her accusations in the process.

Looking back, the rifle blast must have turned Katrina's world completely upside-down. She wasn't exactly naïve—no soldier who's killed and watched her brothers and sisters die can be classified as such, and sure as hell no soldier who stepped foot on Furnace—but she was trusting when it came to her squad-mates. Really, any fleet soldier with the same assignment. I can imagine how much worse it was to have

Aziza of all people turn on her like that, even if it was provoked.

It was a tense situation to say the least, but Aziza *had* to know deep down that Katrina was only riling her up because she couldn't bear the thought of leaving her behind.

Right?

I wasn't sure.

We stood in a loose triangle without uttering a word for a few moments. Aziza and Katrina stared each other down. Neither of them was willing to make the first move. My eyes darted back and forth between them, trying to decide whether or not it was worth it to make a play for Aziza's rifle before hell broke loose. I didn't want to force her hand, though, so I waited for one of them to break the silence.

Just when I sensed Katrina was finally going to cave, however, a shadow passed over the mountain and we all ducked reflexively. A moment later, a giant, winged creature swooped over us. Some odd mix of a dragon and a bat. It screeched loud enough to shake the mountainside.

"Fuck," I muttered. "Find cover!"

Aziza pulled the trigger before I could stop her.

"No!" I shouted. "What are you doing?"

As if the shot she'd fired at Katrina hadn't done enough damage revealing our position and attracting unwanted attention from the creatures below, she now released a whole goddamned round into the bat's torso.

"Stop!" I yelled, but it was pointless. She couldn't hear me over the gunfire and it was too late to make a difference, anyway.

Once her clip ran dry, I rushed out from behind the rock I'd used for cover and grabbed her by the arm. "What the hell is wrong with you?"

"Did you *see* that bastard?" she protested. "That thing was going to kill us!"

"Maybe," I agreed, helping Katrina to her feet. The bat let out an enraged squeal and veered back in our direction. "But it's *definitely* going to now."

Yet amazingly, it hadn't seen us, even with the aid of gunfire. A blessing, surely, and one of few I can count that day.

After a while, the creature moved off toward the crater. I glanced back the way we'd come, trying to determine whether the demons at the lava lakes had realized what was happening or if they were too busy torturing innocent souls to pay us any mind. I thought that if they weren't looking, we might be able to escape back down the mountain and try to navigate the caves to the other side instead.

I quickly realized it wasn't an option.

"Shit," I hissed.

Not only had the bastards seen us, a whole herd of them swarmed the base of the mountain in pursuit. At the rate they were moving, I estimated they'd overtake us within the hour even if we sprinted the whole way. We were in bad shape.

There was no time for debate.

"Move," I told Katrina, pushing Aziza in step behind her. They both stumbled but didn't protest. We all knew we were finally out of options. No matter what awaited us up ahead, at least we'd be moving in a new direction.

"Better reload, Zeez," Katrina said. There was bite to her voice but sincerity, as well. I thought that was very big of her.

The two remaining troopers from Salib's squad led the way down the steep slope and I plodded along after them, glancing over my shoulder every few moments even though movement shot bolts of pain through my neck.

We descended the mountain toward an indistinct field of corpses with an army of nightmares at our heels. The sick part is, I thought we were *lucky* for spotting them first. I guess my concept of luck is just another casualty of the fire planet.

THE DRUGS WEAR OFF: REFLECTIONS

As it turned out, the way down the mountain was a hell of a lot harder than the way up. Not in terms of the cardio workout but in the effort it took to keep our momentum from hurling us down the slope to our deaths, probably slamming into every boulder and dead bush along the way.

Our urgency faded by degrees the further we were removed from the lava lakes, despite the landscape ahead being far more macabre than what we'd left behind. Part of it was because we could no longer actually see the horde pursuing us with blood-spattered mouths. Part of it was probably the way that the rocks on the mountainside blocked the corpse fields from view, as well.

Aside from the three of us, the mountain was utterly lifeless. We couldn't hear the creatures behind us anymore or the screams of their victims, and that made us a little more comfortable. Psychologically, if not physically. Soldiers always feel more at ease when they're marching toward an objective, even in the direst of circumstances. It gives you a sense of control. Sitting and waiting is about as bad as it gets. No action. No control. Only nagging fears.

About two-thirds of the way down, however, we reached a section of the mountain path where the rock wall opened up and we had our first horrifying view of the corpse fields.

"My God..." I muttered.

The scene was like something out of the bizarre old plague folktales. The ones that ran rampant during the first viral outbreak in northern Michigan. There were miles of intersecting pillars with crucified bodies draped over them. All different species. The victims were mired in varying stages of decomposition. Separate, free creatures moved between the rows wearing all black. Guards, maybe. Stewards. Watchmen. Red, wooden masks covered their faces, but they were too far away to distinguish any other remarkable features. The bodies themselves were so densely clustered that it was difficult to differentiate one from the next.

The smell was overwhelming, but the worst part of all was the measure of order in that awful place, which had led to the assembly of thousands of crucifixes as well as the systematic nailing of creatures upon them.

They must be killing constantly to have this many, I thought. *Literally non-stop.*

Somehow, the idea of structured brutality was more unsettling than the blind, sadistic delights of the monsters at the lava lakes. Those creatures had been mindless savages starved for meat and a temporary thrill. The apparent order in the corpse fields, however, hinted at a rudimentary cooperation between the abominations, and some greater—or lesser—purpose to the madness.

No, I thought. It was my only certainty in the moment. An indefinite negation. *No. I'm not going down there.*

"Is it too late to go back?" Katrina panted.

Aziza backtracked until she found a rock she could rest against and plopped down, shaking her head. "I can't believe I let you assholes talk me into this. You should have left me. I'd be done with this shit by now."

Easing herself down with her back to the carnage, Katrina scoffed between deep inhalations. "If you really wanted to die, you wouldn't have run off with us the second that bat attacked. You would have reloaded and kept shooting."

"Stop," I said sharply. I was tired and in a hell of a lot of pain. Mostly, though, I was sick of listening to them bicker. It had gotten old fast. Bottom line, we needed water or it wouldn't matter if any of us *wanted* to live or die. It would be beyond our control. Katrina already looked like she was on her last leg (no pun intended...seriously), and despite Aziza's stubborn vitality, I didn't think she was far behind, either.

Katrina laid her head against a boulder and closed her eyes. "*Is* it too late to turn back?" she asked again.

At first, I hadn't been able to tell whether or not she was serious, but I quickly decided she didn't have enough energy to muster the same sarcastic comment twice. "Yes," I told her, because in terms of the time it would take us to retrace our steps versus the amount of time we had left to live, it *was* too late to turn back, or really to do anything at all. We were pretty much fucked every which way we turned. "We've got to keep going."

"For what?" Aziza asked.

I glared at her, then doubled over and tried to catch my breath like Katrina. Just the sound of her labored breathing made me feel like I was running out of oxygen, too. It also brought on a peculiar, claustrophobic panic that I hadn't felt since my first spacewalk when I heard a hiss in my suit and thought the oxygen was leaking. It was a purely psychological reaction, but that didn't make the panic any less potent in the moment.

"You know what, Zeez?" I said. "If you don't want to come with us, then fucking stay here. You're not doing us any favors tagging along and bitching about it every step of the way." I paused for breath but didn't mind the dramatic effect it created, either. "You can stay right here and get ripped apart by those demon fucks chasing us because of you. Because *you* unloaded a clip on a goddamned mountaintop for no goddamned reason." I took a step toward her and held out my hand. "Just give us your weapon and we'll go on without you."

If one-eyed looks could kill, I would have preferred the corpse fields to Aziza's stare then. But that's all it was. A stare. She didn't have a comeback and she wasn't about to challenge me physically after the hike, even if she thought she would have beaten me under normal circumstances. Any altercation would have killed both of us, and she knew it. We'd either fall down the mountain or exhaust every last ounce of strength in our bodies.

Maybe Katrina was right after all, I thought. Maybe Aziza really *didn't* want to die. Maybe she was all talk, although I couldn't imagine why at the time. Thinking back, I'm guessing it was a defense mechanism, but that borders on psychoanalysis and I'm nowhere near qualified to offer up that sort of judgment.

"Hold up," Katrina protested weakly, raising one trembling hand in supplication.

"No," I said. "I'm your commanding officer now and I'm 'commanding' Zeez to come with us. If she chooses to disobey a direct order, she is immediately suspended from the fleet pending a trial and is not authorized to operate fleet weaponry during that time," I recited. "Her rifle is our property, and we need it."

Aziza shot up, still maintaining eye contact, and held the butt of the rifle out defiantly. "Here," she said. "Take your property back. It won't do you any good."

Katrina struggled up on one elbow. Her eyes remained mostly closed but I could tell by the way her brow furrowed that she was deeply troubled by the course our conversation had taken. "Zeez, please. Stop. I need you to come with us."

"No," Aziza said. "I'm staying here."

"Then keep the gun. *Please.* How will you fight those things when they get here?"

"Didn't you hear?" I cut in, taking the rifle from Aziza. "Why the hell would she want to fight those things off if she just wants them to kill her? It's a waste of ammo, like shooting at a giant fucking bat. And God forbid we spare *one* bullet to put Flaherty out of his misery."

That last bit brought Katrina to her knees, which immediately made me regret telling Aziza off at all. I'd just felt too shitty to keep listening to her bitching. I didn't *really* want her to die.

"Lieutenant," Katrina pleaded.

I turned from them and started back down the mountain. "If she wants to come, she's welcome to, but I'm tired of her bitching and moaning. We don't have enough time left to waste it on anything other than surviving. Now *move*."

Favoring the side where the clown demon had skewered me before Sillinger's miracle surgery, I braced myself and started toward the corpse fields. I didn't look back to see whether or not they followed me, but they did. Evidently, no matter how much Aziza *thought* she was ready to throw in the towel, part of her still hoped for a happy ending. After that, her presence alone encouraged me. If even *she* thought there was a chance we would make it back to the ship, after all, and maybe even make it *home* afterward, then I figured the odds must not have been as bad as they seemed. It was fool's logic, I know, but hearing her mutter to Katrina again on our way down comforted me even more.

After that, it didn't take long to complete our descent despite our fatigue. Or maybe it just seemed like it because I dreaded reaching the bottom even more than I desired it. How long *exactly*, though? I'm not sure. I feel like I should apologize for my imprecise relation of time and distance throughout this account, but I've grown complacent and rely too heavily on our suits' systems to monitor these so-called 'trivial' matters during a ground mission, and I haven't been trained well enough to mark them in real time.

"Let's rest here for a few," I told the others, shambling behind the last bit of cover available before entering the corpse fields.

Katrina didn't bother hiding. She collapsed the moment I gave the order to rest and didn't move until I told her it was time to get going again. I didn't need to ask why she hadn't sought cover first, even ignoring her visible exhaustion. Just like during my dazed journey across the wastelands, we didn't have true cover anyway and wouldn't at all once we ventured into the corpse fields aside from the corpses themselves. She must have figured there was no point exerting herself for the sake of avoiding detection.

Aziza, on the other hand, *did* take cover but she hung back a ways to get it. Probably still pissed at me for chewing her out and 'humiliating' her, although I find it hard to believe she could be that stubborn knowing we were literally hours away from death, maybe less.

"You all right, Katrina?" I asked. It was easy to see she wasn't, but I wanted to help even though I had nothing to offer.

She didn't answer. The three of us fell silent again.

I can't attest to what was running through Aziza and Katrina's heads while we rested there. I would guess Aziza continued her internal debate about death versus suicide, suffering versus relief, and Katrina couldn't think about much of anything at all except her ungodly level of pain. *I* started thinking about home for the first time in a long time, though. And not the *Rockne Hummel* or the fleet stations or even Earth itself.

Home. My *real* home. My parents' house.

Michigan.

Mom and Dad. My brothers and sisters. My tiny apartment in the fleet barracks outside Kalamazoo. I started missing the idle summers of my youth in a physical way. The smells of the wilderness and the Great Lakes waves. The hum of insects at dusk. The movie-set quality of late-night walks on June nights outside Detroit. Those boyhood Junes and Julys were the direct contrast to *everything* on Furnace. I analyzed their imprint on my memory as a barometer of what I'd left behind and just how badly I wanted to get off that planet. To see the green shores of home again.

I hadn't thought about any of that in a long time. I hadn't even thought of my family beyond a general flash of memory that I had, indeed, originated somewhere that wasn't Basic or the lower decks of some fleet warship. Resting there, I couldn't believe how much I'd taken it all for granted while on Earth. Even just the freedom to return home and absorb the familiar smell of the old wooden floors. To remember what it was like sharing a complicated, all-encompassing history with someone that stretched back further than three or four years.

I'm a little ashamed to admit that it took so long for me to start thinking about my family on Furnace, although I'm not really surprised. It has little to do with the depth of feeling for my kin and a lot to do with how uniquely clouded a soldier's brain gets in the thick of battle. There's an assumption, I think, that whenever someone faces a life-or-death situation in the trenches, he or she is immediately reminded of everything they're about to lose and all the loved ones they've left behind. In my experience, it's actually the opposite.

I've faced a few dozen hopeless situations with aliens or gunfire or system-malfunctions beating down on me, and each time, I'm so wrapped up in the surreality of the moment that I have trouble thinking of anything at all. I've heard other men and women say they can see the faces of their husbands, wives, boyfriends, girlfriends, children, parents, siblings, or pets when they're staring down death, but I think that's bullshit. Maybe that's just an indication of a deeper void in my own life and my capacity for true emotional profundity (the girl on Eurpoa is still the only real relationship I've ever had, and I wouldn't exactly describe myself or most other deep space soldiers as emotional or well-adjusted), but I think they just want to make themselves feel better.

That same combat obfuscation was responsible for my lack of sentimentality on Furnace, and I suppose on the battlefield in general. I'm unable to pull myself far enough from the situation to have proper perspective, and there's a big part of me that doesn't truly *believe* the events surrounding me on the battlefield are real or that my life is truly at risk. It's not bravery or combat numbness so much as a lack of comprehension on my part. Even though my rational mind knows the difference between the two, my heart and soul do not. I guess, then, that it's easy enough to see why the deaths of my shipmates didn't affect me the way they should have, ranging from losses in the heat of battle to the sheer ubiquity of death on Furnace (not to mention how most of the crew were relative strangers to me), but I'm paying dearly for it now.

Anyway, thinking about my family and the summers back home (I'm not sure why I defaulted to my childhood memories, but I guess the psychoanalysts and arbitrators of my case would be able to tell you more about that) stirred something in me that I wasn't aware could be stirred anymore. It was a highly-emotional swell of fear and hopelessness which had been completely hammered out of me in Basic. I remembered, for once, that I had something to lose, even if it was only the notion of a past that could never be regained.

I thought of my mother's head thrown across the planet's surface like a tumbleweed in the high winds surrounding the ship, and how I'd thought it was a hallucination or a trick of light at the time.

Mom, I thought. *Is she here?*

It didn't seem possible, but neither did the planetoid or the circumstances preceding our crash.

She can't be, I tried to argue. *There's no way.*

It's difficult to lie to yourself with death at your door.

I started panicking again, and this time I couldn't control it. I couldn't sit still, even though my miraculously healing wounds cried out for rest and Katrina looked three-quarter's dead.

"Come on," I said, practically leaping to my feet. My stomach swelled with pain. I almost fell straight back to the dirt, shrieking, but managed to pull it together at the last moment and spare myself the humiliation. The last thing I wanted was for the other two to think I couldn't even stand when Katrina could hardly open her eyes. At least *one* of us had to lead our group, and I was the highest-ranking idiot with the least amount of pain (which wasn't saying much), so I figured it still had to be me.

"We've got to keep moving," I said through a grimace, more to convince myself than the two of them.

The pain in my stomach, leg, and the back of my neck was returning in one coordinated wave. Probably from sitting down long enough for stiffness to set in. Mostly because whatever miracle drug Sillinger had given me finally ran its course. Maybe that's why Katrina was suddenly so hard up, too. I'd thought it was just exhaustion from the agonizing hike up and down the mountain, but maybe Sillinger had shot her up with something sweet.

Aziza turned back in our direction and started following wordlessly, but it was clear Katrina wasn't ready to get up. There was a good chance she never would be.

Is she dead? I wondered, making my way to her side while attempting to disguise my limp. I don't think either of them would have noticed the hitch in my step or really cared if they had, but I wanted to hide the limitation as long as possible in case someone else was watching us, which seemed likely now that we were out in the open again.

"It's time to get up," I told Katrina gently. I didn't want to startle her in case she'd fallen asleep, but I was suddenly very aware of our exposure in the green-orange haze. I could almost *feel* the breath of the corpses on my stitched neck when I turned from them. The sensation gave me a chill so violent that I couldn't suppress a gasp of pain.

"Come on, Kat!" Aziza shouted. "If I can't die on my own terms, then you aren't allowed to, either. Get your ass up!"

"Quiet!" I snapped.

My eyes darted toward the mountaintop and back to the corpse fields again. I expected to see a whole army advancing, but there was no such force to greet us. I should have realized how truly insignificant Aziza's shout was amid a sea of screaming souls, but I suppose it's human nature to believe we're always being watched by someone waiting for us to either slip up or turn heroic.

"Is she *dead?*" Aziza asked. I took it as a rhetorical question and squatted beside Katrina.

"We're almost there, Kat," I told her, half-believing it myself. "Hold on just a little longer. We'll get you some help as soon as we reach the *Hummel.*"

She whispered something so weakly that I had to strain right up against her fiery breath.

"What did you say?"

She raised her head a little and opened her bloodshot eyes. Each branch of red stood out with alarming clarity. "I'll catch up." She stretched a little. The movement wafted death-stink in my direction from her leg wounds.

I frowned and started pulling her up from the ground. "Sure you will," I said.

Aziza came over to help. We had Katrina on her feet within a few moments, but I knew she wouldn't stand on her own for long, let alone run through open terrain with alien monsters hunting us. The hike had taken everything out of her. Whatever reserve of hope or narcotics had pushed her along until then in spite of her leg wound had finally worn off.

"Let's go," she mumbled drunkenly, then fell forward without even a reflexive attempt to brace herself. Aziza and I caught her a split-second before she hit the ground, but I paid for it when my abdomen flexed with plenty pain of my own.

"Jesus," I winced.

We steadied her against a rock and caught our breath.

Aziza pressed a hand to her cheek and moaned. The gray-yellow infection had spread almost entirely across her face. It was difficult to look at, but I was impressed that she didn't complain about the dizzying pain she was no doubt experiencing. Thank God she didn't suggest we leave Katrina behind, otherwise I think I would have listened to her. I was out of energy and patience. I felt black strands of panic taking root within me. Even then, I knew that there was a specific timeline we needed to follow if we ever wanted to get off the planet, even beyond the demands of our physical forms.

"What do we do now, *sir?*" Aziza asked, putting heavy, sarcastic emphasis on the last word.

I glared at her and took a deep breath to hush the shrieks of agony building in my throat. More than ever, I didn't want to show weakness around her. "We carry her."

Before Aziza could protest—and I could see in her eyes that she was about to do so wholeheartedly—Katrina did it for her.

"Fuck that. I can walk myself."

"I don't think you can," I told her.

I didn't mean for it to be a challenge, but that's how she took it. "*I'll* decide if I can or I can't." She paused and swallowed dry breath. I could tell it took an absurd amount of effort to form words, and she wasn't even the one with a torn-up cheek. "What can it hurt? If I can't make it on my own, I'll get all three of us killed. Neither of you are in any shape to carry me right now."

She was right, and I was glad she was the one to point it out. It made the truth of our injuries better than if we'd admitted them to ourselves. As long as I didn't tell them that I was worried the stitches had torn in my stomach and back, I could pretend everything was fine. The wounds didn't exist at all.

That way, I wouldn't have to think about the creature who'd cut me, either, which was an even greater relief than Sillinger's drugs.

"Fair enough. Then let's get this shit over with."

Aziza nodded and accepted her rifle when I un-holstered it and held it out to her. She was the one who led us into the corpse fields. Katrina followed on unsteady legs that carried her every which way but straight. Each step she took made me wince, especially since I was behind her. I had a front-row view seat to the carnage along the back of her legs. The sight was bad enough, but the smell of her infected wounds made me nauseous to the point that I had to suppress a few gags strictly for the sake of morale.

And still, the smell of her rot was nothing compared to the corpse fields. Once we hit the first row of crucified aliens, I promptly doubled over and emptied the few scraps of nothing-much from my stomach.

And it only got worse from there.

THE CORPSE FIELDS

No matter how prepared we thought we were to walk among the rows of crucified bodies, each of us was shaken when we saw them up close. It was worse than we'd imagined, even after having a bird's-eye view during our descent. The sense of claustrophobia was something I hadn't counted on in such a flat landscape, either. It ate at my nerves and rang alarm bells throughout my head. I felt a tangible weight settling in over my chest. It was difficult to breathe.

The border of the white pillars wasn't far from where we'd stopped to rest. It rose menacingly from the earth like the crooked teeth of a man-eating Titan. Each pillar stood nearly fifteen-feet tall and about three feet wide. Once we were close enough to distinguish the bodies, though, I barely noticed the pillars at all. How could I? Even the oddly appropriated features of the victims were recognizably twisted in agony. Aliens from corners of space humanity hasn't touched outside the imagination of Lovecraft and a few equally sick individuals. The ones on the outskirts were still breathing, moaning, or sobbing softly for the most part, but their bodies were too weak to muster a cry for help.

It made a sick sort of sense for the outsiders to be the freshest, considering the locals (whoever they were) would have started somewhere in the center of the open land and gradually forged their way towards the mountains and hills on either side of the plateau.

The hills, I reminded myself. *Just focus on getting to the hills. The ship's somewhere on the other side of them.*

It may have been wishful thinking, but the further removed I was from the wastelands, the easier it was to believe.

I can't begin to describe how miserable it was stepping onto that field. My nightmares still take me back among the rows of corpses. Each victim watches me pass with an accusatory stare while rainbows of blood flow from their undeserved wounds. Sometimes, they climb down and chase me between the rows until I'm surrounded, then drag me to the ground and tear me apart with their teeth. Once they've eaten their fill, they pin me to the pillars with nails whittled from discarded bones.

Most nights, I'm afraid to sleep. But as bad as the dreams can be, the reality was even worse.

I felt a heavy faze bearing down on me the moment we entered the crucifixion forest. Even the corpses seemed to stare at me from their decomposing husks, which had once been equally unrecognizable alien creatures.

I only managed three steps into the multitude before one of the hanging bodies—this one slightly more humanoid in appearance than most—jerked to attention and shrieked at the top of its lungs. The sound startled me so badly that I lurched backward into a disemboweled Fronov corpse, though how a blue-skinned *Fronov* had wound up there, I can't begin to guess. I gagged when its purple intestines wrapped around my face.

"Fuck!" Aziza shouted.

She started firing into the corpses like a goddamned fool. In the moment, I wanted to kill her, even though I'm partly responsible for her indiscretion. I shouldn't have given the rifle back to her. She'd just seemed so *together* when we'd helped Katrina up that I thought she could handle it. Sulky and wounded, sure, but mentally composed. The situation was so thoroughly fucked, however, that it shouldn't have surprised me to see that even an *elite* fleet soldier was liable to chase shadows and snap under pressure.

Tearing the scarf of entrails from my neck, I struggled free away from the Fronov corpse and ran toward Aziza as fast as my cramped leg would carry me. I could already sense the collective eyes and ears of the corpse fields turning toward us. I didn't want them to settle on us before I stopped her.

"What the fuck is wrong with you?" I shouted over the gunfire. I shoved Katrina out of my way hard to get a clear line. She crumpled helplessly against the base of a pillar.

Desperate, I kept running until I plowed through Aziza full force. I didn't even attempt to pry the rifle from her hands. I didn't just want her to stop shooting. In that moment of terror-induced rage, I wanted her out of the picture. Not *forever*. Just pushed out of the way for a little while.

I think.

She flew with a predictably startled yelp and smacked against the tusk from a humanoid body with the head of an elephant. Her eyes immediately snapped shut and her body went limp.

Damn it, I thought. I'd hit her harder than I'd meant to, but like I said, I was desperate. Anyway, she wasn't dead. I quickly checked her pulse to be sure and there was still a slow beat against my fingertips. I was relieved for the time being, but in the back of my mind, I wondered if she'd put us at risk again. I'm ashamed by how my self-preservation instincts calculated the risk so coldly.

What about Katrina?

I looked back at her collapsed form a half-dozen steps away. My breath stopped. Her left leg had twisted behind her to make a forty-five degree angle with her opposite hip. Her shoulder was visibly dislocated, and not the one that had already been damaged. In other words, she was fucked.

All because of me.

No.

I scrambled to my feet, carefully avoiding the flailing arms and legs of the crucified aliens, and rushed to her side.

"Wake the fuck up!" I shouted, no longer caring about the noise. Our cover, or whatever measure of cover we'd *had*, was already blown.

Katrina was conscious, though. In fact, her eyes were wide open and staring down the row of corpses behind me. "Here..." she whispered. Her jaw dropped with an audible creak. She started gasping repeatedly. She didn't seem to notice her broken leg at all, even though it had fractured severely enough to bend her suit's armor plating.

A chill shot up my spine to my neck so violently that it stung the cuts above my shoulders, then shot back down with greater intensity when her eyes rolled to the whites. Her head dropped back until she was staring at the sky and she started chanting, "Here...here...here..." over and over again. Like she was waiting for something. Or calling to it.

I sensed movement from the corner of my eye and jerked away, dragging Katrina's exposed tibia along the dirt in the process.

It was Aziza. She was slowly gathering herself from our collision, but her reaction was still unsettling.

"Shit!" she exclaimed, looking behind me. She scrambled backward and tangled in the low-hanging tentacles of a pale-skinned bipedal with long, bristled hair. Its soupy blood dripped orange over her face and into her eyes. There was a sizzling sound as the acid burned her already-damaged cheeks, but she didn't seem to notice it any more than Katrina noticed her compound fracture.

Knowing Aziza, whatever specter had worked her up enough to retreat was nothing to fool with. I picked up the pace.

I couldn't avoid looking back, though.

Against my better judgment—not to mention the survival instincts within me that raged at my stubborn audacity—I turned and found myself staring into the eyes of evil incarnate.

It was one of the giant masked creatures with charcoal-black skin that I'd seen from the mountain. A Watchman. Its red mask had been carved into a crude representation of the demon clown's grin. It dragged an axe through the dust with a blade longer than my torso, sending swirls of gray and orange in its wake while its head cocked slightly to the side. I saw black bile worming through its yellow teeth while bubbles of gray-white puss popped along its skin and quickly vanished. It raised its left arm—the one that wasn't dragging the axe—and pointed one gnarled finger at me.

"You," it said in perfect English. Not even Standard, but the language of my native land. My country.

My home.

"Here...here...here..." Katrina gasped in response.

The crucifixion victims that were still alive let out a simultaneous howl of terror. Come to think of it, I'm sure even the dead ones joined their chorus.

"Here...here...here," Katrina chanted.

I couldn't hear her over the howling creatures, but her mouth moved along in the same strangely hypnotic rhythm. I knew exactly what she was saying.

"Here...here...here..."

The red-masked behemoth growled and beckoned me forward, then used both arms to raise the axe over its shoulder for a strike.

"Run!" I yelled. Aziza was already moving and Katrina couldn't move at all, though, so I guess it was more of a reflex than anything.

I leapt to my feet again, ignoring the pain in my stomach, and dragged Katrina through the row as the behemoth picked up steam. It started sprinting toward us, puffing deep, demonic growls with each thunderous step.

I couldn't carry Katrina. Even under the best of circumstances, there was no way I could have lifted her by myself with all our gear and still achieved any measure of speed, and especially not enough to outrun a powerful creature like the masked demon with its mammoth axe slung back for carnage. But I couldn't bring myself to drop her, either, even knowing it meant certain death for both of us. I hesitated for a split-second while I reconciled myself to the idea, but by then it was too late. My indecisiveness had made the decision for me.

"Come on, Katrina!" I screamed in her face, shaking her violently. "Wake up!"

Her eyes were still rolled to the whites. Her breath kept pushing out in the single, moaning exhalation of the word 'here' over and over again, speeding up along with the demon's footsteps as it drew nearer.

I tried—futilely—to continue dragging her, but this time she actively resisted with both legs.

"What the hell are you doing?" I shouted.

Something struck me on the back of the neck and I rolled over top of Katrina, cursing as I fell face-first into the dust. I thought I was dead. In fact, for about the fifteenth time since I'd left the ship, I was *sure* of it. I could practically hear the axe-blade singing toward my head through the haze, but then Katrina contorted so forcefully that I was thrown clear of the strike and landed against the base of another pillar. I felt my ribs crack beneath the armor plating, but I was up and running within moments like nothing had happened.

The axe struck the earth where I'd been laying a moment earlier. The ground rippled outward as the blow landed, spreading dust and blood across the flatlands. I glanced back at Katrina and was relieved to see she was still alive, but the feeling was short-lived. The demon had already muscled its axe from the ground and was less than ten feet away from her. Rather than screaming or running though, she continued chanting, "Here...here...here..." as her eyes rolled slowly forward again and she regained some form of sentience.

"Katrina!" I yelled, desperate to get her attention before the behemoth struck.

But even in waking life, she didn't seem all that concerned by the monster's appearance. She stopped chanting and raised her head ever so slightly, but her expression didn't change and she didn't voice a protest of any kind.

It's too late for her, I thought.

So I started running.

Tears formed in my eyes. I want to say it was from the noxious fumes of the corpse fields and the wind as it whipped against my eyeballs, but the truth of the matter is that I already felt terrible for knocking Katrina over to get at Aziza, even if my intentions had been pure. I don't know what being possessed Katrina once her leg broke and her eyes rolled to the whites, and I don't *want* to know, but it stands to reason that her proximity to death allowed the possession in the first place.

And yet I still had one last reason to be grateful she'd survived the trek through the mountains even as life drained from her body. It's the lone consolation I have when I think back to how I left her at the feet of a crucified alien zombie and an axe-wielding demon-giant.

As awareness re-spawned in her eyes, Katrina struggled onto her broken leg, bracing herself against the pillar at her back and scooting forward until her crooked leg had enough room to avoid pressing against the surface.

I watched over my shoulder, still running, as the demon reared back and prepared to charge me again, and then my legs tangled in the corpse of a bipedal lizard that had slipped to the bottom of its crude cross. I went tumbling yet again.

Fucking idiot, I cursed myself. *You're done now.*

I scrambled to my feet quickly, falling twice among the bones and sinew of a Kalak corpse in the process, but the killing blow that I anticipated never arrived.

"What are you doing?" I heard Aziza screech faintly. "Get out of there!"

Rattled, I started moving again. She wasn't talking to me, though.

The demon roared louder than the entire chorus of crucified aliens combined. I turned back to find out why.

Somehow, Katrina had unholstered her rifle and pointed it at the demon's head.

"One move," she warned. Even if the demon *had* understood English, she wouldn't have needed to complete the threat. The rifle spoke for itself.

Despite the forest of bodies screaming and thrashing and trying to grab hold of me to prolong their miserable lives, I stopped in my tracks to watch the exchange between Katrina and the demon. I wanted to see if she would survive in case I had the chance to atone for abandoning her, but I also wanted to see whether or not the demon was susceptible to pulse rifles. If it was, that would change my whole outlook on the return journey to the *Hummel*. At the very least, it would give me a fighting chance until the ammunition ran out.

Slightly dazed by the hyper-surreality which always permeates life and death situations for me on the battlefield, I watched Katrina unload her pulse charges into the monster's body, tearing it apart like it was no more formidable than a human or some cannon-fodder Kalak. The efficiency of the pulse rifle was incredible. The way the monster's tar-black skin first folded then exploded, spraying its acid-blood everywhere, mesmerized me. The blood itself burned through the skin of the nearest crucifixion victims. All from a few pulse charges.

Now we've got something, I thought, quickly drawing Salib's pulse rifle from the holster on my back. Maybe I had a shot at playing hero, after all.

In the end, though, Katrina's defiant stand was her very last gasp. Streams of acidic gore rained over her bare skin as blast after blast tore through the demon's body, dissolving her organs and exposing her veins to the gray-orange atmosphere.

"Kat!" Aziza screamed.

The crucified aliens suddenly ceased howling. The red-masked demon's body—or what remained of it—crumpled to the ground with a wet squelching sound that coupled oddly with the pop and sizzle of Katrina's skin as she fell to the earth beside it.

And then the whole field fell quiet. All eyes turned to the two shuddering corpses leaking and spraying what was left of their lives at the foot of two crucified giants from another universe.

Damn, I thought. I couldn't tear my eyes away from them, even though the rational part of my brain begged me to run with my pulse rifle at the ready.

After a few tense moments, Aziza was the first to break the quiet stillness. She cried out and stumbled over to Katrina, tears bubbling over the angry infection that had overtaken most of her face.

"No!" she sobbed, dropping to her knees beside her fallen friend. She cradled Katrina's head even as the demon's acid-blood dripped over her hands and peeled away her skin. She didn't seem to notice.

I watched them for a moment, then sensed movement all around me and shifted my attention. The eyes of the damned souls still nailed to the pillars all turned to me. They howled again in eerie dissonance that made my stomach roll, then I saw the Watchmen approaching through the rows of corpses. They came in all shapes and sizes and each carried a unique weapon, yet not one among them was any less terrifying than his brethren. They were Nightmare incarnate.

There wasn't time to check on Aziza again. As far as I was concerned, the corpse fields had officially become an every-man-for-himself shit-show. I started running for the hills opposite the mountains. I couldn't exactly see them since the pillars stretched seemingly forever, but I'd somehow kept my bearings enough during the struggle to know I was headed in the right direction. I may rely too heavily on my suit for calculating time and distance, but my internal compass has always been reliable. I figured as long as I moved away from Katrina and the demon corpse, I would eventually wind up someplace safer. I would settle for someplace else.

Something could kill you before you get there.

I doubted I could avoid running into at least one Watchman before reaching the hills, but I took heart knowing that Katrina had pulverized one of them with her pulse rifle. The fact that it had taken nearly all her ammunition to do it was beside the point.

While I was distracted by the masked demons, several impaled aliens snapped out with their legs, tentacles, or slender, drooping arms to scoop me up. I managed to slip away without being caught, but it grew exceedingly difficult to avoid their grasp the longer I ran between them.

"Here...here...here..." they chanted. All in dissonant English. My native tongue.

Thinking back, I still don't quite believe I lived through this nightmare. These beings came from other galaxies, other universes, perhaps other dimensions altogether, and we were in the deepest, impossible corner of deep space. They were terrified, angry, confused, and wanted to kill me. There was no way they could have known Standard, let alone English, and yet I heard them as plainly as I heard anything on that planet.

'Anything on that planet.'

It's an important distinction. I have to remind myself of the context, because if I truly misheard or hallucinated *their* voices, I may have hallucinated Salib, Katrina, and Aziza, altogether. Maybe even Teemo and the clown demon, too, and I *know* they were real. They *had* to be.

Right?

Within ten minutes of running, my stomach started to burn. I heard the rapid, pounding footsteps of the masked Watchmen in pursuit, along with the howls and chants of the damned in a rhythmic, soul-crushing monotony. I caught flashes of movement between the rows of corpses as the fearsome predators stalked me, then suddenly one of them stood directly in my path. A Watchman, with a hood drawn over its face to cover its mask and horns. Not running. Standing completely still, in fact, with a scythe gripped in the black glove of its right hand. Breath steamed out from the shadow of its hood, and the sheer force of the billowing tendrils froze my heart.

Him, I thought, remembering the overwhelming dread the clown demon had evoked in me the first time around. Except I knew it *couldn't* be him. The sensation was similar, but not exact. This creature served the clown, maybe, but that wasn't the same as *being* the clown.

And the movement continued behind the rows.

My legs refused to stop moving. They must have known it wouldn't do me any good.

"Here...here...here..."

The chanting increased in speed and intensity.

"Here...here...here..."

Hell's empty, I thought, bringing the pulse rifle to bear as I ran. *All the devils are...*

"Here...here...here..."

The red-masked Watchmen closed in. They were worse up close. Taller and stronger than any living thing had a right to be. Gravity didn't seem to affect them at all, unless it made them stronger somehow. I couldn't imagine how heavy their weapons would be on the surface without a gravity-equalizing spacesuit to assist them.

"Here...here...here..."

Somewhere in the distance, a woman screamed at the top of her lungs. The sound lasted a full three or four seconds before she was abruptly silenced by a resounding thud that bulleted across the flatlands. As soon as the echo died down, I realized the scream had come from the dark storm-cloud which had formed behind the Watchman up ahead.

"Let her go!" I shouted, gripping the pulse rifle's trigger.

I watched in horror as three red-masked demons pinned Aziza's limp, semi-conscious body against two fresh pillars.

"Stop!" I screamed.

"Here...here...here..."

One of the crucified aliens whipped out a soggy tentacle that knocked me flat and the impact with the ground forced my finger against the trigger. I wasted four precious pulse charges before I recovered enough to pull free.

Damn it!

I was so irrationally angry when I got to my feet that I wasted three additional charges shooting the ugly bastard in the head. Then I realized there were other Watchmen behind me as well, all with hoods drawn over their red masks.

"Fucking great," I said aloud.

There was no escape.

A storm-front thicker and more potent than any Oklahoma tornado descended over the corpse fields. The screams and chants of the damned souls had morphed from a repetitive monotony of "Here...here...here" into low, indecipherable growls punctuated by barking voices that spoke in a language a lot like ancient human tongues.

So this is it, I thought. *This is how I die.*

I can honestly say that of all the crazy, fucked-up deaths I'd feared as a fleet navigator in deep space, I never in my wildest dreams (or nightmares) imagined something even remotely resembling the grotesque theater I'd unwittingly stumbled upon.

The three Watchmen flanking my main adversary hoisted Aziza onto the pillars with ropes. One of them reared back and hammered a spike through her right hand so hard that it ripped her arm from her shoulder.

"Stop!" I pleaded.

Aziza's body slumped now that the nail and ropes no longer supported the right side of her body. The red masks continued, undeterred. The next nail held true, and so did the one they put through her stomach and then the one they used to connect both feet to the stone.

The voices of the damned grew into a fever pitch, and then morphed into deep, garbled laughter.

I dropped to my knees with the pulse rifle still aimed at the vacant stare bearing down on me. The hooded demon retrieved its scythe from the ground and stomped briskly in my direction.

"Tscharia," the damned souls whispered. Then they all fell again.

I was out of time. The hooded Watchman would reach me in seconds, and its scythe would rip the head from my shoulders so the red-masked demons could eat my brains and desecrate my corpse. The others just watched. Even the ones who'd crucified Aziza stood completely still with their bald heads titled sideways and the eternal grins of their horned clown-masks. Looking at them made me realize there was an empty pair of pillars right beside Aziza, and I didn't need a name plate on either of them to know they'd marked one especially for me. How they'd managed to assemble it so quickly and also smuggle Aziza past me without drawing attention was beyond my understanding. Like a lot of things, I guess.

The hooded demon moved within a dozen feet of me.

Screw this, I thought. *What the fuck am I waiting for?*

I adjusted my aim with the pulse rifle and pulled the trigger.

Eat it, asshole.

The Watchman's head snapped away from the path of the rifle blast without breaking stride and the demon quickly grabbed me by the throat.

Whoops...

It lifted me from the ground in one smooth motion. I gagged. Its rancid breath cooked my face until my eyes watered.

Thank God I had the sense not to try out-muscling its grip, which was well on its way to crushing my windpipe. Even a split-second delay would have changed things. Instead, I jammed my rifle into its neck and held down the trigger, squeezing so hard that I would have snapped off the trigger guard completely if the demon had held onto me a few more seconds. By the time the third pulse blast tore into its throat, though, it dropped me to the ground and stumbled backward.

It was hard to muster the necessary motivation to rise after hitting the ground. Wave after wave of breathtaking agony broke against my stomach, legs, and the back of my neck. Coupled with frantic gasps for air and coughs that were so violent I nearly retched up my internal organs, I barely remained conscious, let alone managed to stagger to my feet and start moving again. But if I hadn't kept going, I would have died then and there. I probably should have.

The pulse rifle shots hadn't done nearly as much damage to the hooded demon as I'd thought, though. The monster was stunned and clearly wounded, but the blasts seemed to have enraged it more than crippled it. Either this was an archduke made of sterner stuff than the one that Katrina tore to shreds, or her weapon was a lot more powerful than mine. Considering they were both standard-issued and banned from combat use unless authorized by fleet command (they were still in the experimental phase; some of the bugs hadn't been 'worked out'), I thought the former was more likely than the latter. Each demon appeared different, after all, so it stood to reason that they belonged to different species and had varying degrees of susceptibility to the concentrated energy blasts of the pulse rifles. I've seen the same phenomenon in the field with Kalak who were born on different planets. Everyone has a different death threshold.

Regardless, the Watchman had recovered quickly and was preparing to make another charge. Luckily, it had lost some momentum. I managed to duck into the next row of corpses before its scythe could cut me in half.

The new row wasn't much of a reprieve. Four red-masked Watchmen awaited me, and the others that had been standing around Aziza's body began to converge.

"Wherever you go," they whispered in unison with the clown demon's voice. "I will find you."

I fired into the onrushing Watchmen with the pulse rifle. The power indicator flashed toward zero but I had no other options. I decided on the spot to save the very last charges for myself, if it came to that. I didn't want to suffer like Aziza.

The first shots went wild, scattering across the crucified corpses towering over the battle. I didn't think much of it at the time—I was a little preoccupied—but those wild shots were the ones that wound up saving my ass. They got the inmates all worked up.

A Watchman clubbed me in the back hard enough to make me bite my tongue. I fell forward, still firing. As I tumbled to the ground, another demon opened me up at the ribs with a thin, hooked rod and yanked downward.

I howled.

Mom and Dad, I love you, I thought as my breath came gulping back. I remembered the smell of boyhood summers along the Great Lakes again. Back then, I'd thought Lake Huron was wild and mysterious. I thought there were adventures to be had on the open water between Michigan and Ontario, where I first became fascinated with the mysteries of deep space.

Space. An infinite cesspool of misery with fresh horrors on every goddamned rock. Why did I ever choose to seek them out?

Remember me.

I rolled onto my back and stared up into the Watchman's hooded, indistinct face.

The end.

I knew it was over.

Just as it was about to strike, however, something tore the creature away from me and threw it high into the air.

What the hell...

Then another demon went flying.

And another.

And another.

"Here...here...here..." the chanting began in earnest.

Another Watchman flailed its arms and roared with anger. They were vanishing before my very eyes.

I struggled to my knees and watched as the crucified undying lashed out, caught, and feasted upon their captors. All that time, it seemed, they'd just been waiting for the right distraction.

Is that all I was?

I didn't stick around to watch the peculiar spectacle. I ran toward the hills as fast as I could, carefully avoiding the grasp of any damned alien with a mind to scoop me up for desert.

When I finally reached the end of the corpse fields and ducked behind a cluster of rocks, I collapsed in the dust. Away from the stench, the violence, and all the stark reminders of mortality. I wept like a five year old for a while, right up until I realized dehydration would kill me if I kept on blubbering. And what a pathetic way *that* would have been to die. Crying myself to death after surviving an attack by the demon Watchmen.

It doesn't get any *less* hardcore than that, even on a planet like Furnace with a field of corpses in your wake.

VENOM

I spent the next fifteen minutes in a daze, moaning softly with my head pressed against the rocky hillside while trying to ignore the hot sting of air against my torn-up chest. I could hardly keep my eyes open, both from sheer exhaustion and the dried out feeling that had usurped my veins from head to toe. I couldn't find the energy to stand.

It was hard to shake the losses of Katrina and Aziza even though I hadn't known either of them very long and hadn't cared all that much for Aziza. To be honest, she'd mostly been a pain in the ass, though I guess her attitude might have been more tolerable under other circumstances. Only guilty tongues condemn the dead though, so I guess I should keep my mouth shut on that front. God knows she helped out as much as she could when push came to shove, especially in getting Katrina to her feet after I'd knocked her over. If we hadn't done *that*, and if Katrina hadn't blown the first masked demon to pieces long enough for us to run away, I'd have had yet another Watchman chasing me through the corpse fields. Maybe that would have been enough for them to hunt me down and end me before I reached the hills. Maybe he would have been the one to slip through the grasps of the damned and nail me to a crucifix.

So I guess what I'm saying is both Katrina and Aziza probably saved my life, at least indirectly, and the fact isn't lost on me now. It wasn't *then*, either, although I couldn't fully process it while I was focused on remaining conscious. I wasn't out of the woods yet, and I still had a bitch of a hill to climb with my ribs bleeding so freely.

I was afraid to move at all knowing I might further expose my wounds, but I could feel the opportunity for escape slipping away. I had trouble believing that the Watchmen had actually been *killed* by the aliens, and if they'd survived as I suspected, I knew they'd gather themselves and catch back up before long.

And there was always the clown to consider.

Forget about him, I thought, forcing myself to sit up. *The others will catch you before he does if you don't move.*

It wouldn't change things much either way. Dead was dead, or to put it more succinctly, unending death was unending death. At that point, with the memory of Aziza's screams still fresh, I didn't really give a shit *who* tortured me. I wanted to make sure it didn't happen at all.

Using the barrel of the pulse rifle for balance, I struggled to my feet and snuck a glance back down at the corpse fields. The rows of crucifixes seemed endless and the mountain impossibly distant though I couldn't have run much more than a few miles. It looked fake from my vantage point, which probably owed to the storm-cloud haze hanging about a dozen feet above the heads of the crucified aliens. It cast an eerie, dream-like glow the color of migraines over the opposite peak.

What now? I wondered.

I had to press on, but I also had to find water. That would become a familiar mantra the rest of the way. I had a massive headache, and although I'd taken a pretty serious blow to the back of the head from one of the Watchmen, I knew at least part of it was rooted in dehydration. Truth be told, I'm sure it was a little bit of stim withdrawal, too. You learn to rely on the little white pills when you've been in the service long enough. It's a hell of a lot easier to make mistakes without corrective chemicals regressing you to the mean, and those kinds of mistakes cost lives. Given my time in stasis—albeit brief—and immediate surface deployment, I hadn't dropped a stim in almost a week, and the effects hit me hard once the adrenaline of the corpse fields filtered out.

As if I needed another reason to find the ship.

What's going to kill me first? I thought grimly. *Dehydration? Blood loss? An alien? Demon? Withdrawal? Falling down the hill and smashing my head on a rock?*

I knew there were about a dozen ways I could die in the next few hours. I started walking anyway, busying my mind with careful analysis of which death seemed likeliest. It helped distract me from the daunting climb and the weight of the pulse rifle now that my chest had been torn to the bone.

Not much farther, I thought.

Until what?

I grimaced and shifted the pulse rifle onto my hip to alleviate some of the pressure. I didn't dare re-holster it after the corpse fields, though. I wanted it ready to go at the drop of a hat (or tentacle) even if I drained some energy reserves keeping it that way. With my legs dragging and my arms practically numb, the chances I'd be able to draw before something crept out from behind the rocks and tackled me were slim enough as it was. Even with the rifle ready, I still might not get a shot off fast enough. It hadn't worked in the corpse fields, so why would it then?

What's the point? You're alone now and you don't know where you're going. You're screwed.

I grimaced again as my right foot slipped out from under me and I fell to a knee. It was hard to decide which hurt worse: my midsection from the belated reaction to dropping or the impact with the ground that rattled my already throbbing brain.

"Fuck it," I muttered. "Fuck this place."

I needed stims. Badly. Amazingly, it was that savage need which got me back to my feet without missing a beat. Nothing else was even capable of doing the trick. The *Hummel* was a dream, an ending too happy to be imagined. Earth likewise seemed unattainable while I scaled the hillside and tried to keep from passing out. Stims, on the other hand, were small. The size of a VP-127 bullet, just about. Maybe a little smaller. Unlike the *Hummel* and Earth, which were just as far away but much bigger and elusive, the prospect of finding stims was realistic. I needed to focus on something small, something that wasn't necessarily a goal so much as a soulless thing. Find stims, I decided, and all my problems would be solved.

I climbed a few more steps before leaning against a boulder and tapping the comm link on a whim. "*Hummel*, this is Lieutenant Chalmers. Is anyone there?"

I waited for a moment with my chin resting against my chest and my eyes closed, knowing there would be no answer but holding out hope anyway. I didn't realize it then, but I guess I was bracing myself for the death of *all* hope. I *knew* the comm wouldn't work—thinking back, I'm convinced I even heard the dead click of the line when I pressed the button—but admitting it in that desperate moment would have pushed me over the brink. Into what? I don't know. Maybe suicide, maybe just a long sleep on the hillside which would likely have ended in some creature or another tearing me to pieces.

I punched the comm again and stood up straight. It made my ribs burn but the pain woke me up.

"*Hummel*, do you read? This is Lieutenant Chalmers from Salib's squad. Our unit has sustained heavy casualties." I swallowed, or tried to. It's difficult to pull that off when your throat is as dry as the surface of Baronsseha. Never heard of it? You wouldn't want to. "I think I'm the only one left alive."

There was a singular crack of static and then I was suddenly launched headfirst into the hillside hard enough to crack my shoulder plating.

What the hell?

I was too stunned to move. A fresh spray of pain fell over my head and arms before settling in my ribs. I tried to catch my breath but the wind had been knocked out of me, shriveling me into a fetal ball at the base of the boulder. I took comfort feeling the pulse rifle pressed firmly against my hip but had no idea whether or not I'd get a chance to use it.

I heard the creature before I saw it. It began as an ominous scratching sound approaching from a long way off, then the scratching turned near and frantic before stopping completely. It was replaced by a *whoosh* then something long and heavy flew through the air and cracked into my back again. This time, I couldn't move at all. Breath came gasping out of me as my lungs saw the writing on the wall and attempted to escape through my lips. At the same time, a white veil of hyper-reality settled over my vision. I saw every detail of the dust around me in exquisite detail. The tiny black pebbles scattered over the ground. The crooked, lifeless weeds springing out from beneath the boulder. The top of an alien skull three-quarters covered by shadow and earth. Time slowed. I still couldn't look back at my attacker, and didn't think I'd see it at all before it killed me.

Before the creature could strike again, though, my momentum did the work I couldn't do myself and rolled me in the opposite direction. A stinger as long as one of the crucifix pillars slammed into the ground beside me but I managed to kick another few feet beyond its reach. A moment earlier, the point of the massive, yellow-and-purple cartilage would have gutted me. Half of my insides would have been driven at least a foot deep into the poison Furnace soil. Yet another comforting thought.

Get up!

My breath returned in gulps. I struggled to my feet, fell back to the ground as the stinger recoiled, and finally lugged the pulse rifle around to point at my assailant. I nearly managed a shot before the creature leapt at me with six sharp appendages aimed at my midsection. It was huge. Within moments, its pulsing, blue underbelly and insectoid scowl filled my vision. It squealed victoriously through yellow incisors, sensing the kill was nigh. I was an easy meal, and I figured meals must have been rare indeed for a creature dwelling on the outskirts of the corpse fields. I doubted the Watchmen allowed many souls to escape their torment.

Most of my body was still recovering from the initial blows, but I managed to propel myself back down the hill with just enough force to clear the creature's stingers. Unfortunately, that meant I was also suddenly hurtling back toward the corpse fields fast enough that I probably would have died if I'd hit a boulder along the way. I hadn't gotten very far up the slope but the path twisted and turned between rocks the size of the *Hummel's* short-range shuttles.

Dig in, I told myself, grinding my teeth with my eyes squeezed shut. Locking my legs to brace against the fall might snap them, but it was better than the alternative. I knew what awaited me back the way I'd come, and even the brief look I'd gotten at the giant bug attempting to impale me with its six-scorpion tails was enough to know I didn't want to run straight back up the hill, either. If I was going to survive both the fall and the monster, I'd have to take a risk.

Screw it, I thought. I sensed the base of the hill nearby and threw out my legs then locked my knees in fast succession. I knew I'd only get one shot.

At first, I didn't think my boots would catch enough traction to stop my momentum, but after a few grinding impacts, I managed to throw my weight just far enough to my left to smash into a boulder. My back and shoulder took the worst of the impact, but it wasn't as bad as I'd expected. Most of the armor on the left side of my body was still intact, or at least enough so that my bones didn't hit straight on.

I'm alive, I thought.

There wasn't time to celebrate. The giant scorpion-bug had rounded on me again with its twisted antennae drenched in alien blood. Two stingers quickly lashed out toward my throat.

This time, I didn't hesitate. I fired even before I'd steadied the pulse rifle and caught both stingers with the same charge. It didn't blow them up—the bug's exoskeleton was too sturdy for it to be *that* easy—but it redirected them from my path. I wiped sweat from my forehead and charged up the hill again, carefully aiming pulse charges into the monster's softer midsection as I approached.

It didn't stop there, though. In fact, the scorpion-bug wasn't dissuaded in the least. The other four stingers swung out all at once from different angles, making it impossible to catch them all before at least one connected with me.

"Damn it..."

I hit two with pulse charges before attempting to duck beneath the others. It didn't work. I avoided the point of one coming low to my left but it still connected with my shin. I went sprawling to the ground just as the last stinger flew high to my right and tore skin from my cheek. The venom started burning before I hit the ground.

"AAAAGGGHHH!" I screamed.

The pain was immense, but I kept firing. I didn't have the luxury of pain or paralysis. The first two stingers were coming right back at me and they seemed faster than before. Like the creature knew it had me right where it wanted. And it did.

I connected with a few charges to slow it down before I had to shoot one of the stingers away and leap over the other with less than an inch to spare, but the shots still didn't seem to do much damage. Purple blood exploded from its stomach and lines of electricity seizured through its massive body, but the creature didn't drop. I started to think there weren't enough charges left in the rifle to do the job, and if a pulse rifle wouldn't kill it, chances were nothing else I'd find on the hillside would, either.

But I was getting closer, and that was a mark in my favor. My legs burned with fatigue but I knew my shots would be more effective once they had a shorter distance to travel. Maybe if I didn't have to contend with its slashing stingers, I reasoned, I might find a weak spot somewhere along its exoskeleton.

You will.

The familiar battle rush had descended upon me, drowning the cries of pain throughout my body. Suddenly, I knew I was going to survive, and not *just* survive. I was going to kill the scorpion-bug motherfucker even if it took my bare hands to finish the job.

You will be my vessel, the clown demon's voice rose in my head unbidden. It stunned me long enough that I nearly tripped over my own feet before regaining my composure and shrieking up at the scorpion-bug's quivering antennae.

Whether it fueled my rage or simply reminded me of the stakes, hearing the demon's voice was like having a branding iron jammed directly into my back. I howled and charged forward with renewed vigor, sensing each swipe from the giant insect's stingers a full second before they hit. I shot away the blows that I could and parried aside the others with the barrel until I was directly beneath the creature, dancing between a half-dozen spike-legs. It squealed so loudly with rage that even in the midst of avoiding impalement at the end of its stingers, I couldn't help but remember the screaming wind that had driven Chara to suicide. It felt like about six months had passed since then, and yet I knew rationally that it couldn't have been more than a few hours.

Could it? I wondered.

The surface was fucking with my head. I knew that much. And it was entirely possible that what I'd perceived as a few hours had actually been years back on the *Hummel*, maybe millennia back in the Milky Way. Aidric Squad—the elite commando unit the fleet deployed on special-forces missions—had dealt with similar temporal anomalies in various points of the galaxy, and it seemed probable that such a spike would be amplified by about a million on Furnace.

I shouldered aside a swinging stinger and felt the remnants of my armor finally give beneath the pressure. It hurt like hell, but it was better than feeling the burn of its venom again. I could already feel it clawing the skin from my face and burrowing into my bones. It was only a matter of time before it melted my brain.

And how long will that take on Furnace?

There was a chance I was still within whatever theoretical bubble existed on the surface.

Assuming there is one at all.

It was a terrifying thought, knowing that anything and everything I knew and loved back home could have died while I limped across the wastelands or fought off the red-masked Watchmen in the corpse fields. Earth itself could have wasted away to nothing. The human race could have died out, and I was still slugging my way up the hill, killing monsters.

Trying to, anyway.

Another swipe from the squealing scorpion-bug smacked into the back of my right leg. It didn't cause any major damage, but each blow still hurt like a bitch. I grimaced and shifted the pulse rifle against its soft belly, but the moment the barrel touched its exoskeleton, the creature changed its tactic. Before I realized what was happening, all six stingers descended on me at once. They didn't slice and dice me, though, and that was especially good because I wouldn't have been able to dodge them all at once. Maybe if I'd had some warning, I could have used the creature's temporary vulnerability to deliver the killing stroke. Instead, it scooped me up and leapt high into the air.

I had a momentary glimpse of the whole terrible scope of the corpse fields, then we were crashing back to the hillside with enough velocity that I still don't know if my stomach has made it back down from my throat.

Can't let it drop me, I thought.

The scorpion-bug was slowly releasing its grip as we dropped closer and closer to the surface. It intended to squash me, I realized. It was tired of trying to pin me down and had decided to let Furnace's gravity do the dirty work. I could tell by the triumphant pitch of its squeals that it considered the battle won and was revving up for a warm meal.

Dropping the pulse rifle, I reached out with both hands and grabbed the stalks of its stingers, careful to avoid their venomous tips. I didn't need my palms burned away on top of everything else. In response, it started separating the stingers more forcefully, and that made it difficult to maintain a firm grip. I held on though, knowing I only needed to keep myself trapped within the relative safety of its stingers for another few seconds at most. Once we hit the ground and the creature took the brunt of the impact, I could retrieve the pulse rifle (provided the fall hadn't destroyed it) and try one last time for the kill shot before I'd have to cut my losses and retreat to conserve pulse charges. I had to think about the aftermath. If I spent all my ammo on this one monster, who knew what I'd have to resort to if I encountered something else on the other side of the hill? Something worse?

Screw that.

Just before we hit the ground, I threw all my weight to the right and turned the stunned creature a full hundred and eighty degrees. The thrust of momentum only sent us flying a few feet off course, but it was enough. Its massive, thousand-eyed head cracked against a boulder and I was suddenly covered in purple blood from head to toe, holding onto the flailing stingers for dear life.

Hold...hold...for chrissakes hold.

I barely resisted the urge to let go and shield my exposed skin from the venom spewing out of the creature's head as the last shuddering arches of life departed its hideous body. It wouldn't have done much good, since its blood was burning through my armor wherever it touched anyway.

After a few moments which seemed to stretch into hours, its stingers finally slowed their desperate lunges. I released my grip and leapt away from the corpse in one clumsy motion, trying to avoid further contact with the giant bug before rolling around in the dust to clear as much of the purple blood as possible. At least the blood wasn't as bad as the venom. It wasn't concentrated in its head the way it was in the stingers.

Once I was satisfied most of my armor was still intact, I rolled onto my back and attempted to catch my breath, cursing the fleet for never creating a combat-sim with a giant scorpion-bug stalking the edge of a corpse field run by demons. They certainly had the means, and they had computers to visualize even the most absurd scenarios, ones which human minds could never have conjured on their own.

My headache returned triumphantly, worsened by the dull ache where the venom had burned my cheek and nose.

Hasn't this been enough? I demanded of no one in particular. Maybe the clown demon, maybe the fleet, maybe God. It doesn't matter who, because no one felt like answering and my skull was pounding worse than ever.

I needed stims. Badly.

INTO THE CITY OF GOLD

Even with the scorpion-bug dead, I knew I needed to move quickly or I may as well have let the demons tear me apart in the corpse fields. My window for escape was closing just as rapidly as my window for survival. I didn't have much wiggle room, but if I could just summon the strength to reach the other side of the hills, I sensed the *Rockne Hummel* would be waiting for me.

Sensed, or maybe hoped. It was possible my skin would burn away from the monster's venom before I got anywhere, although the open wound seemed to get better by the moment. It could have been the effects of the poison, though. Numbing the impact area while it went to work disassembling my brain. Maybe it was the same acid that had burned Aziza's face. Remembering how terrible she'd looked even in relation to our surroundings dropped a lead ball of dread in my guts. As badly off as she'd been, I was probably worse.

But all I needed to do was reach the ship, I told myself, and everything would be all right.

For a little while.

I had no idea what would happen in the long run for those of us marooned on the planet. The natives might eventually find a way to drag us off the ship and crucify us for some imagined infraction or another. More likely, they'd kill us for no reason at all. Maybe we'd hold out long enough to die from starvation or thirst rather than at the hands of demons, but the end result would be the same. I'd held out hope that I would reach the ship again, but even if I did, I wasn't nearly as delusional about our chances of reaching Earth.

Focus on the ship, I reminded myself. *They've got water and med supplies. They can patch you up and send someone else to the surface to watch, assuming they don't already know what's happened.*

I found it hard to imagine that the captain wasn't aware Salib's team hadn't reported back, but I also didn't think he would send out another team after us. If we weren't back within three hours of our projected arrival, he would have considered us dead like any fleet captain and made his strategic decisions accordingly. In other words, we would be omitted from the ration considerations and both our equipment and ranks would be re-appropriated however the captain saw fit. That isn't to say the change couldn't be undone if it turned out that all was well, but I knew the crew would be quicker to write us off as losses on Furnace than they would on a routine mission, where they might have vowed to stay behind until they'd discovered what had become of us.

I rose groggily to my feet, trying not to put too much weight on any one part of my body now that Sillinger's drugs had fully metabolized.

One more goddamned hill, I thought, wincing as the deep gash along my ribcage pressed against the remnants of my armor plating. My chest wasn't even the worst part, either. The back of my head pounded with an ominous, warm beat where I'd been clubbed. I was bleeding—I knew that much— but I didn't have the heart to investigate just how heavily. I figured if it was a cracked skull or something comparably debilitating, I would have been unconscious. I was awake, so I assumed it was just a bad concussion and the fog shrouding my every thought would eventually dissipate.

I took a few painful steps forward, glancing over my shoulder to be sure I hadn't been followed. There was no sign of pursuit, and the corpse fields had fallen eerily silent. I wasn't too worried about the monsters of Furnace skulking along in the shadows until they found the perfect opportunity for a strike. The demons were a lot of things, but subtle wasn't one of them. If any of them were nearby, I figured I would find out sooner than later.

The hill wasn't even a quarter the mountain's height, and yet it seemed at least ten times more daunting now that I'd been so physically and psychologically ravaged in the land of the dead. The first step up the incline sent lightning bolts from my calves all the way to the back of my head. I wound up stumbling three steps backward before my trembling legs caught themselves and locked me in place.

"One more hill," I said aloud, trying to squeeze the last drops of energy from my dried-out husk of a body.

The hoarse croak of my voice startled me more than the pain. I sounded like someone else entirely. It was the mutterings of one of the starved, damned souls I'd left behind, maybe, or the whispering pleas of a powerful ghost. Certainly not the voice of the man, and certainly not *me*. The lack of conviction in my words sobered me up by another degree. I started to think that I would *never* make it no matter how close I was to salvation. My body had simply given out. There was nothing left in the tank to burn and no one around to spur me on.

Wherever you go, I will find you.

The words rose unbidden in my head and made me shudder. But they got me moving again.

There were plenty of footholds and resting points along the slope to help me scale the hillside. Even in my poor condition, it took less than a half-hour to reach the top, but that's where all my hope and momentum abruptly deflated.

"You've got to be fucking kidding me," I muttered.

The good news was that I could see the *Rockne Hummel* resting in a massive crater a ways off, and none of the indigenous monsters appeared to be anywhere in its vicinity. The bad—or rather, *terrible*—news was that the clown demon's ancient city stood between me and relative safety, and the city was now bustling with activity. I couldn't make out specifics yet, though. Some of that owed to the perpetual fog of my post-concussion stupor, but the frantic shadow-play across the wide city avenues filled me with dread nonetheless.

What now? I wondered.

I sat down to think it through, carefully disseminating my despair into manageable concerns.

I couldn't imagine facing even one more man-eating demon before devouring food, water, and an empty bed, let alone an entire city full of them. And that was without acknowledging my physical limitations for crossing another few miles of open land. I've never experienced agony like I felt then. There wasn't a single part of me that *didn't* hurt. Shit, I had just about every possible injury in the trenches during the Kalak War, but it was a whole 'nother animal having all of them at once. In a way, I guess it dulled each individual misery, since it was too difficult to concentrate on any one ailment at the exclusion of others. Was that a silver lining, or just the incomprehensible depths of suffering?

You don't have a choice, my rational brain reminded me. *You have to accept that it's going to hurt. There's no other way out.*

There was, actually, but it wasn't much of one. I didn't want to die with the unenviable view of the corpse fields on one side and the haunted city on the other. At least not any more than I wanted to get off my ass and move on.

Before I could convince myself otherwise or allow indecisiveness to steal yet another critical decision out from under me, I stood and began negotiating my way down the hill. I fully expected to fall to my death each time my weak legs didn't quite find purchase among the rocks, but going down wound up being much faster than coming up. Within ten minutes, I'd reached the bottom without incident, mostly because I didn't stop to rest at all. Stopping would have been the end of me.

The details of the city were a little clearer once I emerged near enough the city walls from the gray-orange haze that even the concussion couldn't obscure my vision. The city looked much different from a new angle. Decrepit, but not dead like I'd initially thought back when Teemo and I had cowered pathetically behind a rock to view the ancient ruins.

The stone wall might have been gray once upon a time, but the grime and dust caked over its crumbling surface had bled to a uniform white which reminded me of Greek antiquity, mostly due to the marble columns and stone edifices for which the Mediterranean is still famous. Every few feet, strange symbols adorned the walls in a variety of colors. I took the rainbow murals for paint at first but quickly realized they were actually comprised of blood from the myriad aliens tortured in the lava lakes and corpse fields.

Sick bastards.

I couldn't make sense of the symbols or the inscriptions carved in bone between them, though I easily located the writing implements in the dust beneath each block of text. They were shaved to a point on one end with dried blood smeared over the other. I didn't want to read the symbols, anyway. In the beginning, back when Teemo and I had first stumbled on the city, I would have been fascinated by the alien script and done everything I possibly could to document the finding. By my second visit, however, I would have pissed all over the symbols if I'd had enough fluid left in me to make it happen. In the grand scheme of things, it would have been a petty gesture at best, but in lieu of nailing a corpse to the wall and desecrating its body, I thought pissing would have sufficed. Besides, brooding over subtle revenge scenarios was the only motivation I had left.

Skulls lined the base of the walls. Not skewered on stakes the way I imagined the Furnace natives wanted them, but casually tossed from the ramparts of the city watchtowers. The nonchalance of the act and the anonymity of the corpses—the very *mundane* nature of their deaths—was harsher to behold, I thought, than the almost understandable intimidation methods of conquering armies displaying their kills as a warning not to fuck with them or else. It wasn't just the mounds that were disturbing, although they were formidable. It was the fact that whoever had murdered those creatures cared so little for life that the remains had been unceremoniously tossed into the gutter. Not trophies, then, but annoyances. A part of everyday existence. A process.

I couldn't imagine living in a world like that, no matter how many battles I've seen.

I shuddered.

Quit stalling, I thought, then forced myself to keep moving.

The gates were open and no demons stood guard, so I crept my way along the wall until I reached the entrance. I made sure my pulse rifle still had charges remaining and peered around the corner to assess the situation.

The stone street leading through the heart of the city was quiet, but there was evidence of recent activity. For one thing, fresh corpses were heaped in front of a short white building, and the few human victims I spotted from Salib's squad among their ranks didn't look like they'd been hit by rigor mortis yet. In case that wasn't enough to warn me off, there were also giant, cloven-hoofed tracks in a zigzag pattern leading down the street. They were wet, so the trail would have been easy enough to follow. I figured it was blood, but didn't really care one way or the other. I'd grown desensitized to the horrors of Furnace, after all. As if combat hadn't steeled me enough to the sight of gore already.

I hesitated for a moment before entering the gates. My training taught me that utter silence on a main street coupled with signs of recent, violent activity screamed of a waiting ambush. But, again, the monsters I'd seen so far hadn't exactly struck me as the type to set complicated traps for one measly human. You can call it overconfidence on their part, I guess, but I think it's more general indifference. Same with the lack of guards along the watchtowers. They simply didn't care if their city was infiltrated by the aliens they captured, because that just made them easier to catch. As far as they knew, there was nothing in the universe capable of overpowering them. They were probably right in that regard.

Just get down that street as fast as you can, I thought. *Stick to the shadows and stay away from any noise you hear, no matter how small.*

I wished I had another trooper with me for extra eyes and ears since my senses weren't as sharp as they needed to be for that kind of mission, but I pushed the idea aside. There was no point worrying about things beyond my control when my energy was already fatally low. I might as well have wished I was back home for all the good it would have done me. Maybe I was actually better off on my own, anyway. Pushing through the city alone was such a bold move that maybe the monsters would be caught completely off their guard. Maybe, I thought, I *could* make it through even if I didn't execute a perfectly stealthy escape, since they would all be either concerned with torturing their recent victims or finding new ones to break from the universe at large.

They're smarter than that, I reminded myself, crossing the threshold and limping to the heap of corpses as fast as my aching legs would carry me. *These aren't goddamned trolls. These things are smart. They can sense you.*

Without warning, the clown's voice whispered inside my head again.

Wherever you go, I will find you.

I shuddered and pressed my body into the pile of corpses, numb to the feelings of revulsion I knew I should have experienced. Those triggers were overridden by the idea that some deceased soldiers from Salib's squad might still have ammunition on them, or water hidden somewhere in their suits. It wasn't likely, considering that I knew any fleet soldier would have wasted every last bullet fighting before being taken if they could manage it, but I couldn't ignore the possibility. There was a good chance I would need ammo somewhere down the road, and I thought maybe one of them had an SX pistol, which surely wouldn't draw as much attention as a pulse rifle.

It was slim pickings, but I found a knife and the SX I'd been hoping for, although there were only thirteen bullets remaining in the clip and it was a smaller model than I would have liked. Once I'd re-holstered the pulse rifle in the half-busted slot on the back of my suit, I shuffled beneath a marble archway to the right of the heap and peeked around the corner for a better view of the street.

Just as before, it appeared deserted as far as I could see, but it *felt* different this time. I sensed another presence nearby. Something familiar, like the clown demon had returned to claim his prey, or like the hooded Watchman from the corpse fields wanted revenge after I'd slipped away. Either way, it felt like something was watching me, and there were seemingly endless windows and doorways along the main road where it could track my movements without exposing itself.

The foot-soldiers of the demon army didn't seem capable of calculated strikes, so that was a small consolation. Everything I'd witnessed to that point assured me the prospect of psychologically torturing their prey didn't hold much allure to them. However, I could easily imagine the clown demon lurking in the shadows, delighting in my imagined security and resourcefulness.

If he's watching, there's nothing you can do to avoid him, anyway. You'll never find him if he doesn't want you to, and you wouldn't be able to kill him even if you did.

As if in confirmation, his voice spoke clearly in my head once again.

Wherever you go, I will find you.

That old mantra.

"I hope you do," I growled spitefully, unsure whether or not he could hear. It was pretty big talk considering that I would probably die if I didn't reach the *Hummel* soon even without further assistance from his disciples.

The moment the words left my lips, I spotted shadows moving beneath one of the larger Greco-Roman monoliths a few hundred yards away.

Stupid, I thought.

Infiltrating the city had been a breeze up until then, and I'd just ruined an opportunity to slip through relatively unnoticed by addressing the clown demon aloud rather than in my head. That, too, I'll write off as the by-product of pain and sheer exhaustion (and maybe a bit of concussion symptoms), but the fact of the matter is I've been trained to know better. I was fully aware of the stakes, too, which makes the slip even more surprising. Even now, I wish I could go back and keep my mouth shut, just to see how things would have played out. I probably would have been worse off, actually, and I certainly never would have learned the bizarre history of Furnace or why the clown drew souls from across the universe to eternal torment.

As the shadows drew nearer and I realized there were more of them than I could count, I scrambled to the other side of the corpse heap for cover. My careless movements unseated the top two bodies—both of them human but mangled beyond recognition aside from the armor plating wrapped around their limp appendages—and caused a chain reaction among the other corpses.

"Shit," I said aloud. I figured tact didn't exactly matter at that point, since anything near enough to hear the curse would surely have noticed the crumbling tower of bodies I'd set in motion.

I'd thought I was completely dry of adrenaline and numb to the all-encompassing fear which would otherwise have been a normal human response to the sight of flesh-eating monsters, but I rediscovered both necessary evils when I heard the howls, growls, and shouts echoing down the city streets when the horde spotted me.

After that, I didn't even attempt to hide. The main road through the city was long and wide with about a hundred empty buildings where I might have ducked inside and prayed for the best. The soldier in me recognized the chances that I could outwait them were extraordinarily slim, though. My instincts also insisted that, if I was going to die regardless of my next move, I should go out in a blaze of glory. So help me God, I would take a few disfigured bastards down with me and end my *own* life before I would ever submit.

Wherever you go, I will find you.

Rising painfully to my feet, I darted between the closest buildings, not knowing whether or not there was an outlet at the end of the alley or if I was backing myself into a corner. All I knew was every demon on Furnace seemed to be descending on me at once and I needed to break their eye-line as quickly as possible. If I was lucky, they wouldn't be able to tell which alley I'd taken from the main road. It helped that most buildings in the city were relatively low to the ground, owing both to age and architectural style. Nearly all of them were in some state of disrepair, and I don't think renovation was high on the list of priorities for the citizens of Furnace.

Leaping onto a fallen block from the building at my right, I managed to climb onto the roof of an empty chapel and scurry across it until I found a better view of my pursuers.

About a hundred of them were still charging straight for me. They knew exactly where I was. I didn't see any Watchmen among them and felt minor relief at that realization, but these hideous beasts were more akin to the lava demons, and that wasn't necessarily good, either. Their mouths curled back in snarls or flapped wild tentacles and external rows of razor-teeth. Those capable of salivating dribbled uncontrollably. Their eyes were lit with unbridled, self-conjured rage.

Leaning over the edge of the roof, I strapped the SX pistol to the remnants of my utility belt, opting for the pulse rifle instead.

"So much for subtlety," I muttered.

The front line of attackers cut through the storm-cloud so quickly that even my training as a marksman struggled to catch them in my sights. They'd nearly reached the building entrance already.

I flipped down the pulse rifle's safety and propped my leg against the decorative column to steady my trembling arms. It didn't help much, though, because my legs were trembling, too.

"Come on, fuckers!" I shouted.

I started unloading into the onrushing horde, thinking to myself that I wouldn't wind up using the SX at all unless it was to off myself. It wouldn't do any good against the bastards from that distance anyway, and I didn't want to risk running out of ammo without all options at my disposal. I've always sort of thought suicide by pistol was a weak way to go during battle when you could easily spare a few fleet brothers and sisters by dropping another enemy soldier with the extra bullets, but Furnace forever changed my opinion on that. Some combat situations are just so fucked up, you need to make absolutely certain the enemy doesn't catch you alive.

My first two shots tore the heads off onrushing attackers, which owed more to the congestion among their ranks than my actual shooting prowess. I'm pretty sure the third pulse found a body somewhere, too, but I didn't spot that one once it left the chamber. I was too distracted by the savage ease with which the clawed monsters at the front of the line began to scale the walls around me.

Damn, I thought. *So much for sniper detail.*

I quickly abandoned my perch as the demons flooded the alleys on either side of me. Others started climbing the walls.

"Shit shit shit shit..." I inhaled sharply.

A rear escape was already blocked. Without hesitation, I sprinted directly toward the front of their line in the nearest alley and pushed off the edge of the roof as hard as I could, throwing myself clear onto the next rooftop in a leap that ended in a paralyzing thud.

"Not now," I gasped, clutching my ribs.

The jump had seemed short but I'd forgotten about the damage to the gravity-equalizers in my suit, which were only functioning at about a quarter of their normal capacity. I hadn't carried as far as I'd hoped. On top of that, Furnace's gravity had increased the severity of my impact. If I'd thought I was in pain while climbing the hill, it was nothing compared to what I felt then. And yet, I remained conscious, even though I wasn't sure I wanted to be.

The sound of the screeching demons spurred me back to my feet even before breath returned to my lungs. I didn't bother looking back to see how close the mob was to catching me. It only would have slowed me down, and the weighted growls were incentive enough to continue.

If I was honest with myself, there was really only one option left for escape. The pulse rifle was relatively effective against the creatures, but I didn't have enough time or enough ammo to pick them off one by one, and I didn't have any grenades to carve a huge swath from their ranks. The buildings were close together, though, and the next three or four stretching back toward the *Hummel* were each roughly the same size. It would be difficult to negotiate the gaps with the extra gravity and the damage to my suit's internal systems, but I thought I could manage. I had to, knowing the alternative was being eviscerated by a hundred demons rather than just a couple.

Grinding my teeth, I pushed to the edge of the roof and leapt to the next building just as the first demon scrambled within a dozen feet of me. I felt its footsteps shake the building on the platform beside me just before my own legs pistoned forward to the next roof.

This time, I was better prepared for the violent pull of gravity and landed with a little more grace. Enough, at least, that I only felt a minor flare in my ribs when my legs braced against the impact. I didn't pause on that roof at all, though. I just used the momentum to leap to the next one, and then the next. By the time I reached the fourth building down, I was too winded to keep it up. I turned and steadied the pulse rifle again, figuring I could at least buy a few moments to catch my breath since there were only three rooftops remaining before a gold-domed church that was two floors taller than I could reach.

Things were looking pretty dire as it was, but then I spotted a whole new threat. Above my attackers, about a dozen giant bat-creatures were flying toward me in a scattered formation. They may have been drawn by the commotion initially, but they had clearly picked up my scent and chosen to join the frenzied mob.

You did the best you could, I told myself, *but it's over.*

After all, even if I made it from one rooftop to the next, I knew I still couldn't outrun or out-climb the bats.

So I did what any good fleet soldier would have done facing insurmountable odds with an enemy army advancing toward their surviving crewmates (assuming, of course, that anyone was left alive on the *Hummel*). I planted my feet on the stone surface of the crumbling rooftop and unloaded Salib's pulse rifle into the motherfuckers' faces.

One by one, I blew off their heads as they approached me, still trying to come up with any alternatives for escape I hadn't yet considered. I drew a blank, but that was fine as long as I had the satisfaction of seeing their brains explode when the energy bursts struck. The shots nearly blinded me as they rippled out in succession, but I heard the outraged roars among the demon ranks and felt the wind beat against my face from the wings of the giant bats, which assured me I was at least making progress. Angering them, if nothing else. I wanted to be sure they remembered me for centuries to come, if not forever. Maybe only a day. There's no accounting for the memory-life of demons.

I fired until the clip ran dry and then I let the rifle drop. It was useless to me then. The only place I could find more ammunition was aboard the *Hummel,* and the ship had far more bullets in its cargo hold than bodies to fire them. The crew would die of starvation long before they ran out of ammo to defend the ship.

The demons finally reached the roof where I braced for my last stand. They began pouring over the edge with incredible, savage grace. I backed away until my boots touched the edge of the roof columns then dropped to one knee, more out of pain than despair. A beast with the muscle definition of a Kalak warlord and the head of a piranha was first in line. It seemed to sense that I was out of ammunition and charged gleefully ahead of the others for a few moments. A cruel smile formed on its otherwise expressionless face as it closed in on me. Behind the piranha-thing—and eventually overtaking it— was what I came to think of as a classic demon, or at least the way they are depicted in classical art. This one had horns, cloven feet, dark red skin, and yellow eyes with black fur dotting its face. Among creatures that either barely resembled beasts from old Earth mythology or fell completely outside my sphere of physiological reference, it was especially jarring to see such a familiar visage bearing down on me.

This is it, I thought.

I drew the SX pistol and placed the barrel against my temple.

Nothing else to do.

The two lead demons were within ten feet of me with the first bat creature visible above their heads. It was time to pull the trigger, I knew. But at the last second, I hesitated. My finger tensed and I pulled the gun away with a trembling hand.

Fuck this, I thought.

Against my better judgment, I turned the SX around and fired through the piranha-thing's mouth, blowing out the back of its head just as it opened wide to tear into my face. Acidic blood and brain matter splattered against me. And just like that, suicide was out of the question. I wouldn't have time to pull the trigger again. I wasn't sure I'd even have time to pull the trigger on another demon before it killed me.

That split-second hesitation all but guaranteed an eternity of suffering, and I knew it. Once the beasts caught you, they never let you go. I took small comfort knowing it had happened too late for me to dread my fate, regardless of how fervently I raged against the dying of the light.

God, please let my family know I love them.

It was an irrational thought considering it was a practical impossibility (even assuming that God exists) but any soldier will tell you that there are few atheists in a foxhole, and thinking back on it, I'm not surprised by my reaction at all.

The dead piranha-thing hit me full force while bits of its brain flew through the air. I tilted my head down and lowered my shoulder to brace for the blow, but the impact still carried me off the roof. Panicking, I kicked the corpse away from me as we flew through the air, then swung the SX back around to fire into the cascading demons I imagined following me over the edge.

Except they didn't follow. The classical demon bowled right over onto the next roof—it must have been easier for them to find purchase along the golden dome with their claws, talons, and inhuman strength—and the confused horde followed right after it.

Holy shit...

The demon hadn't been able to slow up in time, and the others were rushing after it so aggressively that they swept it along before it could alter course or warn them that I'd dropped into the alley.

I landed on my back in something wet and yielding with the piranha's flailing legs atop my chest. Rather than trying to break free and take off down the street, I remained motionless while the monsters passed by overhead. I watched them with a sustained wince of apprehension, amazed by my dumb luck yet thoroughly expecting it to turn any moment. All it would take was one of them realizing what had happened, even the last one, and the end result would be the same as if they'd all seen. I would merely have prolonged the inevitable, and I'm not sure it actually counts as prolonging when you're already dealing with eternity.

But the horde had such a single-minded purpose that every last one of them passed over the alleyway where I laid beneath the piranha-thing's corpse in a wet bed, which I prayed was only wet from garbage and not sewage or decomposing bodies.

You've got to be kidding me, I thought.

I stared up at the black storm clouds for several minutes after they passed, long after the growls and grunts and hammering footsteps faded back into the heart of the city. There was a huge part of me that was relieved, and yet a nearly equal part of me was disappointed. As long as I survived, I had to keep trying to get back to the *Hummel*, and the prospect of untangling myself from both the piranha and the filth beneath me just to slink into the shadows of the Greco-Roman buildings was so daunting that I briefly reconsidered pressing the SX to my temple to save myself the trouble.

No, my conscience countered. *Remember what happened to Katrina. Aziza. Flaherty. Sillinger. Teemo. Chara. Remember how badly you want to get back to your family again. Remember how much you want to be home.*

Slowly, the feeling returned to my arms and legs, though not the energy.

Remember what it's like to be in a warm bed. Remember what it's like to close your eyes and sleep.

I inched out from under the piranha and rolled down the pile to the damp ground.

Just close your eyes, my mind continued. My body obeyed. *Remember what it's like to sleep.*

My face came to rest in the dust and stone safely within the building's shadow.

Sleep.

I was too exhausted to resist the command. My body had bled every last drop of energy without any food, water, or rest, and with considerable injuries to boot. I was still recovering from Sillinger's emergency surgery, after all, and probably needed one or two other minor operations just to get back into fighting shape. The prospect of sleep had never sounded so good in my life.

Just close your eyes.

Now that the immediate threat had passed, I felt my body's internal systems beginning to shut down one by one.

Sleep.

And having brushed within kissing distance of death enough in the prior six hours to have forged an understanding with fate, I allowed myself to sink into the black nothingness on the other side of my eyelids.

Wherever you go, I will find you.

FURNACE

I was out for no less than two hours.

WATCHED

As far as I know, my sleep was uneventful, though I was so knocked out that I doubt even torture at the hands (or tentacles) of Furnace's demons would have woken me before my body was ready. I didn't have any *new* injuries, at least, and that was a good sign. If one of the monsters had indeed seen me lying in a pile of wet garbage beside the headless corpse of the piranha-thing, they must have mistaken me for another dead body and moved on without further investigation.

When I *did* wake, it took a moment to drum up the courage to open my eyes. I hoped I would hear a doctor's voice back on the *Hummel* right away, informing me that while the short-term prognosis wasn't great, I should pull through with a shitload of physical therapy and a can-do attitude. After several moments passed with no sound aside from the steady drip of liquid on stone, however, I accepted that my fortune hadn't extended quite far enough for that happy ending. You might argue I'd been lucky up until that point, I guess. You might say I should have been grateful to be alive. I tend to consider myself ridiculously *unlucky* for having been thrust into the situation in the first place. But that's just me. I still recognize that survival itself makes me a hell of a lot luckier than Salib's team. I just had to accept that no one else was going to carry my ass back to the *Hummel*. I had to do it myself.

Any good soldier will tell you that waiting for the fleet's heroic intervention to save you from the killing floor is about as helpful as pressing a VP to your temple and pulling the trigger. It's even less helpful when the majority of your squad is gone, because that makes it easier for the big-wigs to write you off as an 'acceptable' loss. There's a lot of bullshit in the media about how the fleet (or really any branch of the military) refuses to leave hostile territory until they've recovered all troopers and agents beyond enemy lines because it goes against the military code of ethics. The truth is, though, the fleet only cares about the fleet's interests, and I'm not always one of them.

Millions of soldiers either volunteer or are conscripted from Earth's colonies to afford the RSA the luxury of expendable pieces. They don't give a shit about us as individuals. God bless Gibbons as he's considered one of the few soldiers' captains, but even *he* would have sounded the order to get the hell off Furnace the moment engines and primary systems were back online, regardless of who he left behind. I wouldn't have blamed him if that's the way it played out, considering how horrific the mission turned out to be. In that scenario, it would have been best for everyone involved if he just cut his losses. He was never given that option, of course, but that's beside the point. The point is that no one but your squad looks out for you once the shit hits the fan.

As far as I know, my active squad was all dead, and they hadn't really been *my* squad to begin with. That's one of the downsides of being promoted to a bridge seat. You're not really part of a team anymore. You're assigned to missions, that's all, and sometimes those missions last a while. Sometimes a captain even picks the same crew for multiple missions, and sometimes you make friends along the way and request to serve alongside them as often as possible.

But that all pales in comparison to the brother and sisterhood of an infantry squad, commando unit, or special ops team, where soldiers really look out for one another. Each one of you knows exactly what the others have been through, who they've lost, and how many days it's been since they last saw home. You run every single mission together, and you're hunkering down in the trenches with each other for most of them. Not sitting cozy in your quarters reading a novel or dicking around in SurReal World. Not even locked in a stasis pod while your vessel hurtles across the galaxy. Instead, you're burying each other on alien planets or digging bullets from each other's legs while mortar shells rain down around you. You're vomiting at the sight of decapitated human colonists who've been desecrated by some ruthless alien species solely interested in documenting Human culture. It sucks, and it's cathartic.

In that sense, you lose brothers and sisters who are closer than family when you take a bridge seat, but you also don't have to deal with the day-to-day horrors they experience on the front lines. Unless you're like me. Then, you still do.

The only exception is if you become a pilot, a navigator, a tactical officer, or an engineer on a genuine fleet warship like the *Doorway*, in which case you're pretty much in it for the long haul. Then you get to form those deeply-rooted bonds with your crew. But you've got to work your way up to that. It's a hell of a lot of responsibility to command a warship in any capacity, and I haven't decided yet whether or not I want to take that jump. My guess is it will take a while.

I realize that this may seem like a digression from waking in a city gutter, but that's what ran through my head as I writhed around in the heap of refuse plotting my next step, and I've vowed to be as thorough and accurate with this account as possible. I knew I couldn't count on anyone, and at least in this case, that was a good thing. If I'd waited for the cavalry to swoop in and rescue me, I would still be waiting.

Even after the two hours of rest, my body was weary to the core. I didn't know if I could stand up and keep moving. Also, I didn't have a clue *where* in the city I'd wound up aside from a general recollection of hurdling rooftops. I'd used up all the pulse charges before I'd dropped the rifle and moved onto the SX, which had something like ten bullets left in the chamber by my estimation. On top of all that, I didn't know if the crew of the *Hummel* was still alive or if the ship had been overrun. I assumed they hadn't left the planet yet, but it would have been just my luck if they *had* considering the way things were going that day.

So what was my incentive to get up and venture onto the city's main street?

Nothing. Simply nothing.

I was tired of running. Tired of pain. Tired of thirst. Tired of terror. Tired of the sights and smells of the fucked-up monsters and their appetites, which well exceeded my comprehension as a (relatively) sane human being, even one who has seen some horrific shit in his day (if this account isn't evidence enough, I'm willing to provide additional examples from the Kalak War). In a way, it was peaceful lying in a gutter on an alien planet with the acid of the piranha's blood eating through my suit. It wasn't spectacular, but at least I didn't *have* to run if I didn't feel like it. Part of me wanted to stay there until I died. If any more demons came poking around, I'd just play dead until they wandered off. And if they didn't wander off, so be it.

Is this what Katrina died for? my conscience at last spoke up. *You broke her leg so she couldn't escape those bastards, and then she stood up for all of you while you froze in fear. You owe it to her. She gave you a chance to live.*

It was a harsh assessment, perhaps, but that's the sort of pep-talk I needed at the time. I was beyond the point of reaching the *Hummel* for my own sake. My will wasn't just waning, it was swirling down the goddamned toilet. I had to latch onto a greater cause.

"Fine," I sighed, propping myself up by the elbow and leaning against the domed cathedral. "I'll go."

The reflection from the golden dome illuminated the marble roof across the way even without the aid of starlight. Furnace was self-illuminated, which was impossible but the reality nonetheless, so I guess it made sense that the buildings operated the same way. I don't know. None of it really makes sense when you start dissecting it, and this isn't even the fucked up part. I didn't realize just how much that cathedral (or mosque or synagogue or temple or whatever the populace called it) would stick with me once I returned to Earth.

As I've previously noted, the city was heavy on familiar Greco-Roman architecture, but the cathedral took it to another level. It looked like an exact copy of a building I've seen in datapads from the Second Dark Ages. Long before my time. The Earth structure was destroyed by the now defunct caliphate as a final, desperate punishment to the people who'd risen up to eradicate them, but the image has endured across the centuries. On Furnace, it was big, imposing, and utterly out of place among the decrepit city buildings. My eyes were repeatedly drawn to it.

Why don't you go in there and check it out? a voice asked.

It wasn't that simple. Churches are traditionally viewed as places of sanctuary, but I had no desire to find out what twisted religion the Furnace demons practiced, assuming it could truly be called 'religion' at all. I couldn't ignore the potential for finding answers inside, though, and it was right next to me. I needed a feasible objective to get moving again and I didn't see any immediate alternatives. If I thought too hard about crossing the whole city, descending the crater to reach the *Hummel*, then waiting for the ship's systems to come back online so I could even *attempt* to figure out where the fuck we were in relation to the rest of the universe, I would be paralyzed.

So I pushed myself to my feet, fought the black splotches of unconsciousness that leapt to the forefront of my vision, and shuffled over to the dripping gutter-liquid for a drink. I figured that no matter what it was, the liquid would feel better going down than continuing to swallow with a dry throat. The taste was bitter, but it soothed some of the raw burn. It wasn't pure enough to solve my dehydration problem, but I hoped it would buy me a few extra minutes down the road.

Wiping my mouth, I turned and limped along the wall until I rounded the corner onto the main street.

The road appeared empty, just like it had been when I'd first entered the city. This time, though, I had a feeling it really *was* empty. No one seemed to be watching from the shadows. Even the clown's voice inside my head had fallen eerily silent for some time, and though the view reminded me of the room where he'd briefly held me as his prisoner, I didn't sense he was near.

Don't trust it, I thought. *He's better than that, and this is his playground. If he hasn't taken you yet, it's because he's not ready to, or you aren't ready to go. But he'll find you. Just like he said.*

It wasn't exactly a reassuring thought, so I pushed it away and limped to the marble steps leading to the cathedral doors.

Then I heard a low growl echoing from the alley across the street and froze mid-step.

Shit, I thought. *What now?*

Keeping my breath steady and my arms locked tightly against my body, I pivoted toward the noise. I thought about reaching for the SX pistol but worried the sudden movement might force the hand of whatever was quietly stalking me through the city.

Whoever it is, why hasn't it attacked me yet? I wondered.

No matter how skewed the creature's perception was—and I had reason to believe every monster on Furnace was demented to some extent—it was plain enough to see that I was in dire straits. I didn't have another battle left in me. The way things were going, I thought I might not even have another *step*.

"What do you want?" I asked. My voice cracked over every word. My throat was so dry it felt like I was gargling barbed wire. I didn't get an answer though, and I couldn't see into the darkened alleyway across the street.

By my reckoning, that left me with two options. I could either pretend I hadn't heard anything at all, head straight into the cathedral, and hope some form of black-magic or general good luck would prevent the creature from following me inside, or I could limp across the street and confront my stalker. All things considered, I figured the former was my best bet. I wasn't in any shape to pick fights and there was at least a fifty percent chance I'd imagined the noise in the first place. I was on high-alert, after all, and when you've been buried in the trenches as many times as I have, you tend to distrust silences. Your mind starts to play with you, if only to keep you on your toes for when something bad really demands your attention.

I turned back toward the cathedral door, careful not to rush in case the movement set something in motion I didn't want any part of. You never know what will spook someone when they're intent on spying on you. Also, it hurt to move, and especially quickly. Each step was accompanied by an anticipatory wince.

The moment my trembling hand reached for the door, however, I heard the pound of boots over the road and snapped back to attention.

It was the hooded Watchman from the corpse fields. The one with the scythe, although it didn't look like he was carrying a weapon this time around. Somehow, I'd failed to notice him following me into the city despite having a bird's eye view of both the corpse fields and the city itself on several occasions. I guess I'd been a little preoccupied.

How? I wondered, then realized it was a stupid question. I'd been unconscious for a long time in the alley. Even if the demon was an imbecile, he could easily have followed the trail of corpses I'd left in my wake until he happened upon my general area. After that, even if he hadn't found me, he would only have needed to duck in the shadows and wait for movement to trap me.

Why, though?

It wasn't that I doubted his bloodlust or even his desire to watch me bleed after eluding his grasp in the corpse fields, but the lengths to which he'd gone to find me contrasted with my initial perception of the Watchmen. I'd thought they were mindless brutes who delighted in the capture and torture of innocent creatures. They still were, I supposed, but if one of them was willing to follow me into the city, he must have served some sort of guard function as well. A shepherd, if you will, although with a much more heinous agenda. The notion of an agenda at all was terrifying, just like it had been in the corpse fields. The demons near the lava lakes had been ruthless savages and that was at least comforting in its predictability. The Watchmen in the corpse fields as a whole were ruthless savages with some measure of group coordination, but still seemed more like animals than sentient creatures with complex thoughts and desires.

But the appearance of the Watchman calmly regarding me from the shadows across the way changed all of that. He'd transcended the apparent uniformity of his rank and developed a specific role. A personality. One which valued some catches over others.

It was an unsettling notion, indeed. If I was valuable enough to the demons that this lead Watchman had followed me across the hellacious tundra and sought me out in a gutter on the verge of death, I shuddered to think what they had in store for me once I was caught.

And I *was* caught, I knew. I'd been frozen in place by the sight of the creature. At least he wasn't rushing me. That would have made it difficult to draw the SX in time, assuming he afforded me the opportunity. For the moment, I was too stunned by the frankness of his approach to do anything at all.

"What?" I said weakly.

It still amazes me how easily I'd forgotten the magnitude of his presence over the course of a few hours. Now that he stood before me again, I shrank beneath his massive form. The heat from his breath seared the venom-ravaged flaps of skin along my cheek and lips. I felt like vomiting from the stench, but I didn't have enough in my stomach to upchuck.

"What do you want from me?" I wheezed. By the time he was close enough that I would have trusted my aim with the SX, I'd fallen to my knees and reached out a trembling hand in supplication. "Why?"

I was broken. Utterly broken. Even now, I'm ashamed by it. By how close I came to giving up in that moment. I hadn't bowed before the scorpion-bug, after all. Or the horde of demons that swarmed me on the rooftops. I'd even managed to get away from the corpse fields without succumbing to despair and collapsing in the dust. So why now, I wondered? What was so damned paralyzing about seeing an alien—even a *demon* alien in a red mask with a penchant for torture—walking calmly toward me? I could have run. It would have hurt like a bitch, and he probably would have caught me, but I at least could have tried. I didn't, though. And as I tried to shift my weight again at the last moment, I wondered if *he* had something to do with my paralysis. Not just through his imposing presence, but some other dark power channeled from his lord and king.

When I dropped to my knees before the cathedral steps, I was certain of it. The Watchman had control of my body. That's why he wasn't running. I was merely a passenger.

Keep your head up, I thought.

It was hard not to plead for my life, but I hadn't done it when I was a POW during the Kalak War and I wasn't about to start. Furnace may have broken me and I may have been close to giving up altogether, but I still had *some* pride. If I was going to allow myself to die at the hands of the red-masked demon, I would at least hold onto that.

"KUURUKA NARYEH," the creature growled.

His voice made me recoil, shuffling six-inches backward even through his mental hold. My body convulsed. It was like nothing I'd ever felt before. Hollow and distant, like it was happening to someone else. When he placed his massive, coal-black hands on either side of my head and spat burning saliva in my eyes, I screamed and tried to rise once again. It was no use, though. His dark magic had me locked in place. Not even my overwhelming revulsion could break the trance now that we were in direct contact.

"DEEBAK SCHEN TSCHARIA," he said, then drew back and hawked another thick, black string of phlegm into my eyes.

The burn forced my eyelids shut, which only made things worse. The acidic spit was trapped now and slathered itself over my eyeballs like a living thing. It probably was.

"OPEN YOUR EYES," the creature commanded.

I blinked involuntarily, more because I was startled that I suddenly understood him than I wanted to obey his orders. Three and a half years in the fleet plus the academy have made obedience a knee-jerk reaction for me on most occasions, but I've also learned resistance. I don't cave easily under pressure, no matter what conclusions you may draw from Furnace. Considering it was the worst of all worst-case-scenarios, I'm hoping you'll give me the benefit of the doubt.

Once the burn of the Watchman's saliva began to recede, I took a deep breath and drank in the world around me. I couldn't gulp it all down in one swallow, though. It was the psychological equivalent of having the whole Pacific Ocean dropped on me at once and trying to catch it between my lips. My mind was drowned by incomprehension. I felt my brain swell until I thought my skull was about to burst, and then everything came into focus again. That didn't mean there was much clarity as to *what* I was seeing, but my perception had at least been altered to the point where my surroundings were more than just a blinding white curtain with a migraine buzz in the background.

Out of all the crazy shit I saw on Furnace, this was the only instance in which I'm thoroughly convinced I hallucinated, although maybe 'hallucinated' isn't the right term, either. It was a message specifically targeted at my brain by the Watchman, so I guess it was more of a vision than anything. He dug into my head and left me all kinds of ugly surprises and trap-doors, some of which I suspect were implanted so he could access them at a later date. I find more of them every day. Sound paranoid? Maybe to you, but you weren't there. You didn't feel his burning hands against your temples. You didn't feel the sudden, violent teleportation into a nightmare world created specifically for you.

"Wherever you go," a voice whispered beside me. "I'll find you."

Objects began to fill in around me and I realized I was kneeling in the prison cell where the Kalak had once tortured me within an inch of death. I wasn't strapped to the oversized bed where I'd spent several weeks without moving, but I could feel the sting of a recent interrogation session from my throat to my hips. The Kalak are big on using vipers from their native rainforests whenever they want to make someone bleed without killing them. The bites hurt like hell but centuries of exposure to radiation has diluted their venom just enough to be non-fatal to human physiology, making them valuable assets in interrogation.

By the familiar, pulsing burns beneath my combat-suit, I could tell it had been less than an hour since I'd had a visit from the goon squad. Probably General Kraat had overseen the session himself. He was the worst of the overgrown lizards who'd somehow managed to sweep a dozen human colonies right out from under fleet protection. If it had been less than an hour, that usually meant I had at least three hours before they settled on a more succinct method for information extraction than the vipers. Not a lot of time, but plenty to get my head together.

I was just glad to be off of Furnace, even for a few moments and even when it meant being dropped into another shitty situation.

Am I really here, though? I wondered. *Has the last year and a half been a dream? A new method of torture the Kalak have devised to watch us suffer? Some way to study human psychology?*

I considered the idea as carefully as my fragile mental state would allow, but eventually decided it was impossible. The Kalak were fearsome warriors and they loved developing new ways to inflict pain, but they weren't exactly experts in holographic projection. They were color-blind, for one thing, and I was confident that particular handicap would manifest in some way with any virtual world they built. Maybe that's naïve, since it assumes that no human would ever consider aiding the enemy for a price or to protest the Crown government, but I fail to see the point of such an involved deception. I'm not a general. I'm not a commander. I have no real secrets their spies couldn't uncover on their own.

The alternative, of course, was that my body still was on Furnace and the Watchman had isolated this particular near-memory for a reason. Why? I'm still not sure. Being a POW for weeks on a Kalak station was traumatizing, no doubt, but no more remarkable than being on Furnace or in the trenches of most other operations I'd run in the infantry. Maybe it was the connection of torture alone, which seemed to be a sweet spot for the demons in and around the city. The Watchman could have searched for a specific brand of agony when he tapped into my neural synapses and decided that my POW days was the best place to lay anchor. It would have been natural and recognizable for him, I guess.

Either way, I knew I was in deep shit. Even if the Watchman had locked my consciousness in a memory while my body remained on Furnace, it still meant I would likely miss my window for escape and survival. I had to figure out a way to break free quickly or else either the *Hummel* would leave without me or a wandering demon would swoop in and devour me while I knelt motionless before the cathedral steps.

And how do you plan on breaking out of this?

I scanned the cell for any obvious escape routes, but as I'd verified about thirteen thousand times during my captivity, there was no such salvation hidden along the sterile, steel walls. For a moment, I'd held out hope that the walls themselves were an illusion and if I reached out with my hand I'd discover they were nothing but air. That wasn't the case, however, and I jammed my thumb testing the theory. You'd think I would have been numb to such minor injuries by then, but I spent the next thirty seconds or so shaking my hand vigorously.

If he didn't want you to escape, why wouldn't he have just killed you? Why the theatrics?

On cue, the voice of the clown demon drifted out from the vents in a puff of white smoke. "You will be my vessel," he hissed.

I rose groggily to my feet and backed away from the fumes. Hearing his voice wasn't exactly comforting, but it confirmed to my satisfaction that the intent was not for me to die in the Kalak prison. At the very least, he had something to show me, and I didn't think it was the close walls of the cell or the surveillance pod mounted high above the door. There was still a chance that he was toying with me—in fact, there was a damned good probability of it—but the prospect of invincibility, or really just a safety net, helped convince me to get moving. What did I have to lose? If a Kalak guard gunned me down for attempting escape, so be it. For all I knew, the trick to breaking through the nightmare was simply having the courage to open the door and step into the hallway.

Only one way to find out.

It took all of one step to realize that every single injury I'd accumulated on Furnace had made the jump with me, which made me wonder if I'd miscalculated the amount of time since my last interrogation and whether or not the vipers had been used at all.

Doesn't matter, I decided. *At least I can move.*

Before pain could convince me otherwise, I limped across the room and waved my hand in front of the door controls. If I'd had Kalak blood, the reinforced steel would have gasped open and I would have been home free (more or less). I didn't, of course, and even in this distant memory conjured by the Watchman, I couldn't override the lizards' security protocols simply by willing the door open.

"Great," I muttered, surprised at the sound of my own voice. Now that the physical world had filled in around me, I was startled by how concrete everything seemed. Just like when I'd awoken beneath the bone chandelier in the clown demon's city hideaway. And just like when I'd barely eluded the clown thing's grasp and wound up in the wastelands, I was hoping for a miracle.

I scanned the room frantically. My combat-instincts wanted me to keep moving, like I knew deep down the horrors that would follow, but it was no use. The Watchman had brought me back there for a reason and he meant to see his plan to fruition before I found a way out. I'm convinced that even if I'd somehow managed to break free of my cell and stagger into the main corridor, I wouldn't have gotten far. Either the universe beyond the four walls of my cell would have been completely blank or there would have been an entire platoon of Kalak runners waiting to put me down. Maybe not kill me, but beat me well enough to be sure I wouldn't attempt escape again without some very serious soul-searching. They'd done it to me before and it had worked well enough. For a while, anyway.

I turned back to the oversized bed (which had been converted from a Kalak medical gurney into a crude vehicle for torture and restraint) determined to utilize my lone asset for a grand—and so far undetermined—escape plan. I didn't get far before I heard the clack of boots echoing through the outer corridor. It was a safe bet they were coming for me, whoever 'they' were.

I reached for the SX pistol but there was nothing in the holster and the rest of my utility belt was still missing. I should have expected as much, but my brain was still overloaded with conflicting information. I was a little slower on the uptake with some things than others.

"Here I come," a high-pitched voice mocked me from the hallway. Laughter echoed down the long corridor, pinging off each girder and doorway along the way.

Who the hell was that? I wondered.

It definitely wasn't the voice of a Kalak or any demon I'd encountered on Furnace so far. Worst of all, it sounded vaguely familiar. Human. Female. The longer I thought it over, the more certain I was that I knew the voice.

Mom?

"I've got a present for you," she giggled.

I backed away with my eyes wide, too stunned to position myself for a quick bolt as soon as the door opened and the corridor was exposed. I was trapped in indecision. Did I attack right away based on the assumption that it couldn't *really* be my mother, risking that it somehow *was* and I would be inflicting some measure of physical or psychological damage across trillions of light years?

I didn't decide fast enough. The door slid open and suddenly I was staring up at the most absurd manifestation of my mother I could ever have imagined. Stranger, even, than the sight of her severed head bouncing over the dusty surface of Furnace like a tumbleweed. The body before me was that of a heavy Kalak runner: one of the biggest and strongest among their ranks. It had the same greenish-yellow scales, broad shoulders, and massive hands gripping one of their infamously bulky assault rifles, but the creature's head narrowed into my mother's twisted visage beyond the black and gray hood. She was grinning wide at me and waving the barrel of the assault rifle back and forth, but her teeth were stained black just like the clown demon's and black roots of infection stood out in the veins across her face.

"My boy," she cackled. A long glob of black drool dripped from the edge of her mouth and burned a hole in the steel floor. "It hurts me to see you like this."

Another figure stepped through the doorway. This time, it was the woman from Europa. The navigator who'd explained the new jump theories from Sol Facility.

I was more fundamentally shaken by her sudden appearance than my mother's, likely because I'd already seen my mother's head on the surface and she'd been lurking in the back of my mind ever since. The navigator was so far out of left field for me that it took a moment to realize it was her, although part of that could have been because, like my mother, her form was nearly unrecognizable. Her skin was charcoal black like the Watchmen, except hers looked like it had been burned rather than born. Long, flapping gills lined her ribcage before merging with an open wound on her back where an ugly red creature nested and growled at me.

I whispered her name in horror, still unsure whether or not it was truly *her* since only the eyes seemed to match the woman I'd loved.

"You've been out at sea too long, Mikey," my mother hissed. She took another step toward me and I carefully maneuvered to the other side of the room. It brought me within swiping distance of the burned fish-creature, but since it hadn't addressed me yet and was less physically imposing, I considered it the lesser of two evils.

My mother wasn't deterred. "It's time to come home," she said.

I almost believed the pain in her voice. She reached out to me with her left hand, tucking the assault rifle to her hip with the right.

"No," I said firmly. I was still too shocked to bolt for the door, but I was getting my head about me again and calculating the odds that I could dart through both of them with my heavy limp.

"It's not up to you," the charred fish navigator told me. "We're taking you home."

Both of them moved toward me at once. The red creature hovering over the navigator's shoulder growled again and flashed its pointed, yellow teeth.

"You've been gone too long, Mikey," my mother opined. "We all miss you so much. Your father's inconsolable. You've never even met your niece!"

"I miss you," the navigator whispered. "I dream about you every night."

I shook my head slowly, trying not to gag at the smell wafting from her as the creature nesting in her back shifted within the open wound. My mother's face twisted into deeper rage with each step I took away from her.

"COME HERE!' she suddenly screeched.

I lunged out of her reach and slammed back into the side of the Kalak torture-bed. The impact made me cry out but falling also helped me narrowly avoid the nails of the creature on the navigator's back. It also put me between the two of them, which afforded me a new opportunity. I didn't hesitate. With all the force I could muster, I locked my left leg around my mother's ankle and swept my right along the ground. She fell to the floor hard enough that I heard bones crack somewhere in her upper body, but she was already getting to her feet by the time I released and drove my shoulder into the navigator's midsection. I pushed her just far enough out of the way that I could slip through the door without either of them catching me, then punched the controls as hard as I could and watched them slide away.

"BOY!" my mutant mother screamed as she rushed for the door.

She hit the steel just as it slid completely closed. Hard enough to make me flinch a few steps into the large hallway before my knees caught me.

"Mike!" the navigator pleaded. I could hear the red creature clawing at the door and pictured its nails snapping off from the pressure. The pain wouldn't have stopped it, of course. If anything, it would only have made it angrier. I didn't plan on sticking around to find out.

Feeling a swell of panic materialize in my chest (a sensation which had been blessedly absent in the prison cell), I swung around to start my escape and ran head-first into the chest of the hooded Watchman.

The impact sent me reeling. I could feel the thin veil of reality stretching again, this time so far that my mind was momentarily blinded by the realized depth of my ignorance, and then I tripped over the cathedral steps and the world came back into focus.

I was back where I'd started, at least in terms of the Watchman. I guess the cold marble should have been comforting since it meant I'd somehow wrenched myself free of the demon's control, but the shock of seeing both my mother and the navigator twisted into monsters suddenly crashed into me like a rogue wave.

No, I told myself. You don't have time for that now. Fight it.

I was distantly aware of the red-masked demon crouching over me inquisitively and extending his right hand, presumably to grind more poison into my eye, but I wasn't about to give him the chance. I threw my fist forward into the center of his mask, and when my knuckles immediately screamed with agony, I drew back and hit him again. He didn't fall—not completely—but the force knocked him on his heels and gave me room to regain my footing.

"No!" I roared.

I became a cyclone of wild blows from both fists and feet. Most landed but many were also glancing. Blood from my stripped knuckles shot over my venom-ravaged cheeks, but for once, the pain only spurred me on. I was becoming one of them, I thought. Using the pain to lash out. Maybe that's what the demons wanted all along. To change me into a creature that fed off of pain like them. The more I think about it these days, the more I'm convinced that they care more about turning the things you love against you. Making you question every aspect of your life. Bringing evil into every innocent relationship you've left behind, so that if you ever return to them, you do so with the weighted cynicism of memory. You've seen what Hell looks like, and you've seen how things that seem innocent and comfortable can be warped into your most terrifying nightmare.

I wasn't going to let the Watchman kill me, if only because he was the one who'd put those thoughts in my head. He's the reason I know what my mother would look like if her genes were spliced with a Kalak runner.

I punched and kicked until he lay motionless on the dusty street, and then I pulled the SX pistol, knelt on his chest, and blew a hole through his temple. He didn't resist at all, and I didn't feel any better after re-holstering the SX and staggering to my feet. I guess I knew even then that he'd gotten what he came for and had known the consequences for a job well done.

Once I'd gathered my breath, I turned back to the cathedral and continued on without looking back.

TSCHARIA

The marble cathedral steps were worn from frequent use, which seemed out of place considering the environment. Maybe it was an illusion. Maybe the demons had stolen the building from another species they'd tortured and killed. In any event, it was more plausible than any of those demonic assholes frequenting a house of worship, no matter what indecencies the so-called 'religion' practiced. It was too much order for creatures like them. Too specific, if that makes sense. And though they occasionally displayed some group-think and general cooperation with each other, they didn't strike me as the type to conform beneath one banner.

What about the clown, then? I wondered. *Maybe I've got them all wrong and they're actually extraordinarily misguided zealots of a religion older than Earth itself.*

I didn't really give a shit either way. It was a nice enough distraction from my perilous reality, though, that I didn't soil myself at the belated notion of stumbling into a service when I opened the doors. And if it turned out that a few demons were seated in the congregation worshipping an unknown deity (maybe the clown thing) in their own peculiar way—like raping and beheading innocents in the name of their god—I would either feign allegiance to that deity or collapse on the spot depending on convenience. I didn't care which.

I stood before the large wooden doors with my right hand on the latch for a few moments, studying the grooves along the panels and the inscriptions overhead. Most of it was gibberish to me, but I recognized one word in particular straight away because it was written in English.

TSCHARIA, the inscription read.

Sha-rye-uh, I mouthed.

The word sounded familiar, but it took me a few seconds to place where I'd heard it last.

The bastards in the masks, I realized.

The demons had chanted the word when they'd nailed Aziza to the crisscrossed pillars in the corpse fields. It was also inscribed on the city walls amid a similar grouping of indecipherable symbols.

Tscharia, I thought.

I was familiar with the concept of morality as law and also the curious way morality had been interpreted in the Second Dark Age, but I didn't think the two words were necessarily related. The abominations of Furnace had no moral law—at least none that made sense to me—so I wrote off the repetition as coincidence. Or, more succinctly, a combination of symbols in an alien alphabet which coincidentally resembled the word *Tscharia* in English.

Who gives a damn? I thought. The name didn't matter. What interested me was the other symbols above the door, how they were apparently related to constellations even though the sky was barren of starlight.

Is that a map? I wondered.

The navigator in me was interested enough in the crude symbols that I forgot where I was for a moment, which only made the jolt back to reality more jarring when a scream shook the city street.

I can use this, I thought, quickly scanning the symbols to see if any of them were remotely familiar.

I couldn't be certain that the symbols were stars, or that the word *Tscharia* represented the planet where the *Hummel* had crashed, but I didn't have any better theories and I doubted the *Hummel's* crew had come up with answers while I was away, assuming they were still around.

Another scream. This time, the wind howled in response.

Move.

I decided to revisit the issue once I'd poked around the cathedral for more evidence of where I was and how to navigate the *Hummel* back home, then pushed the oddly circular latch of the door handle and shouldered my way inside.

The interior was dark. The staggered rows of pews, the off-centered altar, and the general dishevelment of the décor all gave the building a funhouse effect. The theatrical atmosphere was only dampened by the human corpses that were nailed to the walls, hung from the rafters, and heaped before the altar. A collection of severed heads was arranged in a loose circle at the center of the room.

I wasn't surprised. Accenting rooms with mutilated bodies and streams of blood was par for the course on Furnace, more or less. It was alarming to see so many *human* corpses, though, since I was sure none of them had come from the *Rockne Hummel* or any other fleet vessel. In fact, the bodies that were actually clothed seemed transported from another time. An era long forgotten in modern Earth politics except among archivist androids with exceptional memory processors. Medieval or earlier, by my guess. No one on Earth dressed in those tattered clothes anymore. Not even tribes in lesser populated regions. In fact, poverty-stricken colonists on other planets wouldn't even have made such inefficient garments unless it was for a dramatic production, which didn't seem likely, either. By my admittedly foggy deductive logic, I figured that meant the bodies had been taken from another time altogether, though how they could have possibly survived so long—even on Furnace outside the normal rules of physics—was beyond me. Mind you, that's a very rough assessment from a navigator with no real background in ancient history, but their attire was at least reminiscent of the Two Dark Ages and the way they're depicted in historical vids.

Luckily for me, the building was otherwise deserted, and though the exterior was in far better shape than most buildings within the city walls, it didn't look like anyone had ventured inside for at least a few days.

If they were brought in that long ago, how are the bodies still intact? I wondered, limping toward the heap of corpses for closer examination.

As I knelt down beside them, hoping to answer the furious swirl of questions inside my head, my attention was abruptly drawn away.

I stopped moving mid-squat. "Hello..." I whispered.

Beyond the altar and beneath a realistically (which is to say, revoltingly) rendered sculpture of a beast defiling a woman stood a large throne. The woman's vacant eyes seemed to lock onto me and nothing at the same time. The effect was chilling enough to make me shudder, but it wasn't until my gaze wandered to the throne that my breath stopped completely and my muscles tensed.

Not again, I thought.

It was the clown demon.

His head hung between his shoulders so that his chin rested against his chest and his horns stood out prominently. He wasn't looking at me.

Yet.

I backpedaled toward the door the moment I saw him but my legs tangled and I wound up falling into one of the wooden pews, as though the clown had pushed me himself.

I don't know how things would have turned out if I hadn't fallen and instead rushed out to the street. Probably I would have died, since a horde of monsters searched the city for me even then. At the very least, I never would have learned what Tscharia was or why I'd been brought there. I didn't piece it all together until I reached home again, but I wouldn't have been able to at all if I'd left prematurely.

I sat in stunned silence for a few moments. Watched the clown demon slouch in his throne. Picked distractedly at my scabbing wounds. Bought time. Every once in a while, I scanned the cathedral to be sure we were alone, ignoring the presence of the human corpses altogether. There wasn't another demon in sight as far as I could tell, though. I think it was meant to be that way, I thought. In the end, it had to be just the two of us. He had a plan for me—I knew that much already—and I thought there was a chance he'd let me live as long as his bloodthirsty disciples scattered across the planetoid didn't spoil our party.

The clown never moved from his throne, though, and after a while, I started feeling a bit more comfortable. Maybe 'comfortable' isn't the right word, I guess, because I was still just about shitting my combat-suit in terror. But I wasn't about to turn tail and flee again. Part of me was tired enough of the whole goddamned business that I *wanted* the creature to engage me, if only because I knew he would give me the answers I needed. Maybe not the ones I *wanted*, but answers that would provide me a fuller perspective of the stakes—and potential loopholes—of my captivity on Furnace.

"Why am I here?" I finally asked.

My voice was even weaker than I remembered. The fluid I'd ingested in the alley hadn't turned out to be the miracle elixir I'd hoped it was, after all.

Minutes passed in complete silence. I was content waiting. It may not have been the cheeriest of surroundings, but I felt oddly safe under the hidden gaze of the demon. The idea that he, out of all the creatures on Furnace, might have some capacity for discernment, some shred of rationale behind his actions, was comforting in its own way. He might eventually order up the same torture I would receive at the hands of other demons, but at least it would come with a measure of consideration. For better or worse, he would make a calculated decision. Otherwise, I would have been dead the moment he bit through my helmet, not whisked away to some private sanctuary with a bone-chandelier where the prying eyes of his disciples couldn't reach me. The demon ghost with the smeared, bleach-white face appeared to have a vested interest in me, and until I demonstrated that I wasn't worth his time or bother, I thought I could count on his peculiar protection.

What the hell is wrong with me? I wondered. *How fucked is this place that I'm looking to the clown demon for protection when he caused this shit in the first place?*

The dose of perspective sobered me enough that I squirmed uncomfortably over the wooden pew. I felt a chill building in the small of my back again.

"What do you want from me?" I asked.

I didn't really expect an answer and I didn't get one. He didn't move at all.

But the bodies nailed to the walls *did* start to move, so subtly at first that I wasn't sure where the creaks, moans, and rustling sounds were coming from. I rose to my feet slowly, trying to avoid eye-contact with the shadows in my periphery so I could pretend that the dead humans weren't actually moving.

It didn't do any good.

Panicked, I limped to the altar as fast as I could. I was determined to get answers before the end, no matter what 'the end' turned out to be.

"Why am I here?" I asked again.

My voice was still hoarse, both from thirst and the hooded demon's grip. By sheer force of will, however, I managed to shout my next question.

"What the fuck do you want from me?" I yelled. The words faltered on my tongue as my vocal cords cut in and out. "What do I have to do to leave?"

There was a loud crash behind me. One of the undead bodies had fallen to the floor from twenty feet above the ground.

And then another.

And another.

They started dropping every couple of seconds. The impacts were so forceful that my bones rattled from head to toe.

"Answer me!" I shouted, stepping around the bodies and severed heads in front of the altar. I worked my way through them until I was covered in shadow just like the clown demon.

Except it wasn't really him, and I should have realized it long before then. There was, indeed, a throne and the clown's visage had been rendered imposingly upon it, casting judgment on a congregation of dead and undead alike. But it was just a bronze statue. Slightly elevated, yet otherwise completely lifelike and built to scale.

Damn damn damn! I thought.

Every second I remained in the cathedral brought me one step closer to a confrontation with the resurrected corpses that lined the walls and piled before the altar. And for what? A good fight? Bullshit. Yet again, I'd risked my life to beg answers from an inanimate object. Not much different than home, I guess.

I turned and saw a few undead humans had either crawled or limped to the cathedral entrance. They began streaming down the aisle ceremoniously. There was nowhere to go. They hadn't noticed me yet but were blocking the only exit anyway. There was no telling what they would do if we made contact, or whether or not they would even be able to *find* me with their degraded senses. I figured a couple millennia was a long time to stay in shape. Most of them probably weren't getting around so well.

I didn't want to find out whether or not that was true, though. Somehow, the idea of undead humans—a comfortable familiarity suddenly corrupted by the Hell planet—was more unsettling than the monsters themselves, if not more terrifying. I knew how the people were *supposed* to look and act, but instead saw the moaning, mutilated wraiths that they'd been twisted into. Numb to the world around them.

Maybe I was more afraid of them because I knew I was staring at my future if I didn't escape the planet before natives destroyed the *Hummel*. Maybe it would even be *those* undead humans who broke it down. Posing as living beings so the crew took pity on them, then offering themselves as sacrifices to the clown god as they sabotaged their brethren. Maybe they envied our vitality. Maybe they wanted to prevent the rest of us from returning to the lives they'd missed. Maybe they just wanted to please *him*.

They're too slow, I thought. Yet they'd still done a hell of a job of cornering me, if that was their intention.

Instinctively, I backed deeper into the shadows surrounding the clown's throne while the undead humans continued their somber, shambling approach. The procession was unnerving. I'd seen similar rituals every Sunday as a boy when the congregation visited the altar to offer a sacrifice or eat the flesh of their crucified savior. Except, on Earth, the parishioners typically hadn't been mired in various stages of decomposition. Some of these ghouls were missing limbs. Some had their heads tilted at absurd angles from broken necks. Some were even worse.

"Here...here...here..." they began chanting.

I shuffled back toward the statue until I was practically in its lap. For whatever reason, I felt more comfortable in front of the throne than the altar, and more comfortable in front of the altar than out on the street. I guess I should have counted my blessings.

"Here...here...here..."

The low murmur from the undead grew louder as they approached.

Desperate, I turned to face the clown.

"What do I have to do?" I asked.

People will tell you the definition of insanity is performing the same action over and over again while anticipating different results, but I think speaking to an inanimate object and fully expecting conversation with a sentient demon creature ranks right up there with a simple failure to learn from mistakes. In fact, I think it's a lot worse.

"Why am I here?" I asked again. In case there's any doubt I'd lost my grip on sanity, you can add the first definition to my resume, as well. Even I didn't have any optimistic delusions about how far I'd fallen.

Which is why I wound up and threw my fist into the clown's face as hard as a I could with a hoarse shriek of rage.

"Answer me!" I shouted.

"Here...here...here..." the congregation droned on, shambling nearer with each futile plea to the demon king. Their deity. The lord of Furnace and all its miseries.

I drew my fist back again, ignoring the hot blast of pain where the bones had been badly bruised (but not quite broken) in the first strike. I punched the clown's head.

"ANSWER ME!"

"Here...here...here..."

I shrieked again. A pathetic, strangled thing which barely escaped my esophagus on its way up. Then I threw my fist into the clown's face one last time.

The head exploded away from me and slammed against the back wall. It landed beneath a painting of a malformed beast congregating with a spherical object, which might well have been a planet or some alien creature beyond my modest understanding of extraterrestrial physiology.

"Tscharia...Tscharia...Tscharia..." the congregation whispered.

I stared at the gaping hole in the clown demon's neck, paralyzed by a mixture of skepticism and wonder.

"Tscharia…Tscharia…Tscharia…"

Leaning on trembling legs which barely kept me upright, I stared down into a vision of the cosmos that was utterly incomprehensible for my human mind. I simply couldn't process it. It was either the essence of God or His utter absence, and both prospects were equally terrifying and magnificent.

Before I could venture deeper or pry open the rest of the statue, however, the entire undead congregation screeched at once and turned their attention my way.

What now?

I slowly pivoted and looked back toward the altar.

Every human had risen. The ones pinned to the walls had wiggled themselves free and assembled before the altar. The squelching heap of corpses had likewise untangled into two-dozen wraiths. Their faces were all covered in shadow, but their white eyes bore into me through the darkness. They sneered as their chant reached a fever pitch.

"Tscharia…Tscharia…TSCHARIA!" they shrieked.

I stepped behind the statue for refuge, terrified beyond rational thought or action.

They all charged at once.

"TSCHARIA!" they howled.

I pulled the SX pistol from its holster and ducked behind the statue, waiting for the first wave to get close so I could use my few remaining bullets as efficiently as possible. There was no indecision anymore. I wanted to get the hell out of the cathedral, and I wanted to get the *Rockne Hummel* the hell off of that planet. I didn't want to become one of *them.*

"TSCHARIA! TSCHARIA!"

I had no idea what the word meant and I wasn't about to ask for an explanation. As soon as the first corpse-woman was within arm's reach, I aimed the pistol between her eyes and pulled the trigger. With the cathedral's acoustics, the impact was deafening. Her skull and rotted brain blew out the back of her head and sprayed the onrushing wraiths. It didn't deter them in the least.

I used the back of the throne to kick myself farther away from the attackers and fired another shot. This one caught the intended target—an adolescent boy—directly in the throat. He staggered backward and fell to his knees, clutching his neck with wide eyes as though he hadn't been dead already.

What are *these things?* I wondered. *Why are they coming after me? I'm human!*

I scrambled backward until I was flat against the wall. The press of the undead was so thick around me that all I could see was caved-in chests, eviscerated stomachs, and twisted legs.

Stay calm, I told myself, making sure each shot I lined up landed a kill. My brain wanted to panic as they closed in around me, but I fought back. *You can still get out of this. They're stiff and slow. Just clear the front line and make a break for it. If you push yourself, you can beat them to the door.*

I took a deep breath and straightened to stand at my full height. Three corpses made a play for me and I threw my whole weight into them, knowing there was no way I could fire three kill shots before one of them managed to pull me to the ground. The strike worked, at least in the sense that it knocked the three of them onto their backs, but it dragged me down, too.

"Fucking shit..." I growled as I slipped over top of them. A sea of hands enveloped me.

The others were quick on the uptake. Almost like they understood what was about to happen before I'd even made contact with the trio, which told me something beyond blind hunger and an overall bad attitude was spurring them on.

But they can't be intelligent, *can they?*

It didn't seem possible, yet they'd filed toward the altar with *some* semblance of order, and then had organized themselves well enough to prevent escape.

A fresh surge of pain exploded through my leg. Then my shoulder. Then my left forearm.

"FUCK!" I screamed.

They'd started biting.

What the hell are *these things?* I wondered again. *Zombies?*

I roared and threw myself backward as hard as I could, dislodging the biters and clearing a few feet of breathing room as I rolled against the wall. I started firing the SX into the crowd again before I landed. There was no point in conserving ammunition if the fuckers were going to *eat* me. I'd been clinging to the faint hope that as former humans (or something like it), they'd listen to reason given enough time. Or at least, you know, not fucking *eat* me. Half of them didn't even have chests or stomachs or throats to process whatever chunks they tore away from my body, so I didn't see the point.

Every shot found a home, but not every shot brought one of the bastards down. They were undead, remember, and nothing but true headshots seemed capable of neutralizing them. I can't even verify that the ones I hit in the head *did* die a second time. The crowd was so thick that, for all I know, they may have resurrected at some point and rejoined the effort to tear me limb from limb.

I dropped two more of them.

Three.

Four.

But they kept right on coming.

"I'm on your side!" I shouted stupidly. I couldn't believe how everything had turned so suddenly.

Another one of them crawled over and bit my foot, shattering a handful of its own teeth but causing little damage to my boots or armor plating. It clamped on hard, though, and wouldn't let go until I put a bullet through the back of its head. I couldn't tell whether it was a man or woman, and I guess that's probably for the best.

After all the shit I went through out there, fucking humans are going to kill me?

I wanted to be outraged, but as my clip finally ran out and there were still a dozen or more of them within ten feet, cutting off all exits, I was only stupefied. It was paralyzing. I couldn't get over the goddamned injustice of it. I was a *human*, just like them! I could help them if they let me! Yet here they were, intent on ripping my head off and feeding on my entrails because some goddamned clown with horns and bad makeup told them to. I was more than outraged. I was personally affronted by the idea.

"Fuck all of you," I spat. "You belong here."

As soon as the condemnation left my tongue, I regretted it. Not because I thought it would make a difference one way or another, but because I realized the only reason they acted that way was they'd lived on Furnace too long. It's the sort of place that changes you fundamentally, no matter how hard you struggle against it. I learned that the hard way in about a day. It *changed* me. It warped the core of my being. In a day. Give me a thousand years? I don't think I would have held up half as well as they did.

I frantically searched the cathedral for an alternate escape, but just like when I'd narrowly avoided a similar fate along the roofs, there was nowhere to go.

Might as well make a run for it, I thought.

I braced against the wall and prepared to sprint head-on into the group of human corpses. I figured I'd take as many of them down as I could with the element of surprise and then book it to the door as if (and because) my life depended on it.

Before I had a chance to test my genius plan, however, my attackers suddenly stopped rushing me and stiffened up. Some even fell face-first into the altar as their muscles locked. They didn't attempt to brace themselves.

The cathedral fell utterly silent, but I didn't trust the quiet. It just meant something more heinous was on its way. Something capable of shutting down the dead in the throes of a killing frenzy.

Slowly, I scooted down the wall until the clown sculpture shielded me from a direct assault. I kept my eyes trained on the corpses just in case they suddenly broke their paralysis and mounted another charge. Their collective inhaled sharply when I passed the clown's throne, but otherwise, they remained frozen. Their vacant eyes tracked my movements, but they didn't prevent me from limping away.

I passed just far enough into the shadow to be certain they couldn't see me, then squatted down and attempted to squeeze between the throne and the wall. As long as I could fit through the opening wearing my space suit, I thought I'd be able to slip past them in the darkness. With their necks locked in place, they would be none the wiser.

I managed to get about a quarter of the way through before reaching the rounded pedestal beneath the throne, and then realized I couldn't go any further. I wouldn't fit. And if I wanted to pass on the inside of the statue, I'd have to climb over it. I didn't like the idea of exposing myself to the sculpture's grip at all, even if it was an inanimate object that had lost its head. Maybe because of it.

Suck it up, I told myself, carefully guiding my ribs back to safety behind the sculpture.

Once I'd maneuvered my upper body away from the wall, I stood to my full height again and glanced at the frozen corpses, just to be sure they hadn't moved since I'd ducked out of sight. They were still locked in place, and now I was beyond the scope of their vision because they couldn't turn.

Why, though? I wondered.

I'd expected something bizarre to happen when they locked up, but so far, the stopping itself was the only thing which could be construed as bizarre. At least, relative to the situation. Relative to the location.

I knew I wasn't out of the woods yet, though. Not by a long shot. Not even in terms of the cathedral. The spooks around the altar could reanimate any moment. Worse, I still felt the presence of the clown king lurking in the shadows.

Where?

I searched the second floor balconies overlooking the marble floors, trying to spot an imposing darkness amid the velvet drapery. There were all sorts of indecipherable statues and paintings leading up to the convoluted mural on the ceiling, but nothing that moved. It still felt like a thousand eyes watched me from perches all along the walls and back near the instruments where the choir would have sat during services (if such a thing as a choir or services existed on Furnace).

And I felt him nearby.

Wherever you go, I will find you, his voice echoed in my head.

I made my way out among the spooks, no longer frightened that they would reach out and throttle me. I didn't even look at them as I shouldered my way toward the pews. My eyes were locked on the upper balconies, certain I would catch his movement eventually. A sign that he was watching me. Waiting for me. Maybe a symbol I could decipher into every answer I needed to leave.

He's my only way home, I thought.

The insanity of the notion made me laugh involuntarily. A short, barking sound that made my raw throat burn anew. How could *that* bastard be my only way home? To even joke about it was ridiculous. He was the reason I'd gone through all the shit on Furnace in the first place! If Teemo and I hadn't spotted him approaching us down the city street, we wouldn't have shot the flare that drew the rest of the squad to our location and got them killed. I don't know the specifics of the initial melee aside from what other surviving crewmembers have filed in their reports, but I know we wouldn't have sent the flare up right away if we hadn't seen the clown demon. And if that son-of-a-bitch hadn't bit through my helmet and dragged me off to his city hideaway, then I wouldn't have had to cross the wastelands, lava lakes, mountains, corpse fields, or the city itself just to get back to where I'd started.

So for my rambling brain to even *suggest* that the clown demon could be anything but a mortal enemy was beyond absurd.

And yet, blame it on the dehydration (or I will for you), but there seemed to be truth to the idea. Why else would he have allowed me to live for so long? Why else would he have lured me into the cathedral and frozen the undead spooks when they were about to gut me (by then, I was sure it was him and not just some blessed coincidence)?

Because it's more fun for him this way. He enjoys watching you suffer. As soon as you die, the game's over and he has to return to his miserable existence on this miserable planet with nothing but corpses and man-eating monsters for company.

That also had a ring of truth to it, probably more so than the idea that this undoubtedly malevolent creature had somehow turned benevolent simply by kidnapping me and then watching me escape. Like a case of reverse Stockholm Syndrome.

"What do you want?" I asked.

My voice was much calmer this time. Steady and patient. If I didn't hear an answer by the time I reached the door, I decided, I would leave the cathedral altogether and see if I could find answers elsewhere in the city. Or maybe I'd just book it to the far gate as fast as I could and pray I didn't cross paths with any other demons along the way. I probably wouldn't get far, but far crazier stunts have worked on the battlefield through the ages. Miracles and tragedies occur every single day.

"Did you bring us here?" I pressed. "Is there a reason we were pulled here or was it just bad luck?"

No answer.

I was halfway to the large wooden doors, spinning in circles to scan each empty balcony. There was still no sign of movement.

Fuck it, then. You're chasing shadows.

I wanted to believe it, but I still felt the clown's eyes on me. They were heavy.

It's all in your head. Of course you feel like something's watching you. Something's been watching you since you stepped out the airlock.

The head of the sculpture was pointed in my direction. Its empty gaze seemed somehow meaningful. I frowned and fought (unsuccessfully) to suppress a shudder, remembering the first time I'd encountered something extraordinary on Furnace aside from the crash itself. The memory filled me with dread.

My mother's severed head. Rolling across the dusty ground like a tumbleweed. Her mouth stretched back in pain.

I clenched my fists and jaw.

"Was that you?" I shouted. The more I thought about it, the angrier I got, and I was already heated. At the rate I was going, I'd snap any moment unless an aneurysm dropped me first.

The spooks in front of the altar still hadn't moved. I didn't see anything on the balconies, either.

"Screw it," I said. To punctuate my disdain, I spat precious saliva on the marble floor. "You're nothing."

The moment I turned my back to the altar, though, the whole congregation roared to deafening life again.

"Jesus!" I exclaimed.

The sound of every corpse screaming at once made me duck reflexively, like the sonic boom was actually a Tikhonov mine.

I probably should have headed straight for the doors then. I scrambled for cover behind the pews instead.

This is what you wanted all along, isn't it? I thought bitterly.

The spooks turned toward me but started dismantling the décor around the altar—ropes, string, nails, and banners—and separating the materials one by one rather than engaging me. They unwound the fabric in tandem, each completely focused on the task at hand. Like they didn't notice me at all.

I stood and rapped my swollen knuckles on the back of the pew, just to see if I'd draw their attention again, but they kept on sorting. One of them even turned toward the sound, but not to look at me. Instead, he scooped up the head of the clown king and placed it back atop the sculpture's neck.

Crowning the king, I thought.

When I was certain their attention was otherwise occupied, I wandered back down the aisle toward the altar, careful to keep the pews nearby in case I needed a quick blockade.

The resurrected humans finished sorting the décor and started dragging the piles over to the sculpture in unison. They didn't speak, yet somehow operated in perfect synchronization anyway.

"Here...here...here..." they chanted.

Not this bullshit, I thought.

"Tscharia...Tscharia...Tscharia..."

They laid the fabric over the sculpture's shoulders and draped bits of string over his face, making the detached head wobble to the point that it seemed like it would drop and shatter against the floor with any additional weight. For my part, I didn't think that would necessarily be the *worst* end to the bizarre ritual, but somehow the head stayed put. Just to spite me.

When they finished dressing the sculpture, each damned soul returned at once to reclaim their stations. Those who'd been tangled at the front of the altar when I'd entered crawled back together, contorting their bodies enough so others could fit in the macabre puzzle they formed with their rotting limbs. Those who'd been pinned to the walls staggered over to a simple wooden table behind the altar and retrieved large stakes along with a blunt steel instrument. A group of them worked together to toss the knotted end of a rope onto the balconies and somehow managed to make it stick on the first try. They pulled themselves up the wall with the rope, then pinned themselves in tiny, wooden slats between stones with the stakes they'd brought from the altar.

"What the fuck..." I muttered under my breath for probably the hundredth time since I'd arrived on Furnace.

I watched with numb fascination as one by one they climbed to willingly impale themselves against the cold stone.

By my estimates, the process took the better part of five minutes. When it was over, the last corpse holding the rope walked it over to the altar, swung the slack over a dim chandelier I hadn't noticed until that moment, and methodically hung himself above the corpses. There was a loud *crack* as he leapt and the drop caught him, nearly ripping his head from his body in the process. He started a pendulum swing in front of the clown king statue, which looked every bit like the Lincoln Memorial in its somber, slouched appraisal.

Before the hanged corpse stopped swinging—before, in fact, I could even process my surroundings well enough to realize I should get the fuck out of there as fast as possible—shadow enveloped the altar and consumed the tangle of bodies.

I sensed movement in the cloud. I also sensed that the others were gone and only two eyes watched me, but they were *powerful* eyes. Eyes that made my legs tremble. A stare that slithered into the core of my being. Violating. Every injury I'd sustained in the prior twenty-four hours stood out in maddening clarity.

I'd gotten my wish, I realized, and he'd kept his side of the bargain.

The clown had come to parley.

There was no escape now that I'd lingered long enough for the sculpture to become possessed, so I stayed where I was and prepared the best I could for an audience with the Devil himself. Unlike during the wild shootouts I'd had with lesser demons on the planet's surface, I figured I'd get a good opportunity for distracting banter before the creature decided what to do with me.

Wherever you go, I will find you, his voice called out. Not through the air, though. Fired directly to my brain. Maybe it was my imagination. Maybe it was memory. I still don't know.

A moment later, his ghastly form emerged from the billowing cloud of shadow. Nothing of the sculpture remained, although bits of string still hung over his diseased face and a jagged line circled his neck where his head had been knocked off.

His presence was even worse in the flesh than I remembered. Bigger. Stronger. Uglier. His eyes were more menacing than the rest of the demons combined, even the Watchmen from the corpse fields. It was the feeling of cruel knowledge in his stare. The cold, calm assessment. The raw power. Like he knew exactly what he was doing and didn't care at all.

If I hadn't already known it, the sight of him emerging from shadow in full regale would have been enough to convince me he was the monarch of Tscharia. The king, chief, emperor. Whatever you want to call it, that's what he was on Furnace. It was clear not just in the way he carried himself, but in how the whole room seemed poisoned by his presence. The cathedral itself shrank to avoid his gaze, yet I was locked in place by wonder and indecision.

How could I have ever thought that he was on *my* side, I wondered? Did I really want to stay and see what horrible fate he had in store for me?

Ever since I crossed the corpse fields, I'd been trying to convince myself that he wasn't as bad as the others simply because he hadn't killed me right away. He'd carried me off and toyed with me, which, truth be told, suggested whole new levels of psychotic tendencies but was still preferable to immediate torture and mutilation for the delight of Furnace's demons. I guess if they'd taken me before the clown king had, though, I would have been dead already or at least suffered my *first* death. It was still unclear how many lives each soul had to lose on Furnace, or if life was truly unending and each victim was sentenced to eternal torment in the interstellar version of Earth's Hell. Like a holo-game. Re-spawn after re-spawn, forever and ever. But the point is, if I'd avoided the clown king altogether, I would only have been an anonymous corpse suffering the same fate as thousands (perhaps hundreds of thousands or even millions) of other innocent souls.

But I was marked. That was the trouble.

I didn't fully understand it until I watched the clown king beckon me forward from the darkness with one long, gnarled finger, but it began to come together in my head. He had a plan. He'd set me aside for a greater purpose.

The shit was hitting the fan.

All along, I'd taken solace in the fact that he *hadn't* torn me apart when he bit through my helmet or when he had me locked away unconscious. But as much as I'd hoped for a loophole to salvation, I suddenly decided it wasn't in the cards. I couldn't appeal to the abandoned sense of goodness in him or some crude, psychotic desire to make my life a game solely for the chance to survive.

The truth was much more heinous than my contrived, naïve hopes. He didn't just want my soul, he wanted me to be his personal gateway to the suffering of entire worlds. I hadn't been spared because he thought I was an all right guy. He *needed* me.

"Here...here...here..." the dead bodies instructed.

With a silent swell of relief, I realized the clown king had stopped walking. The cloud of shadow billowing around him began to dissipate. He stood slightly hunched over at the front of the altar with the pile of corpses at his feet and the hanged body still swinging over his head, waiting for me.

"Tscharia," the corpses told me.

Weary, I approached the altar. What else could I do?

No matter what I've told you before or what I tell you hereafter in this account, I assure you that I've never been more scared in my life than in that moment, and I can't imagine any scenario where I ever will be again.

Yet I limped on anyway, because that's what fleet soldiers are taught to do. Keep marching, one foot in front of the other, come Hell or high water. I had the Hell part taken care of, but I could have done with a wave of high, fresh water right about then. Drowning didn't sound so bad. Comparatively.

GATEWAY

The sculpture hadn't disappeared. I figured that meant the clown must not have been in the cathedral the whole time, and if he had, it was up among the balconies like I'd initially suspected. The idea that he might have been channeled through the sculpture itself somehow and yet remained physically separate only occurs to me now, but it makes a hell of a lot of sense. People all over the universe worship relics and talismans based on the idea that some measure of power is contained within the objects. I wouldn't be surprised if that belief was a reality on Furnace. The clown king was worshipped through blood and souls, after all, so by all accounts of black magic and the Old Testament, his power was sufficient to manifest through the icons of the macabre rituals. He could have materialized from any piece of the cathedral at any time.

When I reached the last row of pews before the altar, I stopped walking and bit my lip. I couldn't force myself any closer to the demon. His hot breath hit me from fifteen feet away and was punctuated by the smells of rot and infection that comprised his physical form in lieu of bones and sinew. His black eyes bore heavily down on me. His razor-toothed mouth was drawn back in a snarl. I didn't need to venture any closer to know he could kill me with a flick of his wrist.

Steeling myself, I cleared my throat and asked the question I'd decided most important. "Why am I here?" I said.

"Here...here...here..." the corpses mocked.

Neither my question nor the obedient prayers of his acolytes had any effect on the clown king of Tscharia, however. He hissed sharply, though not in a particularly menacing way. It was still terrifying. His voice somehow managed a grinding squeal and throaty growl simultaneously. The sort of voice that rattles you from the boots to the eyeballs.

It was obvious within moments that he didn't intend on answering the question.

Maybe you're not asking the right one, I thought.

Either way, I couldn't allow the silence to stretch any longer. I figured the more I engaged him, the greater chance I had to survive. If silence persisted and he decided he wasn't getting what he wanted from me, there was a strong possibility he would torture me out of sheer boredom.

"How do I get home?" I asked.

It was a desperate question and I didn't expect him to answer it. How would *he* know what I had to do to get back? As far as I could tell, he didn't even know what *galaxy* I came from, let alone which individual planet. Still, I had to ask it on the slim chance that he'd brought me, specifically, to the planet for a reason, not just marked me for torment once we crossed paths. I shuddered to think what my purpose could possibly be within his greater plan, but if it got me home, I was willing to hear him out.

Once again, though, he didn't answer, so it was a moot point.

I couldn't stop talking anyway. I didn't know what silence meant.

"What do you want from me?" I asked.

"Tscharia...Tscharia...Tscharia..." the corpses whispered in unison.

Still, the clown king said nothing. Maybe it was just my imagination, but the perpetual half-grin, half-sneer he wore across his rotting lips had deepened with each question I posed.

I was just about ready to give up when he took a sudden, jittery step forward like his whole body had been rocked with electricity. Maybe it was just poorly controlled rage. Maybe hunger. I shuffled back toward the door, knowing there was no way I'd reach it in time if he decided to rush me. I also knew I had to continue filling the silence, but none of my questions had worked so far and I was running low on mental ammunition.

Keep trying.

"What is this place?" I asked quickly. "What is Tscharia?"

He stopped walking and tilted his head to the side.

"Here...here...here..." the voices said.

With slow, haunting grace, the clown king pointed toward the sculpture. I didn't need to ask whether or not he wanted me to approach it.

"Tscharia."

I glanced back at him warily. I couldn't decide whether or not I should trust him. Once I was convinced he wouldn't snatch me up before I obeyed his order, I stepped out from the aisle and approached the right side of the altar. The sculpture stared down at me in solemn appraisal. It was only a journey of about fifteen steps, but it felt like a thousand. I'm sure the clown king made it that way just to watch me squirm. Even under the most mundane of circumstances on Furnace, he still wanted to see me suffer. Suffering, after all, was the most precious commodity on the planet.

"Here...here...here..." the corpses chimed in.

"Shut the fuck up," I snapped. It was pointless, but it felt good. I was tired of hearing them drone on, especially now that they'd been safely pinned away from me.

At some point while the cloud of shadow had enveloped the altar, the head of the sculpture had been reattached. The line where it had split was still visible. When I reached out and tapped its brow, driven by a foreign compulsion which I can only surmise was forced upon me by the clown king, it fell backward again. This time, it completely shattered on the floor.

I turned back to the demon with mild trepidation, wondering whether or not he would be outraged that I'd desecrated his likeness. His stare was so weighted and intense that my stomach churned, but he didn't appear any more or less agitated than he had been before.

"What do you want me to see?" I asked, averting my eyes and trying to make it seem like I'd only done so because I was interested in the sculpture itself. Not because he terrified me, in other words.

In response, a cloud of gray smoke floated out from the sculpture's neck, drifting towards me with an oddly familiar smell. I leaned carefully over the throne for a closer look.

At first, I couldn't make sense of the shapes beneath the fog, but my eyes gradually focused on a rectangular shadow that seemed close enough to touch. The opening was dark even when the smoke began to clear, but even so, I knew a stone staircase when I saw one. I also knew it couldn't *be* a stone staircase leading down from the neck of the sculpture. There wasn't enough room and the floor beneath me was solid.

I stared into the darkness for a few moments, trying to decide what I was expected to do next. Now that I'd bought what time I could, I wanted to avoid interacting with the clown as much as possible, and that meant keeping questions to myself. However, once it became apparent that I couldn't figure it out on my own (I couldn't see anything but the steps themselves, after all, and there was no way I could fit through the neck of the sculpture to descend), I was forced to seek clarification.

"I don't understand," I said. "What am I supposed to do?"

With a crooked grin which could have easily been mistaken for a grimace, the clown king pointed back to the sculpture.

I shrugged, uncomprehending, and reached an arm down the sculpture's throat. I rotated my wrist, checking to see if there was anything within reach of my fingertips. An artifact. A scroll. Anything that might have some arcane significance to this arcane culture I'd stumbled upon. In retrospect, it probably wasn't a great idea to stick an extremity into utter darkness anywhere on Furnace. But nothing would have been able to drag me through the opening, I assured myself, and if something unfathomable actually *could* have, the contortions necessary to compact me down to size would have killed me before I met whatever lurked in the shadows. I'd probably lose an arm at worst, and the alternative was crawling back to the mercy of the clown king.

As I searched around the top two steps, though, the sculpture began to melt around me. Slowly at first, and then so quickly that I had to withdraw my hand and leap backward to avoid the burning liquid.

Within moments, the throne was empty. The melted remnants of whatever alien element the natives used for sculpting was rapidly cooling into a paste over the seat. The throne itself was still intact, having been made of harder stuff (maybe gold) than the sculpture. A lever had appeared at the back. How I could no longer see the staircase with the statue gone was beyond me, but I didn't ask any more questions. In fact, I was done asking questions for a long time.

Without hesitation, I pulled the lever and the seat of the throne creaked forward, dropping with a loud clap against the hollow base.

"Here...here...here..." the voices groaned.

I glanced back at the clown king one last time. His wide, mischievous grin spurred me down the steps so quickly that I nearly took my own head off ducking into the darkness.

"Tscharia," he said. His voice echoed after me down the narrow stairway. "Wherever you go, I will find you."

A wild panic gripped me. Something like claustrophobia, except in reality, it was the need to descend *further* into the confined space. Anything to get away from the clown king before he decided instruction from afar wasn't enough and he had to give me a hands-on lesson to make sure I saw things his way. I could still hear the voices of the corpse-chorus raising exaltations to their deity and briefly worried that they would follow. What if I wasn't supposed to go down the stairway, I thought? What if I'd fucked everything up and now they were going to make me pay for it?

Before I could digest the idea of crawling back into the evil cathedral, however, the seat slammed back into place and I was suddenly alone in total darkness. *Comforting* darkness. At least in the darkness, I realized, I wouldn't have to see death coming. I wouldn't have to behold whichever deformed creature finally ended me. I supposed that alone was worthy of celebration, but I also supposed I might as well attempt to find the bottom of the stairs while I waited. The urgency I'd felt to return to the *Hummel* had all but disappeared, but I still preferred to make it back. In one piece, if it could be helped. The only logical progression, therefore, was to keep pushing on until I either hit a dead end or found my way to the fleet ship at the bottom of the crater.

So I kept going, running my hands along close, damp walls that stank of heat and sulfur. It was easy to keep straight because the path never deviated. I only felt whispering creatures brush past me a handful of times through the whole walk. I was too tired to care.

I couldn't see anything in the cramped tunnel aside from a few shadows here and there which were either a degree brighter or duller than the perpetual darkness. It took about forty-five minutes before the familiar smells started hitting me, though I failed to place them right away. It wasn't until the familiar *sounds* started up that I realized where I was going, and then the psychological torment began in earnest.

My mind became fixated on the steady, maddening drip of liquid on a hard surface. After a while, I sort of tuned it out, though it continued to register in the periphery of my thoughts. I repeatedly caught myself matching rhythms to it in my head. There's another definition of insanity for you: humming along with the drip of liquid in a pitch-black underground tunnel (which may well have been sealed on both ends) on an alien planet with an army of demons above me. I guess that's a little long-winded for Merriam Webster.

As soon as I realized where I'd wandered, however, the sound died abruptly in my throat. In its place, I heard the unmistakable, ambient growl of a spaceship. I guess I'd been smelling the lubricants and oils and electrical casings for a while, but it wasn't until I heard the familiar *thrum* of energy somewhere in the distance that I was able to place it.

A *ship*, I thought, my heart rising cautiously in my chest. *Maybe I will get the hell out of here, after all.*

I wasn't convinced quite yet, but it was the first time I'd felt genuine hope since leaving Europa. As I ventured deeper and deeper into the ground and the temperature rose to nearly unbearable levels, though, suspicion started growing faster than hope and eventually strangled it completely.

Whose ship is this? I wondered.

If it was underground with the entire decrepit city built atop it, the chances that it would ever unbury itself and be spaceworthy again were nil. I didn't think it was the crashed ship of an alien species in the corpse fields, either. I couldn't imagine their vessels pre-dating the city itself.

Then whose is it? And why does the clown king want me to see it? Is he going to bury me alive down here?

The idea didn't fill me with as much dread as perhaps it should have. In fact, the prospect of a quiet death in the privacy of the underground ship, especially without a sadistic demon in sight, seemed peaceful. Maybe the demon clown had taken mercy on my soul after all.

Or maybe you're in for an even bigger shit-show down here. What do you really think's waiting for you at the end of this tunnel? Pizza and beer?

I shuddered. If abominations like the Watchmen were able to live above ground in the Furnace wastelands, I couldn't imagine what manner of beast lived *underground* amid the oppressive heat and toxic fumes of a dying spaceship.

Maybe it's the real *king of this place. Maybe the clown just provides its meals.*

"Screw it," I muttered.

It's not like I had options. The only alternative to following the tunnel until I reached an outlet—or more likely spotted something that made me shrivel up and die at the mere sight—was to spend another hour or so retracing my steps in the darkness, only to return to a bunch of confused, masochistic corpses and the evil clown who'd fucked everything up for me in the first place.

So I kept moving.

Gradually, I noticed a faint light ahead. It was so dull that I thought it might be another mysterious shadow passing by, but its stationary persistence quickly made me realize that the light belonged to something other than a living creature.

Please tell me it's a door, I thought.

Something inside me knew that this was *exactly* what the clown king had sent me down to find, and whether it turned out to be a good or bad thing in terms of my survival, I wanted to see what was so goddamned important that a creature as evil as he would forsake a tasty meal and a great deal of pleasurable torture so that I could encounter it.

I started jogging a little. I'm sure anyone who saw me would have laughed at the pathetic, limping gait I managed while ducking repeatedly in case something jutted from the ceiling or walls. But I *had* to run, because it seemed every time

I slowed up even a little bit to give my body a break, the light stretched farther and farther away from me. If I didn't pull out all the stops, I realized, it might disappear. And who knew if I'd ever find it again? Who knew if it would ever even reappear to *be* found? It was a chance I couldn't take.

By the time I saw the pedestal with its glowing orange pentagram, I felt on the verge of physical collapse. Not for the first time, mind you, but this particular feeling was rivaled only by the pain of scaling the hill at the border of the corpse fields. I'd sworn I would accept death rather than subject myself to that torture again, but that wasn't true. It's a wonder. I'm continually shocked and somewhat humbled by my body's dominant will to survive, which apparently supersedes all concerns of physics and psychological fortitude.

Now that I had some light by which to view it, I could see the interior of the ship around me. It looked like I'd been walking through some kind of long maintenance shaft ever since I'd descended the cathedral steps. The sheer enormity of the vessel implied by this realization was startling. Fleet warships like the newly-christened *Doorway* are big enough to walk through for days, but I'd envisioned a much smaller ship beneath the cathedral until I calculated how long I'd been walking and what portion of the tunnel comprised the maintenance shaft. The height of the tunnel told me that the ship was built for creatures much taller than the average human. Maybe the size of the clown demon and his Watchmen, in fact. It stood to reason, therefore, that the full scope of the ship was absolutely colossal. I might never have found an end to it.

I stepped away from the glowing pentagram to assess the height of the ceiling, guessing whether or not the clown king could have walked upright without difficulty. By my estimation, it fit perfectly.

All right, I thought, leaning against the pedestal and staring into the dull orange pentagram. *I found it. What now?*

I leaned over as far as I could before the gash in my ribs prevented me from dipping lower, trying to see if there were buttons somewhere to activate the artifact. I figured there might a message inside. Coordinates. Pictures. Anything that would make locating it in the bowels of the dinosaur ship seem at least *somewhat* worthwhile. After all, I'd basically signed my life away by venturing so deeply underground without verifiable exits for miles. Even if I retraced my steps to the cathedral and found it staffed by a rescue team with cold drinks, med kits, and comfortable beds to rest in, there was a strong possibility I would expire before I ever reached it.

I fumbled around the pedestal for a while. Cursing. Kicking. Pressing my swollen knuckles against the pentagram. Doing anything and everything to get it up and running. In the end, though, it snapped to life on its own, or at least I think it did. I may have set off a chain reaction with one of my ingenious attempts at hacking into the device, but I wasn't moving at all when it finally ignited and descended into the pedestal with a whirring sound.

I stepped back and watched the walls of the shaft around me light up like the mess hall on the *Hummel* after a long night of heavy drinking, which is only remarkable when you consider the brightest light I'd seen in nearly a day had been the barroom-dull reflection of the cathedral dome in the hazy Furnace atmosphere.

The most astounding thing about the lights was how they displayed on pre-grooved tracks, not just sockets or bulbs. I didn't realize they formed a moving picture until they swept down the shaft behind me and the images roared to life in vibrant red.

TSCHARIA, the first panel read.

Beside the declaration was a detailed etching of the clown king at the city's center, which had been painstakingly depicted at the height of its prosperity and opulence. I've mentioned several times that it reminded me of an ancient Greek or Roman city, and I think that impression has stuck with me more from what I saw in the maintenance shaft than anything I observed on the surface.

As I stared at the etching and began to piece the tale together, it occurred to me that the clown king *wasn't* Tscharia like I'd initially thought. Tscharia was the name of the city. The capital of Furnace, not its king. I wasn't sure if that answered more questions than it raised, but at least it *was* an answer.

Continuing down the tunnel, I observed a historical reenactment of the day that the clown king and his disciples arrived on the planetoid. If I understood the panels correctly, they hadn't stumbled on Furnace by chance. They'd been banished from some Earth-like world in a gigantic spaceship, which I assumed was the vessel surrounding me. I couldn't decipher the justification for their banishment by the supreme deity—who was symbolized by a clenched fist and one emphatic index finger—but it was clear that the panels had a sympathetic bend to the monsters' plight and I therefore interpreted the remaining etchings with a grain of salt.

Forlorn, the hideous creatures (who apparently hadn't been so hideous once upon a time) had built the city of Tscharia and filled it with beautiful fountains, statues, paintings, libraries, and even looping holographic displays of moving artwork, albeit perverse. The technology they'd developed apparently rivaled that of modern humans, and this had been a long, long time ago. Thousands of years at least, perhaps millions. Who knows where they would have wound up without complete isolation? After all, what good was a fleet of spaceships if your physical body couldn't leave the surface?

Clearly, they'd tried to forge a life out of the wastelands for their forsaken people, but the planet itself eventually transfigured them into something far worse than the monsters they'd been on their home worlds. Their architectural wonders had fallen to ruin, the living artwork had likewise faded, and their collective mind had fractured. There was still some semblance of order and cooperation among their ranks, it seemed, but it was mostly fueled by blind, dogged belief in the poisonous teachings of the clown king of Tscharia.

I was surprised to realize that the plight of the demons resonated with me beyond an obligatory, surface-level expression of pity. It didn't take much imagination to see how I could wind up in the same situation if the Crown government suddenly decided I was a liability and it was better to send me off somewhere to rot than deal with me themselves. I'm well aware that my story is a serious threat to their expansionist propaganda should it ever be made public. I've seen them dispose of countless other political threats in the same manner for lesser offenses, declaring them ideal colonists uniquely suited for life in deep space and then banishing them with a wave of the royal scepter (at least, metaphorically speaking). Exile is often more convenient for governing bodies than genocide, I've found, since there are now seemingly endless colonies where problems can be quietly tucked away to be ignored. Sometimes, I wonder if that's the only reason we're hell-bent on interstellar Manifest Destiny in the first place.

It's generally a good PR move to at least feign mercy towards a disparaged people, though, even if you are providing them comically insufficient resources on uninhabitable balls of rock. That's why they don't kill them outright. As far as the Crown is concerned, the troublemakers can denounce the government all they want from soapboxes hundreds of millions of light-years from the ears of the voting citizenry. They'll never be able to relay the actual reasons they've been cast out to sea, and they'll be forgotten altogether once enough time has passed to render their social and political causes irrelevant.

While my experiences on Furnace to that point gave me the gut feeling that the banishment of the clown king and his subjects was justified (or at least more so than the political radicals the Crown allegedly deports at the slightest whiff of dissent), I can understand how the exile had driven them insane. This wasn't just a distant colony in the same galaxy, remember. As far as our scanners and naked eyes could detect, Furnace was a whole universe unto itself. The natives were cut off from every other aspect of the humanoid reality, and judging by the state of the city, it had been that way for a very long time.

In their shoes, I may have cracked the same way, much like I assume I would on Pluto Station. Maybe even worse. To cope with a completely fucked-up world, I may have begun to worship the most fucked-up creature I could find and accept his lunatic ramblings as genuine enlightenment. It's happened throughout history, human and otherwise. An opportunist arises from the downtrodden masses with a convenient scapegoat for their ubiquitous misery, and forsaken people fill their mouths and hearts with the misdirected hatred he spews to channel their desperation into some tangible, destructive force. They are suffering, after all, so why shouldn't others suffer, as well? They are victims of circumstance, so why not create new victims so that they can reclaim some measure of power in their own lives? Carve out a place in the universe, in this case through the literal carving of flesh? And it can't be done merely for the sake of carving. It must be done in the name of a greater cause or else their conscience will object.

I don't think that idea is particularly misleading or, for that matter, revolutionary. At least using Earth as an example, the theory has significant historical basis. How many holy wars have been manufactured out of sheer restlessness, despair, and the feeling that our lives are worthless within the greater whole? How many soldiers of God across countless religions have willingly gone to their deaths solely for the prospect of immortality, whether in a literal, transcendent sense or through the legacy of their championed cause? And the more corruptible the cause, the easier it is to recruit the young and disenfranchised. They don't have a voice or a purpose, so they'll seek both wherever they can be found.

Reading through the history of the demons, I pitied them, but only for a moment. Only until I was forced to take a hard look at whether or not I was a cog in that same misguided machine. The Crown may have more credibility on a secular level than there was during the Crusades, or centuries of European and American Imperialism, or the Second Dark Ages, but I have reason to at least be suspicious that it's merely a more refined version of the same cultural angst and desire for immortality.

Saying so may put me at risk for immediate exile and dishonorable discharge from the fleet for manufactured reasons, but this is supposedly a classified document (which, I should point out, is inadmissible in a DOIA court since it is not a public trial and I have not exposed military secrets) and it doesn't change the facts. It's always startling to see an enemy in a new light, and although I won't even attempt to argue that finally having proper context made me question whether or not the demons truly *were* an enemy (they were still trying to kill me or at least make me suffer and have to be afforded some accountability for their actions), it didn't seem nearly as black and white as it had before. For all I knew at the time, they could have seen us as invaders trying to take their land, or denizens of that most supreme deity who'd sentenced them to eternal deaths millennia ago. It all could have been a colossal misunderstanding.

I knew better than that, of course, and upon further reflection, decided they must have had some form of access to our reality even if it was access through a state of consciousness rather than physical form. That's what ultimately swayed me away from complete empathy and regret. They knew about us, or at least the clown king did, and therefore knew our vulnerability. I can see no other way that their legend or their nightmarish forms could have permeated human culture from so far away. Even if they'd inhabited Earth once upon a time, I find it hard to believe that the collective memory of their presence would have endured across mass extinctions and rebirths. They must have manifested in our reality throughout the ages.

I continued to study the etchings. The panels mesmerized me enough that I forgot where I was for a while, but pain eventually overwhelmed curiosity and I found I didn't have the time or energy to read any more. The history stretched back down the shaft as far as I could see, after all, and I was already on the verge of collapse. I think I managed to decipher the gist of the story anyway, and that's how I discovered what I consider the true identity of the wasteland planet, at least in human terms:

Hell.

Furnace was Hell. Literal Hell. Gehenna, not just outside of Jerusalem but outside of the universe altogether. In other words, utter separation from the universal entity called God. It may seem like I'm being melodramatic, and you may have trouble believing me, but it's true. Not just a personal hell, either, or a really awful place that *resembled* Hell. It was *Hell*, with a capital H, and the evidence was all around me. The Judeo-Christian tale of the fallen angel was right there on the wall of the maintenance shaft, woven into the history of the lonely planetoid in exquisite detail. In this case, the fallen angel was an evil clown creature who'd been banished from an idyllic planet to a wasteland along with his legion disciples, but that still sufficiently aligns with my understanding of Lucifer's fall. Since then, his people have been doomed to spend eternity separate from the rest of the universe except for the souls they lure to share in the unending misery.

Like me, for instance, and the entire crew of the *Rockne Hummel*. Because of one innocuous course alteration, we'd been assimilated into the damned forever.

"We're fucked," I said aloud. The words took on a new meaning the longer I considered the evidence.

Hell is a real place, I continued to remind myself. A planetary-mass object (not truly a planetoid since it orbits nothing at all) you can reach by ship, although you'll need some help along the way.

Hell exists, I mouthed. *Hell exists*.

I repeated the words over and over again in my head. Chewed them back and forth to get the full flavor without truly digesting their meaning.

Hell exists.

Hell is a real place. And not filled with invisible demons who spend their entire existence convincing people to do bad things. Hell is a planet. A tangible body. And the Devil—Lucifer, Satan, clown king, whatever name you prefer—is not a fallen angel but an exiled alien of tremendous, maniacal power. Namely, the power to extract ships from open space and transport them to Furnace so he and his minions can feed upon their misery.

It sounds very gothic (perhaps downright Christian) to say that he uses suffering for sustenance, but when you've been out in deep space as often as I have, you realize that there are endless metabolic demands and endless methods for extracting energy from organic matter. My guess is that these creatures are able to metabolize the chemicals many humans and aliens release when they experience significant amounts of pain, and that the clown king could sense these species (smell them, if you will) from great distances. Somehow, our flight path had skirted within range of the clown king's influence, and that's how we'd wound up in the middle of absolute nowhere...or perhaps the center of everything.

That's not an excuse for my failure by any stretch of the imagination. I still know that I must have fucked up the calculations somehow, and that if I hadn't tinkered with the flight plan to test my theories and shave a little time from our journey, we never would have been culled in the first place. The clown king—Satan, if you prefer—would have located another doomed ship and extracted its crew in our stead. Food would still have been plentiful on Furnace and we would be safely on our way to Marvek so Gallagher could take care of her political business. Chara would still be alive. Sillinger, too. Flaherty, Salib, Aziza, Katrina, and countless others. I have all of them on my conscience, and much more. Fuck-ups like this one are different than mistakes made in the heat of battle, or even taking the life of another creature that's trying to kill you in open warfare. They stick with you. They keep you up at night because they could have been avoided so easily. The 'ifs'.

If I'd stuck to the flight plan. If I'd never slept with my ex on Europa Station. If I'd let Teemo shoot the flare as soon as we'd found Tscharia.

If any of that had happened, things would be different, and that kills me. We wound up in Hell because of me. It doesn't get much more spectacularly traumatizing than that.

No matter how eagerly people on Earth attempt to exonerate me, or tell me there was no way I could have anticipated our abduction simply because we'd re-routed, it doesn't make a difference. In fact, it makes things worse. Especially when someone suggests there's no way to know what could have happened if I *hadn't* altered course. We could have been hijacked by pirates. Blown to pieces by a Kalak cruiser. Abducted and sold as zoo animals or slaves to any number of planets. We could have botched the landing on the colony and everyone would have died, destroying the

Hummel in the process. But that's all bullshit to me. At least in those situations, the pain would have been over in the blink of an eye for those we lost. On Furnace, their spirits are eternal, as are the twisted souls of their tormentors. It wouldn't be just a flash of suffering, then, or even a lifetime of it. A thousand lifetimes. A million.

"Why did you want me to see this?" I asked the humming drone of the spaceship. I wondered briefly how long it had been buried there, and how long it had been since the clown king visited our solar system. How else would his legend have reached the green hills of Earth?

Of course, there was no answer. Or if there was, it was hidden in the decoding of the panels along the maintenance shaft, and I didn't have time to follow them down to the cathedral and back again. I didn't even have time to ask rhetorical questions of the ghost ship. I had to keep moving, even faster now that I knew the clown king's true identity. I guess I'd suspected it all along, but in a tongue-in-cheek way which fell well short of belief until the evidence was right in front of me.

Stepping carefully around the pedestal, I limped deeper into the ship without looking back. There was enough light to see ahead for a while, although the red lights disappeared the moment I crossed to the other side of the pentagram (and who knew the significance of that little artifact; could it have been the coat of arms for the clown king's people back before they'd been exiled? A symbol of their planet?).

I walked for a while in a half-dead stupor, favoring my right side where my ribs were exposed to the stale air, stumbling drunkenly over drainage grates and exposed wiring from the long, steel tubes overhead.

It's too late, I thought to myself over and over again. It became my mantra as I pushed away from the satanic cathedral. My prayer. *It's too late. Everyone on the* Hummel *is either dead or dying. We're all damned.*

But I couldn't shake the core question underlying the revelations of the ancient ship, which seemed to be of tremendously greater import than the hopelessness of my situation. Namely, if Hell exists and Satan is a twisted alien banished from creation, does that mean God exists, as well? And if there is an all-powerful entity capable of exiling an entire culture from the known universe as punishment, who should I fear most? The degenerates of the system, or the system itself? When I direct prayers skyward in my hours of most desperate need, whether in a foxhole somewhere or when dealing with private tragedies in my humble apartment back in Detroit, who is listening? Will an omnipotent being concern itself with my best interests? I suspect not. I suspect it has its own agenda which extends eons beyond the pathetic reach of my lifespan.

It's a disturbing line of thought to say the least, and I'm still not sure I've arrived at satisfactory answers.

After a while, the shaft turned pitch-black again, but I kept walking. I didn't know what else to do. Ten minutes later, I emerged on the bottom deck of the *Rockne Hummel*, and my heart nearly broke from shock and exhaustion. My mind had already been shattered.

FURNACE

HUMMEL

The horrors didn't end there, of course. I was still on Furnace, and as far as I knew, the ship was still incapacitated, possibly even overrun by the monsters who swore allegiance to the clown king of Tscharia.

All I wanted to do was stay exactly where I was and allow sleep to serve up pleasant dreams of another world. I needed water first, though, or the sleep that took me would be death. I was hungry enough to eat conduit shells, too. But I'd been trained well enough to know water was my most pressing need. If I got water from the mess hall there'd be food nearby anyway, unless they'd started locking down resources for rationing since I'd left. It was possible, but I thought it more likely that Gibbons would have devoted all hands to ship repairs. He had to know any food and water that remained on the ship would run out if we didn't leave the planet as soon as possible. We needed to find another rock with more abundant resources right away to have any chance at surviving an FTL jump toward home.

Gallagher might have protested (Crown politicians are always looking for pseudo-democratic solutions to these sorts of problems without any concept of the big picture or the stark realities of survival) but, ultimately, she would have been overruled. Captain Gibbons always toed the line in terms of following orders from Crown Representatives, but he was also a realist with the unwavering loyalty of his crew...even when some of us weren't sure he was doing the right thing.

Water.

I focused on breathing, calculating the amount of energy it would take to stand.

You can't quit now. Not when you're this close to making it.

I wasn't sure what 'making it' meant or whether it would even be worth the trouble, but I knew I at least had to *try* after everything I'd been through.

Water.

I opened my eyes and shifted my weight slightly, suddenly aware that my muscles were stiffening at an alarming rate. I was dehydrated. The longer I waited to find water, the worse the pain would get.

Don't worry, my mother's voice called out from the corridor directly across the way. Her severed head was propped on the grated walkway, staring at me.

Wherever you go, I will find you, she mouthed. Her lips curled back in a cruel smile. Black bile seeped through her teeth.

No...

I blinked and she was gone.

I struggled to my feet using the wall for support, only crying out once when I put too much pressure on my swollen knuckles, then turned back toward the darkness. I was convinced I'd be staring back down the maintenance shaft of the ancient spacecraft. The one that had carried the Devil to eternal exile. But there was nothing. Just a solid, steel wall with the *Hummel's* fleet designation stamped across it and an arrow to the nearest emergency medical supply kit.

Water, or bandages? I wondered.

I decided yet again that water had to be my primary objective. Once I had a drink, I could collapse somewhere and patch myself up with the med kit as thoroughly as possible until I located one of the three doctors aboard the *Hummel.* They weren't all trained for medical emergencies but I figured I was better off enlisting their help than one of the rough fleet officers, who usually didn't know what to make of a med kit unless they were treating a common battlefield injury like a sprained wrist. Even then, I didn't trust their 'expertise'.

I aimed for the corridor where I'd seen my mother's head and tried—unsuccessfully—to block the image from creeping into my thoughts. I was too exhausted to be frightened or even repulsed by it, though. Those nightmares didn't start until I was safely within the boundaries of our solar system again.

Even now, I don't know how I managed to navigate the three hundred feet of banking corridors to the mess hall without falling over dead or unconscious. Maybe it was the idea that the clown king might appear from the shadows behind me and decide he'd changed his mind: I *would* have to hang myself over the altar of the golden-domed cathedral, after all, or stake myself to the wall like the others.

He never appeared though, and eventually I reached the mess hall. The lights over the food processing stations were blinding after such prolonged darkness, but I was glad for the clarity even if it gave me a migraine (which it did). My luck didn't end there, either. Apparently, even if the captain *had* assigned crews to gather resources for rationing, they hadn't reached the bottom decks yet. There was plenty of water left in the still-tank and a mountain of nutrient bars stacked in a bin by the sink. I binged on both. In fact, I drank so much water that I vomited on the mess hall floor, and then drank some more to offset the lost fluids.

The next twenty minutes or so passed in a fog. I heard faint explosions high overhead, probably on the bridge level, but they didn't concern me all that much. I was just happy to be alive, on a fleet ship, and with an opportunity to rest for a moment even if it meant I'd be worse off in the long run. I couldn't go any further until I'd rested. I was sure of it. I could feel death creeping up on me in every shadow, every breath.

You made it, I thought.

I could picture the clown king grinning at me with his black gums and razor-sharp teeth. Shaking his head.

Not yet, he mouthed.

I closed my eyes and shuddered.

Explosions suddenly rocked the bottom deck a few hundred feet from my position. I heard frantic shouts. Someone barking orders. It didn't mean shit to me.

But it will. Soon.

"Damn it," I groaned, getting to my feet for what I swore would be the last time before I slept a week straight.

Brushing the caked dirt and blood from my face with the arm of my suit, I limped over to the emergency weapons locker near the mess hall entrance and used my code to break the latch. Alarms started ringing immediately, but I didn't think anyone would notice or care with everything else happening aboard the *Hummel* just then.

I carefully selected an SX-70 from the trio of weapons and checked to make sure it was loaded. It was. I flipped the safety off and shuffled back into the corridor, aiming toward the shouts and explosions that continued rattling the ship's bowels.

Chalmers' last stand, I thought to myself, feeling every bit a gunslinger as I stumbled down the passage.

Within moments, a group of fleet soldiers started running toward me. They didn't acknowledge me at all except as an obstacle in their escape path. Indistinct shapes trailed them from the darkness, but none of the soldiers were firing.

Elizabeth Gallagher—the Crown Representative who didn't have a sneeze of combat experience anywhere on her otherwise impressive resume—brought up the rear of the group. She was the only one firing at the pursuing shadows and all she had to work with was a YK pistol, which was the weakest weapon on board. One specifically issued to Crown Representatives on deep space missions with the caveat that they weren't to be used unless 'all other options had been exhausted'. It was a suicide weapon, in other words. An insurance policy so that valuable Earth intel could not be leaked through torture or other methods of extraction.

God, I loved her in that moment. Not in a romantic way, necessarily. Not even platonic. I don't know how or why exactly, whether it was the futility of firing a YK into an onrushing horde that wanted to tear her apart and desecrate her corpse, or the fact that she was the only one among a group of trained fleet soldiers who was firing *anything* at the enemy. It took balls, and I respected the hell out of her.

She nearly tackled me as she ran past, still staring back into the growling shadows at the end of the corridor which had at last begun to flood into view. The impact startled her so badly that she squeezed the trigger and nearly pasted me through the eye, but I was too tired to care.

For a lingering moment, she stayed pressed against me, studying my face as if she were decoding every misery that had befallen me since leaving the *Hummel* and couldn't believe what she saw. Then the distance cleared from her eyes and she locked onto me with startling clarity. With relief.

"The engines just came back on line but the ship's overrun."

I nodded weakly and directed her behind me.

"Run," I told her.

She did, but not before firing another three shots into the onrushing demons.

I stared them down as they approached. Their expressions were indistinct in the dim illumination of the ship's bowels, and that was oddly disappointing. I wanted to see their faces twist in agony when the SX bullets ripped through them. I wanted to see them hurt.

Oh well, I thought. *I'll settle for pissing on their corpses afterward.*

I opened fire with the semi-automatic and blew those bastards to hell before they were within ten feet of me. Damn, it felt good, even though the recoil against my chest made my vision treble and my legs weaken.

Once they were all dead (or something like it), I staggered down the corridor in the general direction Gallagher and the others had retreated. Gallagher was waiting for me, standing with legs locked, arms down at the sides of her official Crown uniform, the YK pistol gripped firmly in her right hand like some action hero of a bygone era. Back before the stakes had been so high.

"How many more?" I asked. My voice sounded a little better than it had before. I don't think it will ever be quite the same.

"I don't know," she said. "Comms just went down again, but engines are running. We have crews on every deck trying to clear them out."

By 'them' she meant the natives, and it was encouraging to hear there was a coordinated effort to drive them off the ship. Although, if the example I'd just seen from our soldiers was any indication of the level of efficiency with which the monsters were being engaged, I thought our chances of survival were slim.

It was heartening, at least, to see how thoroughly the SX 70 had done away with them. After being on the surface so long, I'd gotten this notion that the creatures were practically invincible simply because they were beings of mythological import. I couldn't kill a goddamned *demon*, right? Is that even *possible*? I can say now with utter certainty that yes, you *can* blow a demon's head off with a pulse rifle and tear it to shreds with an SX 70. They won't get back up again. Not unless their clown king touches them. He's the one who keeps them going, you know. The account in the ancient ship says they get weak as soon as they leave the planet's surface, too, which explains why I was able to kill them with relative ease on the roofs of Tscharia and in the bowels of the ship. They draw power directly from the soil of their cursed planet. And as much as they must despise captivity, the land is their lifeblood. It sustains them. It gives them strength.

Rifles don't work on all of them, of course. The red masks—also known as the Watchmen—for instance, must be higher up on the food chain, and some of the bigger, eviler ones are probably a bitch to bring down. But the demons on the ship were no worse than Kalak, which doesn't necessarily mean they were *weak*. Far from it. Just that the playing field had been leveled, or at least minutely tilted back in my favor.

"You'd better get to the bridge," Gallagher told me, pulling me back from my thoughts. She eyed me curiously, gently touching the swollen knuckles of my right hand. "Or maybe you should sit this one out."

"No," I shook my head. "They need me." I meant for clearing out the demons, but she didn't take it that way.

"They don't need a navigator yet," she said. "They just want to jump off the planet."

I turned and started down the corridor in the opposite direction. The way the demons had come. The elevators weren't far from there.

"Wait," Gallagher said, jogging after me. "I'm coming, too."

I didn't try to stop her despite her political rank, which mandated that I lock her in a safe room until the ordeal was over. But I did stoop and grab a rifle from the corpse of a fleet soldier slouched in front of the elevator. I tried not to look at the demons too closely but it was hard to turn away. Death wasn't much of an improvement for them, aesthetically speaking.

I pressed the call button on the lift and we waited in silence until the blast doors opened, then I stepped into the cylindrical capsule and she quickly followed.

"You forgot to check in with me before you left," she said, eyeing the gore that covered me from head to toe. The burns on my face from alien blood must have looked hideous, but she didn't seem repulsed. And the scars *did* heal, by the way. It just took a hell of a long time and a hell of a lot of ointment. "I could have pulled you off the surface team. You didn't have to go through...all of that."

I shrugged and checked the ammo register on the SX. "I don't think it would have made a difference." I cleared my throat and leaned back against the wall of the capsule. "Besides, if it wasn't me, it would have been someone else. I wouldn't want that on my conscience. I have enough already."

Her eyes wandered to the floor thoughtfully and she sighed. "I know."

The elevator doors sprang open and I saw the carnage on the bridge for the first time.

DEPARTURE

I may never know exactly how close the ship came to being overtaken, but I deduced from the piles of corpses—human and alien—surrounding the elevator that it had been a very near thing, indeed. It surprised me that most of the corpses weren't human *or* demon. They were alien races, many of which I'd glimpsed around the lava lakes and in the corpse fields. Evidently, some had broken free and were just as desperate to get the hell off of Furnace as we were. Maybe the crew would have been open to them hitching a ride if we'd found a way to communicate within our accelerated timeline, but I don't blame either party for the gory mess on the bridge. It was the planet's fault. In their desperation to leave, the aliens had stormed the ship. The fleet soldiers had misunderstood their intentions and opened fire on them, which led to the aliens themselves attacking. A battle to the death ensued between two miserable peoples with a common enemy.

Nobody's fault. We all just wanted to survive.

"Chalmers!" someone shouted as I surveyed the carnage.

A figure rose from the pilot's chair with one abrupt wave. *Teemo,* I realized. *No shit.*

He didn't look any worse for wear, and the sight of him in his normal seat was a welcome surprise.

I looked around and made a quick inventory of the remaining officers. All fleet personnel who held any level of command had be on the bridge then, I thought, or else they were already dead.

The thought made Gibbons' absence all the more troubling.

"Where's the captain?" I asked, limping toward my station behind the pilot's chair.

Gallagher and Rosie Iglesias exchanged a quick, weighted glance.

"The captain's not himself," Gallagher answered.

I collapsed into the navigator's chair and groaned. "Is he dead?" I asked.

"No," she said flatly.

I wanted to ask more but knew it wasn't the right time. Whether the skeleton crew thought they needed a navigator or not, I was supposed to be there with them.

"Start her up, Rosie," Teemo called from the pilot's chair while he made the adjustments only helmsmen and captains truly understand.

"Are sensors back online?" I asked, beginning my own pre-flight checks to make sure we wouldn't blast directly into a passing meteor or worse. It didn't do much good. I was still more or less blind, unless the scanners were right and there was truly nothing above the planet but space itself. I still had trouble believing it.

"Somewhat," Rosie answered as she powered the FTL drive.

I've never been happier to hear an engine-roar in my life. Maybe we weren't going to make it home, I thought, but we just might get off of Furnace. That was enough for me. I'd have rather taken my chances in deep space with nothing in sight—probably dying within weeks—than spend another moment on that godforsaken planet. At least out in space no one would be hunting us.

But you'll still be within the clown king's influence, I realized with horror. *He can still pull you back. You won't get away fast enough.*

I hadn't given the demon's sphere of influence much thought until then, but it was true. If he could pull us out of our own galaxy, what could stop him from pulling us out of his own planet's orbit?

"Shit!" I hissed, slamming my fist against the control panel.

"What is it?" Teemo asked.

"Nothing," I said. After a moment, I resumed my pre-flight checks. No matter what happened, I decided, we had to at least try. Maybe the clown king had transported me back to the ship because he'd decided to let us go. I didn't trust his motive if that was the case, but it was too late to ask questions.

"Engines are a go," Rosie said from the engineering station.

"Pilot is a go," Teemo confirmed.

"Doesn't look like we'll run into anything," I said.

"Then let's get the hell out of here," Gallagher piped in. She'd assumed command while I was on the surface, which wasn't all that surprising considering the captain was tucked away somewhere. Probably the brig. She was the only one left on the ship with any real diplomatic authority once the captain was removed from command. The other officers on board were either dead, occupied, or stuck on the surface. In the chain of military command, I technically should have been in charge, and then Lao Gang if something happened to me, and Rosie if something happened to both of us, but I didn't want command. Not then. I was too goddamned tired to be the one making decisions.

"Ten seconds," Rosie announced from the engineer's station. "Get ready, Teems."

"Understood," he replied.

Once the engines were fully on line, timing the pilot controls for the initial thrust to propel the ship off the surface was a delicate art. Teemo is one of the best at it, though, and Rosie has her own sterling reputation which I can finally vouch for. The two of them executed a seamless transfer as soon as the engine prep hit zero and the first thrust dug us out of the crater.

"We're in the air," Teemo confirmed.

I quickly locked in coordinates just beyond the planet's orbital field. I didn't want to push us too much farther than that until I knew exactly what the ship was capable of handling. No one had briefed me on the precise condition of the *Hummel* yet and I didn't want to plot a jump that would fry another set of systems and maybe send us hurtling back toward the surface. Once we were out in the black sea again, we could re-evaluate our position and see if there was any way to catch a signal relaying our coordinates or at the very least, point us in the general direction of the nearest civilization. The prospects still weren't good, but we had to tackle one problem at a time.

"Lao," Gallagher called to the Master Gunner, who nodded silently and left the bridge.

"What's he doing?" I asked as we separated from the planet.

She crossed the bridge and put her hand on my shoulder, leaning over to get a look at the navigation screens. "He's going to blow up the city," she said.

I finished making course corrections, which were pretty standard for the time being. Certainly not the on-point calculations the Master Navigator who'd trained me would have liked, but even punching in the commands made my whole body cry out in agony. Somewhere on the surface, a demon was getting his meal.

Maybe we're out of range, I thought.

But not from the clown king. I didn't think I'd *ever* get far enough away from his reach. It was all a matter of whether or not he decided to exert himself to that degree.

"Steadily gaining altitude," Teems announced. His voice rose in pitch the longer we stayed in the air. He couldn't mask his excitement. I don't think anyone really wanted him to.

"Switch to main screen," Gallagher commanded, seating herself in the captain's chair. I don't think it was a calculated move so much as one of convenience (it was the only empty seat remaining on the main bridge area) but I imagine it wouldn't have sat well with most of the crew if they'd seen it. However, most of the crew was dead by then, anyway, so I guess it didn't matter.

"Yes, sir," Rosie answered.

The display screen switched from a direct view of the crater to a live feed from the aft bow. A perfect view of the city of Tscharia, in other words. Even seeing it through the screen made me shudder.

"Master Gunner, are you ready?"

"Yes, sir," Lao confirmed over the crackling comm line. Evidently, it wasn't completely fixed yet.

"Fire when ready," Gallagher told him.

"Yes, sir."

I didn't see the point in leveling the city for any reason but spite, which I guess is understandable enough except that you never want to waste your ship's heavy explosives when you don't absolutely need to. Unlike small arms, med supplies, and foodstuffs, charges for pulse blasts that meet fleet specifications are extremely hard to come by outside Earth's solar system. I kept my mouth shut, though, because I wanted to see the city blown to dust just like the rest of them. Probably even more so. *I* was the one who'd been down there, after all. The one who'd witnessed the atrocities perpetrated in the ancient city. I was sure they'd seen their fair share of fucked-up shit onboard the *Rockne Hummel* (I wouldn't realize just *how* fucked up until I met with Gallagher, Rosie, Teemo, and Lao on the way back) but it still pales in comparison to what I experienced on the surface.

"Jesus Christ," Teemo gasped. "Look at that."

He pointed toward the view screen as if the rest of us weren't already looking.

I heard Gallagher swallow hard behind me. "Any time now, Master Gunner."

The view was spectacular, in a disturbing way. Beyond the crater on the side opposite the city of Tscharia, there was a graveyard of ships that stretched for miles. Skeletons, most of them. Ravaged by the harsh surface winds. Some had retained their general shape despite centuries spent in the elements. None of them looked functional.

"How many do you think they've trapped here?" Rosie whispered.

No one answered. No one needed to. The answer was right in front of us in the endless graveyard. I still didn't think the view was an accurate representation of Furnace's victims, though. I knew there were a lot more somewhere, perhaps buried beneath the capital city like the clown king's vessel.

That could have been us, I thought. *We were next in line.*

I chewed my lower lip thoughtfully, watching the landscape fill the view screen.

So why is he letting us go when none of the others escaped?

I didn't know for certain that no other ship had gotten away, though, so I saw no point in worrying about it.

Even more disturbing than the graveyards was the sight of the lands beyond Tscharia. The corpse fields. The lava lakes. The wastelands, and then the nightmares beyond it. Empty castles with scores of bodies on slow-roasting pits that unraveled each victim's intestines as they spun. A writhing mob of the damned slogging their way along a valley of snakes. Innumerable aliens stoking massive, industrial fires far in the distance.

I shuddered.

"My God," Rosie whispered.

Somehow, it was worse seeing it all from above. More imposing. In fact, looking down on all the carnage in a miniature scale which was still too big to ignore, I couldn't believe I'd made it through everything and lived to tell about it. There were many who hadn't. Millions. Billions. Gallagher put her hand on my shoulder again, as if to apologize for all that I'd been through even though I hadn't elaborated on my experiences yet.

I tore my eyes away from the view screen and focused on the navigation controls. I didn't need to watch any more. I'd *lived* it. And who knew what other senseless horrors occurred elsewhere on the planet? Maybe Tscharia wasn't even the only city on Furnace with a clown king and an army of exiled nightmares. Maybe Tscharia was the *smallest* city on Furnace with the most lenient, civilized demons. There was no way to tell with our sensors just coming back online. It wasn't important, and we weren't about to stretch the systems for a planet-wide scan when it risked frying them all over again. That may have grounded us if we weren't careful, and certainly would make breaking orbit and getting home a hell of a lot more difficult than it already was.

"Lao, what's the hold up?" Gallagher asked over the comm line. She walked up to the view screen as though she'd somehow gain insight just by examining the landscape.

"Locking on target now, Representative. I want to make sure we hit the heart of the city. I don't want anything left, and I don't want to shoot twice."

Folding her arms across her chest, Gallagher turned and walked back to the captain's chair. "Fair enough," she said. "But hurry up."

"Yes, sir."

"For fuck's sake," Teemo said softly. "He's *looking* at us."

My eyes leapt back to the view screen. I couldn't help myself. I knew deep down who he was talking about and what I would see, but I still couldn't prevent it.

It was the clown king, staring straight through the monitor like he knew exactly where the camera was. He probably did.

"Zoom in," Gallagher said, walking directly back to the view screen. "It's saying something."

Rosie isolated the horned demon and focused in on his position. Seeing him up close again drained the color from my face. I knew he was speaking directly to me.

Wherever you go, he mouthed. *I will find you.*

In my head, I heard the voices chanting, "Here...here...here..."

Tscharia.

I blinked and he was gone.

"We'll break through the stratosphere in just a few moments, sir," Teemo reported.

"Lao?"

"Firing in five, four, three, two, one."

We watched silently as the pulse beam sprang out from the ship, disappeared in the heart of the city momentarily, and then was replaced by a rapidly-expanding wreath of fire and debris.

Teemo whistled. "So long, assholes."

I'd never seen such a huge pulse blast before from such close range. No wonder Lao Gang had taken so long arming the blast and picking his target. I think he probably had a better idea than the rest of us how big the explosion would be and wanted to make sure we were at a safe distance before detonation.

"We're gaining altitude. Should be out in open space within two minutes," Teemo said.

I checked the readings again even though I knew he was right. It gave me something to do other than stare at the explosion and think of all the fallen soldiers we'd left behind. Not just dead, but sentenced to a hundred thousand years of torture. If I'd realized that was the reality back when they'd died, I never would have left their bodies. Not that I could have done much, of course. I was in bad shape. I'd barely made it back to the ship, and it had taken more than a miracle to get there. Worst of all, I'd indebted myself to the clown king in the process.

Sold my soul to the Devil, I thought sourly.

I'd never thought I'd use the phrase literally.

Wherever you go, I will find you.

His face kept appearing in my head, even as the pulse blast swept out from Tscharia and blanketed the surface in dust and fire as far as the eye could see.

He's gone, I told myself.

I wasn't so sure, though. How can you kill the Devil? How can you kill evil itself?

"Brace yourselves," Teemo said. "This is going to be a rough one."

I strapped into my seat and closed my eyes.

Please, God, get us home, I prayed as the ship rattled around me. The shields hadn't been fully repaired after we crashed. There simply hadn't been enough time or resources to finish everything that needed work, so Rosie's team had focused on getting them strong enough to withstand space and a turbulent departure, but we wouldn't be able to land anywhere until we patched the rest of it. Apparently, all but two of her team members had been killed as the first wave of demons swept through the ship.

"Hang on," Teemo shouted over the howling atmosphere. "Almost through."

"Break orbit and cloak immediately!" Gallagher yelled.

I understood the sentiment, but she hadn't met the clown king. Cloaking the ship would mean jack-shit with him. He didn't use sensors to locate his prey. At least, not the kind that could be tricked by a rudimentary cloaking device designed specifically to pass beneath the scans of Kalak warships.

As we broke orbit and shot into space, I opened my eyes and stared with wild relief at the black expanse.

Please, God, I prayed again. *Please, get me home.*

"We're clear," Teemo announced with a heavy sigh. He slunk back into his chair and wiped sweat from his brow.

Tears formed in my eyes and I fought them back, embarrassed. I didn't know if it would last long, but for that moment, I was free.

Free, I thought, unstrapping my safety harness and stumbling toward the elevator, not paying any attention to Rosie or Gallagher as they held out their arms with concern.

"Let us help you," Rosie said.

I shooed her away. "I'm fine." I've never lied so deeply in my life.

"Where to?" Teemo asked.

Gallagher helped me into the elevator despite my protests. "We wait a while," she said. "Lieutenant Chalmers needs medical attention."

I limped into the elevator and pressed the button for Deck Three and my personal quarters. Gallagher watched me carefully, likely debating whether or not she should accompany me. "I'm going to go sleep for a couple weeks," I told her.

She grinned weakly. "Good. I'll send a doctor if any of them are still alive."

I didn't think they were, and at least two of the three didn't have medical expertise any greater than the field training the rest of us had in Basic, but I didn't feel like explaining that to her. "Yes, sir," I said instead.

The elevator door closed and I collapsed against the far wall as the decks dinged by.

Free, I thought.

Wherever you go, I will find you.

I didn't make it to my room. When the doors opened on Deck Three, I simply crawled out to the common area and slept on the warm steel for a long, long time.

While I slept, the Devil worked his dark magic again. He wasn't done with us yet.

RETURN

I wasn't awake when it happened so I can't necessarily confirm that the clown king of Tscharia was the one who transported the *Rockne Hummel* back to the point in the Milky Way from which he'd extracted us. But as a navigator and someone who's had firsthand experience with his transportation magic on two separate occasions (entering the wastelands and arriving in the bowels of the *Hummel* just in time for takeoff), I can tell you it is the only reasonable (ha!) explanation. Either way, we suddenly appeared right where we'd initially lost contact with fleet command like nothing had happened. The only difference was that our ship was pointed in the opposite direction.

Back towards home.

Once I realized we were back where we'd started, I wondered fleetingly if it had all been a dream. A grotesque nightmare birthed by the combined evils of the so-called 'Visions of Parin' (space madness) and the chemicals involved in the hyper-sleep stasis pods. That would have been a convenient explanation both for us and the fleet, but physical evidence of our time on Furnace is everywhere. The most glaring corroboratory items are corpses of alien species that don't exist in the fleet database, of course, but our ship's log shows that we traveled an impossible number of light years. Utterly impossible. Something in the duocentillions. Perhaps into another universe altogether. All we can do is shake our heads and accept it.

In all, twenty of us survived. Myself, Teemo, Gallagher, Rosie, Captain Gibbons, Martavius the Cook, Lao Gang, two of the doctors, and eleven other personnel members I'd never had contact with prior to the voyage home. Nearly all the officers made it. All except Salib. That's the shit of it, I guess. There's no reason why the higher-ranking officers should have made it instead of the grunt workers. No *rational* explanation, anyway. Especially for Teemo and me, who were both on the surface for hours.

I do have a theory, though. I think there's a reason the pilot, navigator, master gunner, Crown Representative, chief engineer, and doctors survived. I think the clown king *wanted* us to. I think he picked *us* specifically because he knew we were the ones who could get the ship back home. Back to Earth.

I think he had a plan.

The question was raised whether or not we should attempt to complete our diplomatic mission, but there was no real debate. Even Representative Gallagher had to admit that it was foolish to even consider such a thing given the heavy losses we'd sustained. Besides, we needed extensive repairs on the ship before we could land and we were already way behind schedule for pickup. That's to say nothing of the message we'd be sending disparaged colonists by extracting a high-ranking Crown politician in our beat-up vessel.

Instead, I plotted a course for Pluto Station and we roamed the ship restlessly for days, trying not to think too much about what had happened or the soldiers we'd left behind. Teemo and I cleaned up the bodies the best we could, just so we wouldn't have to pass them every time we performed systems checks in the lower decks or got up in the middle of the night for a snack from the mess hall. It didn't erase the bad memories—far from it—but it spaced them out so we could at least breathe a little without remembering.

Despite my reservations, one of the doctors patched me up pretty well. My wounds were mostly superficial, after all, and were cured with ointment, dermal regeneration, and a whole lot of rest. By the time we reached the research labs on Pluto, I was almost good as new.

Captain Gibbons, however, is another story. I didn't catch all the details because the crew is still being questioned about the events that transpired on the *Rockne Hummel* while I was on the surface, but the gist of it is that things were a lot tenser between Gibbons and Gallagher than I'd realized. More to the point, Gibbons was a lot closer to the edge than I'd suspected. They say that career astronauts often snap when they've spent too much time in the void, but I guess I hadn't known the captain was capable of falling into the deep end until just before he sent me out on the ground mission. Even then, I'd thought he was just a little (understandably) tense given the nature of the situation.

Gibbons hadn't just snapped, though. He'd gone bat-shit crazy.

He started the massacre aboard the *Hummel* by turning a pulse rifle on his own soldiers, and finished by using a fire ax and his bare hands. In all, he was responsible for the deaths of twenty-four crewmembers aboard the ship, and if you add the ones from Salib's squad who he sent to their deaths on a fool's errand, that number just about doubles. There are also reports that he purposely damaged a significant number of key systems upon our arrival on Furnace, making Rosie's job much more difficult than it had to be. Which, I guess, is fortunate for me. If Rosie had gotten the systems up and running even ten minutes sooner, I would have been stranded on the planet.

I shudder to think what it would have been like to be stuck there forever. I dream about it almost every night. Whenever I'm able to fall asleep.

Eventually, Gallagher had enlisted the help of Rosie, Lao Gang, and several other soldiers to sedate Captain Gibbons, at which point he was locked in the brig and wasn't released until the Patrol ship Pluto Station sent to intercept us docked and escorted him to another cell. I'm sure there's one hell of a dark and harrowing story there, but like I said, the members of the crew with information pertaining to Captain Gibbons' mental collapse and subsequent killing spree haven't been released from fleet headquarters. Maybe Gallagher will tell me about it sometime. Maybe it will help ease her guilt, if she carries any. She doesn't exactly strike me as the guilt-bearing type, but people surprise you sometimes.

I guess it's really her story to tell, anyway. Or his. Maybe one of them will share the details with the committee the same way I have. A detailed written account. It should save me from repetitive questions going forward (I hope), and it's certainly helped to get the ordeal off my chest. I guess we'll find out eventually if one of them chooses to do the same, although I don't know that it's in the best interest of the public to leak details about Furnace.

By the way, Gallagher's the one who started calling it 'Furnace' after I explained the history of the planet and its inhabitants. The name seems to fit well enough. Not *Hell*, exactly, because it has a unique place separate from the religious mythology on our home planet. Furnace, where everything burns.

I've kept my mouth shut for the most part, even when my mother asks why I've suddenly been granted six months of paid leave. It's important to keep it secret, at least for a while. We might never get another colony established if people feel they need to worry about getting sucked into Hell itself on top of all the other dangers involved with a deep space mission and settling a terra-formed planet. Besides, if I breathed a word about any of this, I'm sure the Crown would have soldiers dragging me to a Psychiatric Convalescence center within hours, or a penal colony on another godforsaken rock. Probably on the moons of Jupiter. Maybe Haley Penn, otherwise known as the Pit.

I still can't sleep at night, and it's not just the nightmares of what I've seen that haunts me. Since passing out during our escape from Furnace—a rest better described as an exhaustion-induced coma than a normal sleep cycle—I lie awake every night, staring at the ceiling and reflecting on how I screwed up the whole mission. How I'm responsible for the loss of so many lives. Good people, all of them. In their own ways.

I can blame Captain Gibbons for killing members of his own crew and for insisting Salib's squad return to the surface even after we'd agreed repairing the engines was our number one priority. The truth is, though, Gibbons is another casualty on my conscience. If it hadn't been for my goddamned course alteration, he wouldn't be locked away facing twenty-four counts of second-degree murder, along with the fleet's in-house disciplinary measures for the laundry list of protocols he broke along the way.

Without that one course alteration, all his suffering could have been avoided.

In the end, you see, it all comes back to me, no matter how vehemently everyone exonerates me.

And it tears me apart.

The depression comes and goes, but when it arrives, it's absolutely paralyzing. I think long and hard about suicide. Sometimes I even get to the point where the VP barrel is pressed against my temple, and I swear I'm about to pull the trigger. No note, no apologies, nothing. Just darkness. Nothingness. Sweet relief.

But then I think of all the times I could have ended it on Furnace and didn't. I think about all the soldiers suffering in Tscharia and how trivializing their unending deaths by voluntarily ending my own life is a slap in the face to them. *I* made it, after all. I'm a survivor of the *Rockne Hummel*. And if I kill myself after surviving impossible odds on the Hell planet, then what was the point of all their sacrifices? Of Katrina standing up to the Watchman in the corpse fields? Of Sillinger being killed by his commanding officer for saving my life?

I think of all that, and the depression only gets worse. Because I'm ashamed.

And so, I choose to keep living. Not for myself, but for the memories of those I left behind. I guess spite fuels the choice a little, as well. Knowing that every breath I take represents a crushing defeat for the demons on Furnace. My existence is their failure, and it makes me smile to think how it would enrage them to see me walking through the soft grass of my home planet, almost completely healed from the injuries they inflicted upon me.

It's still a part of me, though. *He* is still a part of me. The clown king of Tscharia. A horned demon exiled from this galaxy by a mysterious deity who may very well be the Judeo-Christian God, or maybe not. I guess in any war, we bring back the evil that's touched us. It just runs a little deeper after a place like Furnace. It's harder to root out.

He talks to me at night, you know.

He takes the form of my mother's severed head. Sometimes I wake and the gristle from her neck has smeared red over my chest. Sometimes she's resting on the windowsill, watching me with vacant eyes and a grin that's too wide for her mouth. Sometimes she's on my dresser or in my closet or speaking to me from the hallway.

Wherever you go, he tells me through her mouth. *I will find you.*

It terrifies me. But the worst part of all is feeling that he's telling the truth. He *wanted* us to leave, after all. He selected each survivor specifically, based on our roles in the ship's crew. I have no doubt about that. Lao to protect us, Teemo to fly us home, Rosie to fix the engines and life-support systems, the doctors to patch us up and discover which alien corpses were edible for humans on the way back when our food-stores ran out (I'm not proud of that, but our communications systems were extremely short range and we couldn't have landed on an alien planet for trade even if there'd been one nearby), Gallagher to command the ship once the captain was unfit for duty, Marty to prepare the food, and me to do the navigation that would lead us back to friendly space once we were in the Milky Way. I can't guess what the other eleven soldiers stuck around for. Maybe just some extra muscle in case of trouble along the way. Regardless, I know it was all part of his plan.

And in the cold, lonely hours of the night, I know *why*, too.

Because he came back with us. He used us as vessels to return to the planet from which he'd been exiled. After all those eons without catching a reliable human ship, he'd finally gotten lucky and seized the opportunity. And soon, he will break free.

Wherever you go, I will find you, my mother's head tells me.

So I lock my door at night and dread the day he comes knocking.

Tscharia, she tells me.

Her shrill voice stops my heart, and sometimes I call her in the small hours of the morning just to make sure it wasn't really *her* visiting me as the Devil's mouthpiece. She's always happy to hear from me, and always invites me back to visit the shores of Lake Huron and relive the days of my youth with the rest of my family. The sound of her actual voice always makes me feel better. It makes me feel at home.

But I know someday, she'll answer the phone and start chanting, "Here...here...here..." in that monotonous drawl of the undead.

That's how I'll know I'm done.

ABOUT THE AUTHOR

Joseph Williams is an author of science fiction, dark fantasy, and horror who lives in Farmington Hills, Michigan with his wife and three daughters. He has previously released four short story collections and eight novels.

www.ingramcontent.com/pod-product-compliance
Lightning Source LLC
Chambersburg PA
CBHW020319160726
47992CB00004B/1614